More praise for *The Empty Family* and Colm Tóibín

"Tóibín's attention to language equals the empathy he pays his thoroughly authentic characters, so summarizing their stories only threatens to blunt their exquisiteness, because half the pleasure of reading them comes from absorbing the complicated structures he weaves. . . . He is in top form here."

—*San Francisco Chronicle*

"Rich with tender surprises . . . Tóibín's voice [is] more assured with every new book he brings out." —*The Economist*

"Love in all its guises—nostalgic, unabashedly erotic, perhaps even autobiographical—can be found in *The Empty Family,* including a deft reimagining of Lady Gregory's tryst with the poet Wilfred Blunt, recounted with more than one Jamesian flourish."

—*Vogue*

"The full-blooded triumph of the collection is 'The Street.' "
—*The Boston Globe*

Tóibín lures us into stories with characters who experience true revelation, no matter how quiet or small. With masterful restraint, he lays bare the drama of everyday life." —*Houston Chronicle*

"The Empty Family" reminds us that a *short story* is something altogether different: a work of art, like a painting or a beautiful song.

Ernest Hemingway famously said that in fiction nine-tenths of the story should lie below the surface . . . Tóibín masterfully achieves this goal."

—*The Cleveland Plain Dealer*

"Tóibín generates drama and suspense without ever sacrificing the intensely lyrical writing that he has always delivered."

—*Milwaukee Journal Sentinel*

"Remarkable . . . triumphant."

—*Library Journal,* starred review

"A literary triumph . . . This book, then, is short story writing as dazzling yet serious as it is practiced today."

—*Booklist,* starred review

"Tóibín is a lyrical, melancholy writer, but his stories swiftly gather momentum; they are openly erotic, deeply wrenching."

—The Daily Beast

"With a spare, eloquent style, [Tóibín] guides us through hotel lobbies and pensiones from Dublin to Barcelona. He directs our attention to estranged family members, divorcées and Muslim immigrants, catching each of them at the moment in which they are forced to reckon with their pasts."   —*Los Angeles Times*

"Mr. Tóibín is at his best dealing with matters of the heart and soul. . . . A satisfying test of intellect and sympathy."

—*Pittsburgh Post-Gazette*

"On the evidence of the stories collected in *The Empty Family,* Colm Tóibín must be seriously considered one of today's great short story

writers. . . . Tóibín is shaping up to be the . . .
tury's E. M. Forster." — *.rica..*

"Colm Tóibín is one of the best storytellers writing today. . . . His prose is pitch perfect, each word, each phrase carefully chosen and aptly applied. In this collection Colm Tóibín is at his masterful best." —*Toronto Sun*

"The work of a supreme writer who only improves."
—*The Times* (U.K.)

"A collection that will only further fuel Tóibín's ascent through English fiction." —*The Independent* (UK)

"Exquisite." —*The Daily Telegraph* (UK)

"Reconfirms his mastery of the short story . . . Tóibín raised his profile with the exquisitely bittersweet *Brooklyn,* and this collection is every bit as rich." —*Kirkus,* starred review

"Nine pristine stories . . . These stories go a long way toward establishing Tóibín as heir to William Trevor."
—*Publishers Weekly,* starred review

"Narratives of remarkable scope and variety . . . Tóibín describes the experiences of the young and the very old, homosexual and heterosexual, Irish and Spanish, all with equal assurance."
—*The Spectator* (UK)

"When Tóibín pulls a fully convincing twist on the convention, it's like witnessing a magician pull off an especially deft trick. . . . The work of a modern master." —*The Gazette* (Canada)

Also by Colm Tóibín

FICTION

The South

The Heather Blazing

The Story of the Night

The Blackwater Lightship

The Master

Mothers and Sons

Brooklyn

NONFICTION

Bad Blood: A Walk Along the Irish Border

Homage to Barcelona

The Sign of the Cross: Travels in Catholic Europe

Love in a Dark Time: Gay Lives from Wilde to Almodóvar

Lady Gregory's Toothbrush

All a Novelist Needs: Colm Tóibín on Henry James

PLAY

Beauty in a Broken Place

The Empty Family

STORIES

Colm Tóibín

SCRIBNER

NEW YORK LONDON TORONTO SYDNEY NEW DELHI

SCRIBNER
A Division of Simon & Schuster, Inc.
1230 Avenue of the Americas
New York, NY 10020

First Scribner trade paperback edition January 2012

SCRIBNER and design are registered trademarks of The Gale Group, Inc., used under license by Simon & Schuster, Inc., the publisher of this work.

For information about special discounts for bulk purchases, please contact Simon & Schuster Special Sales at 1-866-506-1949 or business@simonandschuster.com.

The Simon & Schuster Speakers Bureau can bring authors to your live event. For more information or to book an event contact the Simon & Schuster Speakers Bureau at 1-866-248-3049 or visit our website at www.simonspeakers.com.

Manufactured in the United States of America

1 3 5 7 9 10 8 6 4 2

Library of Congress Control Number: 2010032931

ISBN 978-1-4391-3832-8
ISBN 978-1-4391-9596-3 (pbk)
ISBN 978-1-4391-4983-6 (ebook)

Some of the stories in this collection have appeared elsewhere. See page 277.

For Anthony Cronin

Contents

Silence

34 DVG, January 23d, 1894

Another incident—"subject"—related to me by Lady G. was that of the eminent London clergyman who on the Dover-to-Calais steamer, starting on his wedding tour, picked up on the deck a letter addressed to his wife, while she was below, and finding it to be from an old lover, and very ardent (an engagement—a rupture, a relation, in short), of which he never had been told, took the line of sending her, from Paris, straight back to her parents— without having touched her—on the ground that he had been deceived. He ended, subsequently, by taking her back into his house to live, but *never* lived with her as his wife. There is a drama in the various things, for her, to which that situation—that night in Paris—might have led. Her immediate surrender to some one else, etc. etc. etc.

—from *The Notebooks of Henry James*

S ometimes when the evening had almost ended, Lady Greg- ory would catch someone's eye for a moment and that would be enough to make her remember. At those tables in the great city she knew not ever to talk about herself, or complain about anything such as the heat, or the dullness of the season, or the antics of an actress; she knew not to babble about banalities, or laugh at things that were not very funny. She focused instead with as much force and care as she could on the gentleman beside her and asked him questions and then listened with attention to the answers. Listening took more work than talking; she made sure that her companion knew, from the sympathy and sharp light in her eyes, how intelligent she was, and how quietly powerful and deep.

She would suffer only when she left the company. In the carriage on the way home she would stare into the dark, knowing that what had happened in those years would not come back, that memories were no use, that there was nothing ahead except darkness. And on the bad nights, after evenings when there had been too much gaiety and brightness, she often wondered if there was a difference between her life now and the years stretching to eternity that she would spend in the grave.

She would write out a list and the writing itself would make her smile. Things to live for. Her son, Robert, would always come first, and then some of her sisters. She often thought of erasing one or two of them, and maybe one brother, but no more than one. And then Coole Park, the house in Ireland her husband had left her, or at least left their son, and to which she could return when she wished. She thought of the trees she had planted at Coole, she often dreamed of going back there to study the slow progress of things as the winter gave way to spring, or autumn came. And there were books and paintings and how light came into a high room as she pulled the shutters back in the morning. She would add these also to the list.

Below the list each time was blank paper. It was easy to fill the blank spaces with another list. A list of grim facts led by a single inescapable thought—that love had eluded her, that love would not come back, that she was alone and she would have to make the best of being alone.

On this particular evening, she crumpled the piece of paper in her hand before she stood up and made her way to the bedroom and prepared for the night. She was glad, or almost glad, that there would be no more outings that week, that no London hostess had the need for a dowager from Ireland at her table for the moment. A woman known for her listening skills and her keen intelligence had her uses, she thought, but not every night of the week.

She had liked being married; she had enjoyed being noticed as the young wife of an old man, had known the effect her quiet gaze could have on friends of her husband's who thought she might be dull because she was not pretty. She had let them know, carefully, tactfully, keeping her voice low, that she was someone on whom nothing was lost. She had read all the latest books and she chose her words slowly when she came to discuss them. She did not want to appear clever. She made sure that she was silent without seeming shy, polite and reserved without seeming intimidated. She had no natural grace and she made up for this by having no empty opinions. She took the view that it was a mistake for a woman with her looks ever to show her teeth. In any case, she disliked laughter and preferred to smile using her eyes.

She disliked her husband only when he came to her at night in those first months; his fumbling and panting, his eager hands and his sour breath, gave her a sense that daylight and many layers of clothing and servants and large furnished rooms and chatter about politics or paintings were ways to distract people from feeling a revulsion towards each other.

There were times when she saw him in the distance or had occasion to glance at his face in repose when she viewed him as someone who had merely on a whim or a sudden need rescued her or captured her. He was too old to know her, he had seen too much and lived too long to allow anything new, such as a wife thirty-five years his junior, to enter his orbit. In the night, in those early months, as she tried to move towards him to embrace him fully, to offer herself to his dried-up spirit, she found that he was happier obsessively fondling certain parts of her body in the dark as though he were trying to find something he had mislaid. And thus as she attempted to please him, she also tried to make sure that, when he was finished, she would be able gently to turn away from him and face the dark alone as he slept and snored. She longed to wake in the morning and not have to look at his face too closely, his half-opened mouth, his stubbled cheeks, his grey whiskers, his wrinkled skin.

All over London, she thought, in the hours after midnight in rooms with curtains drawn, silence was broken by grunts and groans and sighs. It was lucky, she knew, that it was all done in secret, lucky also that no matter how much they talked of love or faithfulness or the unity of man and wife, no one would ever realize how apart people were in these hours, how deeply and singly themselves, how thoughts came that could never be shared or whispered or made known in any way. This was marriage, she thought, and it was her job to be calm about it. There were times when the grim, dull truth of it made her smile.

Nonetheless, there was in the day almost an excitement about being the wife of Sir William Gregory, of having a role to play in the world. He had been lonely, that much was clear. He had married her because he had been lonely. He longed to travel and he enjoyed the idea now that she would arrange his clothes and listen to him talk. They could enter dining rooms together as others did, rooms in which an elderly man alone would have appeared out of place, too sad somehow.

And because he knew his way around the world—he had

been governor of Ceylon, among other things—he had many old friends and associates, was oddly popular and dependable and cultured and well informed and almost amusing in company. Once they arrived in Cairo, therefore, it was natural that they would stay in the same hotel as the young poet Wilfrid Scawen Blunt and his grand wife, that the two couples would dine together and find each other interesting as they discussed poetry lightly and then, as things began to change, argued politics with growing intensity and seriousness.

Wilfrid Scawen Blunt. As she lay in the bed with the light out, Lady Gregory smiled at the thought that she would not need ever to write his name down on any list. His name belonged elsewhere; it was a name she might breathe on glass or whisper to herself when things were harder than she had ever imagined that anything could become. It was a name that might have been etched on her heart if she believed in such things.

His fingers were long and beautiful; even his fingernails had a glow of health; his hair was shiny, his teeth white. And his eyes brightened as he spoke; thinking made him smile and when he smiled he exuded a sleek perfection. He was as far from her as a palace was from her house in Coole or as the heavens were from the earth. She liked looking at him as she liked looking at a Bronzino or a Titian and she was careful always to pretend that she also liked looking at his wife, Byron's granddaughter, although she did not.

She thought of them like food, Lady Anne all watery vegetables, or sour, small potatoes, or salted fish, and the poet her husband like lamb cooked slowly for hours with garlic and thyme, or goose stuffed at Christmas. And she remembered in her childhood the watchful eye of her mother, her mother making her eat each morsel of bad winter food, leave her plate clean.

Thus she forced herself to pay attention to every word Lady Anne said; she gazed at her with soft and sympathetic interest, she spoke to her with warmth and the dull intimacy that one man's wife might have with another, hoping that soon Lady Anne would be calmed and suitably assuaged by this so she would not notice when Lady Gregory turned to the poet and ate him up with her eyes.

Blunt was on fire with passion during these evenings, composing a letter to *The Times* at the very dining table in support of Arabi Bey, arguing in favour of loosening the control that France and England had over Egyptian affairs, cajoling Sir William, who was of course a friend of the editor of *The Times,* to put pressure on the paper to publish his letter and support the cause. Sir William was quiet, watchful, gruff. It was easy for Blunt to feel that he agreed with every point Blunt was making mainly because Blunt did not notice dissent. They arranged for Lady Gregory to visit Arabi Bey's wife and family so that she could describe to the English how refined they were, how sweet and deserving of support.

The afternoon when she returned was unusually hot. Her husband, she found, was in a deep sleep, so she did not disturb him. When she went in search of Blunt, she was told by the maid that Lady Anne had a severe headache brought on by the heat and would not be appearing for the rest of the day. Her husband the poet could be found in the garden or in the room he kept for work, where he often spent the afternoons. Lady Gregory found him in the garden; Blunt was excited to hear about her visit to Bey's family and ready to show her a draft of a poem he had composed that morning on the matter of Egyptian freedom. She went to his study with him, not realizing until she was in the room and the door was closed that the study was in fact an extra bedroom the Blunts had taken, no different from the Gregorys' own room except for a large desk and books and papers strewn on the floor and on the bed.

As Blunt read her the poem, he crossed the room and turned the key in the lock as though it were a normal act, what he always did as he read a new poem. He read it a second time and then left the piece of paper down on the desk and moved towards her and held her. He began to kiss her. Her only thought was that this might be the single chance she would get in her life to associate with beauty. Like a tourist in the vicinity of a great temple, she thought it would be a mistake to pass it by; it would be something she would only regret. She did not think it would last long or mean much. She also was sure that no one had seen them come down this corridor; she presumed that her husband was still sleeping; she believed that no one would find them and it would never be mentioned again between them.

Later, when she was alone and checking that there were no traces of what she had done on her skin or on her clothes, the idea that she had lain naked with the poet Blunt in a locked room on a hot afternoon and that he had, in a way that was new to her, made her cry out in ecstasy, frightened her. She had been married less than two years, time enough to know how deep her husband's pride ran, how cold he was to those who had crossed him and how sharp and decisive he could be. They had left their child in England so they could travel to Egypt even though Sir William knew how much it pained her to be separated in this way from Robert. Were Sir William to be told that she had been visiting the poet in his private quarters, she believed he could ensure that she never saw her child again. Or he could live with her in pained silence and barely managed contempt. Or he could send her home. The corridors were full of servants, figures watching. She thought it a miracle that she had managed once to be unnoticed. She believed that she might not be so lucky a second time.

Over the weeks that followed and in London when she returned home, she discovered that Wilfrid Scawen Blunt's talents as a poet were minor compared to his skills as an adulterer. Not only could he please her in ways that were daring and astonishing but he could ensure that they would not be discovered. The sanctity of his calling required him to have silence, solitude and quarters that his wife had no automatic right to enter. Blunt composed his poems in a locked room. He rented this room away from his main residence, choosing the place, Lady Gregory saw, not because of the ease with which it could be visited by the muses but rather for its position in a shadowy side-street close to streets where women of circumstance shopped. Thus no one would notice a respectable woman who was not his wife arriving or leaving in the mornings or the afternoons; no one would hear her cry out as she lay in bed with him; no one would ever know that each time in the hour or so she spent with him she realized that nothing would be enough for her, that she had not merely visited the temple as a tourist might, but had come to believe in and deeply need the sweet doctrine preached in its warm and towering confines.

At the beginning, she didn't dream of being caught. Sir William was often busy in the day; he enjoyed having a long lunch with old associates, or a meeting of some sort about the National Gallery or some political or financial matter. It seemed to make him content that his wife went to the shops or to visit her friends as long as she was free in the evenings to accompany him to dinners. He was usually distant, quite distracted. It was, she thought, like being a member of the cabinet with her own tasks and responsibilities with her husband as prime minister, her husband happy that he had appointed her, and pleased, it appeared, that she carried out her tasks with the minimum of fuss.

Soon, however, when they were back in England a few months, she began to worry about exposure and to imagine with dread not his accusing her, or finding her in the act, but what would happen later. She dreamed, for example, that she had been sent home to her parents' house in Roxborough and she was destined to spend her days wandering the corridors of the upper floor, a ghostly presence. Her mother passed her and did not speak to her. Her sisters came and went but did not seem even to see her. The servants brushed by her. Sometimes, she went downstairs, but there was no chair for her at the dining table and no place for her to sit in the drawing room. Every place had been filled by her sisters and her brothers and their guests and they were all chattering loudly and laughing and being served tea and, no matter how close she came to them, they paid her no attention.

The dream changed sometimes. She was in her own house in London or in Coole with her husband and with Robert and their servants but no one saw her, they let her come in and out of rooms, forlorn, silent, desperate. Her son appeared blind to her as he came towards her. Her husband undressed in their room at night as though she were not there and turned out the lamp in their room while she was still standing at the foot of the bed fully dressed. No one seemed to mind that she haunted the spaces they inhabited because no one noticed her. She had become, in these dreams, invisible to the world.

Despite Sir William's absence from the house during the day and his indifference to how she spent her time as long as she did not cost him too much money, she knew that she could be unlucky. Being found out could happen because a friend or an acquaintance or, indeed, an enemy could suspect her and follow her, or Lady Anne could find a key to the room and come with urgent news for her husband or visit suddenly out of sheer curiosity. Blunt was careful and dependable, she knew, but he was also passionate and excitable. In some fit of rage, or moment where he lost his composure, he could easily, she thought, say enough to someone that they would understand he was having an affair with the young wife of Sir William Gregory. Her husband had many old friends in London. A note left at his club would be enough to cause him to have her watched and followed. The affair with Blunt, she realized, could not last. As months went by, she left it to Blunt to decide when it should end. It would be best, she thought, if he tired of her and found another. It would be less painful to be jealous of someone else than to feel that she had denied herself this deep fulfilling pleasure for no reason other than fear or caution.

Up to this she had put no real thought into what marriage meant. It was, she had vaguely thought, a contract, or even a sacrament. It was what happened. It was part of the way things were ordered. Sometimes now, however, when she saw the Blunts socially, or when she read a poem by him or heard someone mention his name, the fact that it was not known and publicly understood that she was with him hurt her profoundly, made her experience what existed between them as a kind of emptiness or absence. She knew that if her secret were known or told, it would destroy her life. But as time went by, its not being known by anyone at all made her imagine with relish and energy what it would be like to be married to Wilfrid Scawen Blunt, to enter a room with him, to leave in a carriage with him, to have her name openly linked with his. It would mean everything. Instead, the time she spent alone with him often came to seem like nothing when it was over. Memory, which was once so sharp and precious for her, was now a dark room in which she wandered longing for the light to be switched on or the curtains pulled back. She longed for the light of publicity, for her secret life to become common knowledge. It was something, she was well aware, that would not happen as long as she lived if she could help it. She would take her pleasure in darkness.

When the affair ended, she felt at times as if it had not happened. There was nothing solid or sure about it. Most women, she thought, had a close, discreet friend to whom such things could be whispered. She did not. In France, she understood, they had a way of making such things subtly known. Now she understood why. She was lonely without Blunt, but she was lonelier at the idea that the world went on as though she had not loved him. Time would pass and their actions and feelings would seem like a shadow of actions and feelings, but less than a shadow in fact, because cast by something that now had no real substance.

Thus she wrote the sonnets, using the time she now had to work on rhyme schemes and poetic forms. She wrote in secret about her secret love for him and then kept the paper on which she had written it down:

> *Bowing my head to kiss the very ground*
> *On which the feet of him I love have trod,*
> *Controlled and guided by that voice whose sound*
> *Is dearer to me than the voice of God.*

She put on paper her fear of disclosure and the shame that might come with it; she hid the pages away and found them when the house was quiet and she could read of what she had done and what it meant:

13

Should e'er that drear day come in which the world
Shall know the secret which so close I hold,
Should taunts and jeers at my bowed head be hurled,
And all my love and all my shame be told,
I could not, as some women used to do,
Fling jests and gold and live the scandal down.

When she asked, some months after their separation, to meet him one more time, his tone in reply was brusque, almost cold. She wondered if he thought that she was going to appeal to him to resume their affair, or remonstrate with him in some way. She enjoyed how surprised he seemed that she was merely handing him a sheaf of sonnets, making clear as soon as she gave him the pages that she had written them herself. She watched him reading them.

"What shall we do with them?" he asked when he had finished.

"You shall publish them in your next book as though they were written by you," she said.

"But it is clear from the style that they are not."

"Let the world believe that you changed your style for the purposes of writing them. Let your readers believe that you were writing in another voice. That will explain the awkwardness."

"There is no awkwardness. They are very good."

"Then publish them. They are yours."

He agreed then to publish them under his own name in his next book, having made some minor alterations to them. They came out six weeks before Sir William died. Lady Gregory did her husband the favour in those weeks of not keeping the book by her bed but in her study; she managed also to keep these poems out of her mind as she watched over him.

As his widow, she knew who she was and what she had inherited. She had loved him in her way and sometimes missed him. She knew what words like "loved" and "missed" meant when she thought of her husband. When she thought of Blunt, on the other hand, she was unsure what anything meant except the sonnets she had written about their love affair. She read them sparingly, often needing them if she woke in the night, but keeping them away from her much of the time. It was enough for her that all over London, in the houses of people who acquired new books of poetry, these poems rested silently and mysteriously between the pages. She found solace in the idea that people would read them without knowing their source.

She rebuilt her life as a widow and took care of her son and began, after a suitable period of mourning, to go out in London again and meet people and take part in things. She often asked herself if there was someone in the room, or in the street, who had read her sonnets and been puzzled or pained by them, even for a second.

She had read Henry James as his books appeared. In fact, it was a discussion about *Roderick Hudson* that caused Sir William to pay attention to her first. She had read an extract from it but did not have the book. He arranged for it to be sent to her. Some time after her marriage, when she was visiting Rome with Sir William, she met James and she remembered him fondly as a man who would talk seriously to a woman, even someone as young and provincial as she was. She remembered asking him at that first meeting in Rome how he could possibly have allowed Isabel Archer to marry the odious Osmond. He told her that Isabel was bound to do something foolish and, if she had not, there would have been no story. And he had enjoyed, he had said, as a poor man himself, bestowing so much money on his heroine. Henry James was kind and witty, she had felt then, and somehow managed not to be glib or patronizing.

Since her husband died she had seen Henry James a number of times, noticing always how much of himself he held back, how the expression on his face appeared to disguise as much as it disclosed. He had always been very polite to her, and they had often discussed the fate of the orphan Paul Harvey, with whose mother they had both been friends. She was surprised one evening to see the novelist at a supper that Lady Layard had invited her to; there were diplomats present and some foreigners, and a few military men and some minor politicians. It was not Henry James's world, and it was Lady Gregory's world only in that an extra woman was needed, as people might need an extra carriage or an extra towel in the bathroom. It did not matter who she was as long as she arrived on time and left at an appropriate moment and did not talk too loudly or compete in any way with the hostess.

It made sense to place her beside Henry James. In the company on a night where politics would be discussed between the men and silliness between the women, neither of them mattered. She looked forward to having the novelist on her right. Once she disposed of a young Spanish diplomat on her left, she would attend to James and ask him about his work. When they were all dead, she thought, he would be the one whose name would live on, but it was perhaps important for those who were rich or powerful to spend their evenings keeping this poor thought at bay.

It was the Spaniard's fingers she noticed, they were long and slender with beautiful rounded nails. She found herself glancing down at them as often as she could, hoping that the diplomat, whose accent was beyond her, would not spot what she was doing. She looked at his eyes and nodded as he spoke, all the time wondering if it would be rude for her to glance down again, this time for longer. Somewhere near London, Wilfrid Scawen Blunt was dining too, she thought, perhaps with his wife and some friends. She pictured him reaching for something at the table, a jug of water perhaps, and pouring it. She pictured his long slender fingers, the rounded nails, and then began to imagine his hair, how silky it was to the touch, and the fine bones on his face and his teeth and his breath.

She stopped herself now and began to concentrate hard on what the Spaniard was saying. She asked him a question that he failed to understand so she repeated it, making it simpler. When she had asked a number of other questions and listened attentively to the replies, she was relieved when she knew that her time with him was up and she could turn now to Henry James, who seemed heavier than before as though his large head were filled with oak or ivory. As they began to talk, he took her in with his grey eyes, which had a level of pure understanding in them that was almost affecting. For a split second she was tempted to tell him what had happened with Blunt, suggest that it occurred to a friend of hers while visiting Egypt, a friend married to an older man who was seduced by a friend of his, a poet. But she knew it was ridiculous, James would see through her immediately.

Yet something had stirred in her, a need that she had ruminated on in the past but kept out of her mind for some time now. She wanted to say Blunt's name and wondered if she could find a way to ask James if he read his work or admired it. But James was busy describing the best way to see old Rome now that Rome had changed so much, and the best way to avoid Americans in Rome, Americans one did not want to see or be associated with. How odd he would think her were she to interrupt him or wait for a break in the conversation and ask him what he thought of the work of Wilfrid Scawen Blunt! It was possible he did not even read modern poetry. It would be hard, she thought, to turn the conversation around to Blunt or even find a way to mention him in passing. In any case, James had moved his arena of concern to Venice and was discussing whether it was best to lodge with friends there or find one's own lodging and thus win greater independence.

As he pondered the relative merits of various American hostesses in Venice, going over the quality of their table, the size of their guest rooms, what they put at one's disposal, she thought of love. James sighed and mentioned how a warm personality, especially of the American sort, had a way of cooling one's appreciation of ancient beauty, irrespective of how grand the palazzo of which this personality was in possession, indeed irrespective of how fine or fast-moving her gondola.

When he had finished, Lady Gregory turned towards him quietly and asked him if he was tired of people telling him stories he might use in his fiction, or if he viewed such offerings as an essential element in his art. He told her in reply that he often, later when he arrived home, noted down something interesting that had been said to him, and on occasion the germ of a story had come to him from a most unlikely source, and other times, of course, from a most obvious and welcome one. He liked to imagine his characters, he said, but he also liked that they might have lived already, to some small extent perhaps, before he painted a new background for them and created a new scenario. Life, he said, life, that was the material that he used and needed. There could never be enough life. But it was only the beginning, of course, because life was thin.

There was an eminent London man, she began, a clergyman known to dine at the best tables, a man of great experience who had many friends, friends who were both surprised and delighted when this man finally married. The lady in question was known to be highly respectable. But on the day of their wedding as they crossed to France from Dover to Calais, he found a note addressed to her from a man who had clearly been her lover and now felt free, despite her new circumstances, to address her ardently and intimately.

James listened, noting every word. Lady Gregory found that she was trembling and had to control herself; she realized that she would have to speak softly and slowly. She stopped and took a sip of water, knowing that if she did not continue in a tone that was easy and nonchalant she would end by giving more away than she wished to give. The clergyman, she went on, was deeply shocked, and, since he had been married just a few hours to this woman, he decided that, when they had arrived in Paris, he would send her back home to her family, make her an outcast; she would be his wife merely in name. He would not see her again.

Instead, however, Lady Gregory went on, when they had arrived at their hotel in Paris the clergyman decided against this action. He informed his errant wife, his piece of damaged goods, that he would keep her, but he would not touch her. He would take her into his house to live, but not as his wife.

Lady Gregory tried to smile casually as she came to the end of the story. She was pleased that her listener had guessed nothing. It was a story that had elements both French and English, something that James would understand as being rather particularly part of his realm. He thanked her and said that he would note the story once he reached his study that evening and he would perhaps, he hoped, do justice to it in the future. It was always impossible to know, he added, why one small spark caused a large fire and why another was destined to extinguish itself before it had even flared.

She realized as the guests around her stood up from the table that she had said as much as she could say, which was, on reflection, hardly anything at all. She almost wished she had added more detail, had told James that the letter came from a poet perhaps, or that it contained a set of sonnets whose subject was unmistakable, or that the wife of the clergyman was more than thirty years his junior, or that he was not a clergyman at all, but a former member of parliament and someone who had once held high office. Or that the events in question had happened in Egypt and not on the way to Paris. Or that the woman had never, in fact, been caught, she had been careful and had outlived the husband to whom she had been unfaithful. That she had merely dreamed of and feared being sent home by him or kept apart, never touched.

The next time, she thought, if she found herself seated beside the novelist she would slip in one of these details. She understood perfectly why the idea excited her so much. As Henry James stood up from the table, it gave her a strange sense of satisfaction that she had lodged her secret with him, a secret over-wrapped perhaps, but at least the rudiments of its shape apparent, if not to him then to her, for whom these matters were pressing, urgent and gave meaning to her life. That she had kept the secret and told a small bit of it all at the same time made her feel light as she went to join the ladies for some conversation. It had been, on the whole, she thought, an unexpectedly interesting evening.

The Empty Family

I have come back here. I can look out and see the soft sky and the faint line of the horizon and the way the light changes over the sea. It is threatening rain. I can sit on this old high chair that I had shipped from a junk store on Market Street and watch the calmness of the sea against the misting sky.

I have come back here. In all the years, I made sure that the electricity bill was paid and the phone remained connected and the place was cleaned and dusted. And the neighbour who took care of things, Rita's daughter, opened the house for the postman or the courier when I sent books or paintings or photographs I had bought, sometimes by FedEx as though it were urgent that they would arrive since I could not.

Since I would not.

This space I walk in now has been my dream space; the mild sound of the wind on days like this has been my dream sound.

You must know that I am back here.

The mountain bike that came free with the washing machine just needed the tyres pumped. Unlike the washing machine itself, it worked as though I had never been away. I could make the slow dream journey into the village, down the hill towards the sand quarry and then past the ball alley with all the new caravans and mobile homes in the distance.

At the end of that journey I met your sister-in-law on a Sunday morning. She must have told you. We were both studying the massive array of Sunday newspapers in the supermarket in the village, wondering which of them to buy. She turned and our eyes locked. I had not seen her for years; I did not even know that she and Bill still had the house. Bill must have told you I am here.

Or maybe not yet.

Maybe he has not seen you. Maybe he does not tell you every bit of news as soon as he knows it. But soon, soon, Bill and you must speak and he will tell you then, maybe just as an afterthought, a curiosity, or maybe even as a fresh piece of news. Guess who I saw? Guess who has come back?

I told your sister-in-law that I had come back.

Later, when I went down to the strand, using the old path, the old way down, when I was wondering if I would swim, or if the water would be too cold, I saw them coming towards me. They were wearing beautiful clothes. Your sister-in-law has aged, but Bill was spry, almost youthful. I shook hands with him. And there was nothing else to say except the usual, what you often say down here: you look out at the sea and say that no one ever comes here, you say how empty it is, and how lovely it is to be here on a bright and blustery June day with no one else in sight, despite all the tourism and the new houses and the money that came and went. This stretch of strand has remained a secret.

In strange, odd moments I have come here over all the years. I have imagined this encounter and the sounds we make against the sound of the wind and the waves.

And then Bill told me about the telescope. Surely, he said, I must have bought one in the States? They are cheaper there, much cheaper. He told me about the room he had built with the Velux window and the view it had and how he had nothing there except a chair and a telescope.

Years ago, as you know, I had shown them this house, and I knew that he remembered this room, the tiny room full of shifting light, like something on a ship, where I am sitting now. I had cheap binoculars to watch the ferry from Rosslare and the lighthouse and the odd sailing boat. I cannot find them now, although I looked as soon as I came back. But I always thought a telescope would be too unwieldy, too hard to use and work. But Bill told me no, his was simple.

He said that I should stop by and check for myself, anytime, but they would be there all day. Your sister-in-law looked at me warily, as though I would be needing her for something again as I needed her all those years ago, as though I would come calling in the night once more. I hesitated.

"Come and have a drink with us," she said. I knew that she meant next week, or some week; I knew that she wanted to sound distant.

I said no, but I would come and see the telescope, just for a second if that was all right, maybe later, just the telescope. I was interested in the telescope and did not care whether she wanted me to come that day or some other day. We parted and I walked on north, towards Knocknasillogue, and they made their way to the gap. I did not swim that day. Enough had happened. That meeting was enough.

Later, it became totally calm, as it often does. As the sun shone its dying slanted rays into the back windows of the house I thought that I would walk down and see the telescope.

She had the fire lighting, and I remember that she had said their son would be there, I cannot remember his name, but I was shocked when he stood up in the long open-plan room with windows on two sides that gave on to the sea. I had not seen him since he was a little boy. In a certain light he could have been you, or you when I knew you first, the same hair, the same height and frame and the same charm that must have been there in your grandmother or grandfather or even before, the sweet smile, the concentrated gaze.

I moved away from them and went with Bill, who had been standing uneasily waiting for me, to the small stairs, and then down towards the room with the telescope.

I hate being shown how to do things, you know that. Wiring a plug, or starting a rented car, or understanding a new mobile phone, add years to me, bring out frustration and an almost frantic urge to get away and curl up on my own. Now I was in a confined space being shown how to look through a telescope, my hands being guided as Bill showed me how to turn it and lift it and focus it. I was patient with him, I forgot myself for a minute. He focused on the waves far out. And then he stood back.

I knew he wanted me to move the telescope, to focus now on Rosslare Harbour, on Tuskar Rock, on Raven Point, on the strand at Curracloe, agree with him that they could be seen so clearly even in this faded evening light. But what he showed me first had amazed me. The sight of the waves miles out, their dutiful and frenetic solitude, their dull indifference to their fate, made me want to cry out, made me want to ask him if he could leave me alone for some time to take this in. I could hear him breathing behind me. It came to me then that the sea is not a pattern, it is a struggle. Nothing matters against the fact of this. The waves were like people battling out there, full of consciousness and will and destiny and an abiding sense of their own beauty.

I knew as I held my breath and watched that it would be

best not to stay too long. I asked him if he would mind if I looked for one more minute. He smiled as though this was what he had wanted. Unlike you, who has never cared about things, your brother is a man who likes his own property. I turned and moved fast, focusing swiftly on a wave I had selected for no reason. There was whiteness and greyness in it and a sort of blue and green. It was a line. It did not toss, nor did it stay still. It was all movement, all spillage, but it was pure containment as well, utterly focused just as I was watching it. It had an elemental hold; it was something coming towards us as though to save us but it did nothing instead, it withdrew in a shrugging irony, as if to suggest that this is what the world is, and our time in it, all lifted possibility, all complexity and rushing fervour, to end in nothing on a small strand, and go back out to rejoin the empty family from whom we had set out alone with such a burst of brave unknowing energy.

I smiled for a moment before I turned. I could have told him that the wave I had watched was as capable of love as we are in our lives. He would have told your sister-in-law that I had gone slightly bonkers in California and indeed might, in turn, have told you; and you would have smiled softly and tolerantly as though there was nothing wrong with that. You had, after all, gone bonkers yourself in your own time. Or maybe you have calmed down since I left you; maybe the passing years have helped your sanity.

On Saturdays before I came back, through the winter and right into early June, I would drive out from the city to Point Reyes, my GPS with its Australian accent instructing me which way to turn, which lanes I should be in, how many

miles were left. They knew me by now in the Station, as the
GPS called it, in the cheese shop there, where I also bought
bread and eggs, in the bookshop, where I bought books of
poems by Robert Hass and Louise Glück, and one day found
William Gass's book *On Being Blue,* which I also bought. I
bought the week's fruit and then, when the weather grew
warm, sat outside the post office eating barbecued oysters
that a family of Mexicans had cooked on a stall beside the
supermarket.

All this was mere preparation for the drive to the South
Beach and the lighthouse. It was like driving towards here,
where I am now. Always, you make a single turn and you know
that you are approaching one of the ends of the earth. It has the
same desolate aura as a poet's last few poems, or Beethoven's
last quartets, or the last songs that Schubert managed. The air
is different, and the way things grow is strained and gnarled
and windblown. The horizon is whiteness, blankness; there are
hardly any houses. You are moving towards a border between
the land and sea that does not have hospitable beaches, or guest-
houses painted in welcoming stripes, or merry-go-rounds, or
ice-cream for sale, but instead has warnings of danger, steep
cliffs.

At Point Reyes there was a long beach and some dunes and
then the passionate and merciless sea, too rough and unpredict-
able for surfers or swimmers or even paddlers. The warnings
told you not to walk too close, that a wave could come from
nowhere with a powerful undertow. There were no lifeguards.
This was the Pacific Ocean at its most relentless and stark,
and I stood there Saturday after Saturday, putting up with the
wind, moving as carefully as I could on the edges of the shore,
watching each wave crash towards me and dissolve in a slurp
of undertow.

I missed home.

I missed home. I went out to Point Reyes every Saturday so I could miss home.

Home was this empty house back from the cliff at Ballyconnigar, a house half full of objects in their packages, small paintings and drawings from the Bay Area, a Vija Celmins print, some photographs of bridges and water, some easy chairs, some patterned rugs. Home was a roomful of books at the back of this house, two bedrooms and bathrooms around it. Home was a huge high room at the front with a concrete floor and a massive fireplace, a sofa, two tables, some paintings still resting against the walls, including the Mary Lohan painting I bought in Dublin and other pieces I bought years ago waiting for hooks and string. Home also was this room at the top of the house, cut into the roof, a room with a glass door opening onto a tiny balcony where I can stand on a clear night and look up at the stars and see the lights of Rosslare Harbour and the single flashes of Tuskar Rock Lighthouse and the faint, comforting line where the night sky becomes the dark sea.

I did not know that those solitary trips to Point Reyes in January, February, March, April, May, and the return with a car laden down with provisions as though there were shortages in San Francisco, I did not know that this was a way of telling myself that I was going home to my own forgiving sea, a softer, more domesticated beach, and my own lighthouse, less dramatic and less long-suffering.

I had kept home out of my mind because home was not merely this house I am in now or this landscape of endings. On some of those days as I drove towards the lighthouse at Point Reyes I had to face what home also was. I had picked up some stones and put them on the front passenger seat and I thought that I might take them to Ireland.

Home was some graves where my dead lay outside the town of Enniscorthy, just off the Dublin Road. This was a place where I could direct no parcels or paintings, no signed lithographs encased in bubble wrap, with the address of the sender on the reverse side of the package. Nothing like that would be of any use. This home filled my dreams and my waking time more than any other version of home. I dreamed that I would leave a stone on each of those graves, as Jewish people do, as Catholics leave flowers. I smiled at the thought that in the future some archaeologist would come to those graves and study the bones and the earth around them and write a paper on the presence of these stray stones, stones that had been washed by the waves of the Pacific, and the archaeologist would speculate what madness, what motives, what tender needs, caused someone to haul them so far.

Home was also two houses that they left me when they died and that I sold at the very height of the boom in this small strange country when prices rose as though they were Icarus, the son of Daedalus, warned by his father not to fly too close to the sun or too close to the sea, Icarus who ignored the warning and whose wings were melted by the sun's bright heat. The proceeds from those two houses have left me free, as though the word means anything, so that no matter how long I live I will not have to work again. And maybe I will not have to worry either, although that now sounds like a sour joke but one that maybe I can laugh at too as days go by.

I will join them in one of those graves. There is space left for me. One of these days I will go and stand in that grave-yard and contemplate the light over the Slaney, the simple beauty of grey Irish light over water, and know that I, like anyone else who was born, will be condemned eventually to lie in darkness as long as time lasts. And all I have in the meantime is this house, this light, this freedom, and I will, if I have the courage, spend my time watching the sea, noting its changes and the sounds it makes, studying the horizon, listening to the wind or relishing the calm when there is no wind. I will not fly even in my deepest dreams too close to the sun or too close to the sea. The chance for all that has passed.

I wish I knew how colours came to be made. Some days when I was teaching I looked out the window and thought that everything I was saying was easy to find out and had already been surmised. But there is a small oblong stone that I have carried up from the strand and I am looking at it now after a night of thunder and a day of grey skies over the sea. It is the early morning here in a house where the phone does not ring and the only post that comes brings bills.

I noticed the stone because of the subtlety of its colour against the sand, its light green with veins of white. Of all the stones I saw it seemed to carry most the message that it had been washed by the waves, its colour dissolved by water, yet all the more alive for that, as though the battle between colour and salt water had offered it a mute strength.

I have it on the desk here now. Surely the sea should be strong enough to get all the stones and make them white, or make them uniform, as the grains of sand are uniform? I do not know how the stones withstand the sea. As I walked yesterday in the humid late afternoon the waves came gently to rattle the stones at the shore, stones larger than pebbles, all different colours. I can turn this green stone around, the one that I carried home, and see that at one end it is less than smooth as though this is a join, a break, and it was once part of a larger mass.

I do not know how long it would have lasted down there, had I not rescued it; I have no idea what the life span is of a stone on a Wexford beach. I know what books George Eliot was reading in 1876, and what letters she was writing and what sentences she was composing, and maybe that is enough for me to know. The rest is science and I do not do science. It is possible then that I miss the point of most things—the mild windlessness of the day, the swallows' flight, how these words appear on the screen as I enter them, the greenness of the stone.

Soon I will have to decide. I will have to call the car hire company at Dublin Airport and extend the time I am going to keep the car. Or I will have to drop the car back. Maybe get another car. Or return here with no car, just the mountain bike and some phone numbers for taxis. Or leave altogether. Late last night when the thunder had died down and there was no sound, I went online to look for telescopes, looking at prices, trying to find the one that Bill had shown me, which I found so easy to manipulate. I studied the length of time delivery would take and thought of waiting for this new key to the distant waves for a week or two weeks or six weeks, watching out from my dream house for a new dream to be delivered, for a van to come up this lane with a large package. I dreamed of setting it up out here in front of where I am sitting now, on the tripod that I would have ordered too, and starting, taking my time, to focus on a curling line of water, a piece of the world indifferent to the fact that there is language, that there are names to describe things, and grammar and verbs. My eye, solitary, filled with its own history, is desperate to evade, erase, forget; it is watching now, watching fiercely, like a scientist looking for a cure, deciding for some days to forget about words, to know at last that the words for colours, the blue-grey-green of the sea, the whiteness of the waves, will not work against the fullness of watching the rich chaos they yield and carry.

Two Women

As the taxi driver failed to notice that the lights had changed and seemed locked in a dull dream of his own, Frances wondered if it would be too rude to alert him, tell him he should move, get going. There was no car behind them to sound the horn impatiently; Dublin at six in the morning was a grey, empty place; it was the city she remembered and began to recognize once they had driven along the almost comically short motorway and were on the Upper Drumcondra Road.

What surprised her now was the speed with which she had resolved, on arrival at Dublin Airport, that she would never come here again, that this would be her last visit. The previous evening at JFK, on the other hand, she had found herself longing for Ireland, chatting with an Irish family as she waited to board; the idea that they were her people and that she was among them again had filled her with warmth. But now, as she was driven across the city towards her hotel, she felt that she was travelling through alien territory, low, miserable and grim. As long as she was open to such mood swings, she thought, then she must not be old.

It was important to behave briskly in the hotel lobby, keep an eye on all her bags and set her jaw firmly as though she were about to make a difficult decision. She had paid for the night before in case they would not have her room ready and she reminded the receptionist of this as the young woman fumbled with the keyboard of the computer, unable to find her reservation.

She pointed to the sheet of paper on the counter.

"Rossiter, Frances," she said. "The name is Rossiter. Look under R."

As the woman glanced up at her, Frances knew how intimidating she could be, and she made no effort to hide the hard impatience for which she was known by those who had worked with her over the years.

The receptionist finally found the booking and handed her a card to fill out, which she did quickly, almost perfunctorily.

"Do you have luggage to take to your room?"

"Yes, it's here. Can it be brought up immediately?"

She kept close to her the large briefcase full of her drawings and specifications and made sure that she carried this herself. And once she was installed in the room she knew what to do—a quick shower to wash the grime of the night's flying from her, fresh clothes left out on the chair beside the bed, and then darkness, lying there pretending that she was young and it had merely been a long night out somewhere and she had fallen home at dawn. In five or six hours she would be ready for a new day and her first meeting.

At one o'clock, when Gabi, the young woman who was to be her assistant, called from the lobby, she was dressed and had made out a list of the things they would need to discuss. Having told Gabi to come up, she moved the tray of half-eaten food from the sitting-room table of her suite and placed it outside the door. She checked herself in the mirror knowing that Gabi would, in all likelihood, never before in her life have worked with a woman almost precisely halfway between seventy-five and eighty. Since she was old, she thought, it was her duty to look busy and bright.

Once Gabi arrived in her room it struck her that the scene being enacted was directly from a script. Gabi was fascinated by the size of the suite, the view over the Green, and then told her how much she admired her work and how many people in Dublin envied her for getting the job as assistant to such a famous designer.

"I am not a designer," Frances said. "I dress sets. Now we have to concentrate because we have problems."

"I just didn't think they had suites this big," Gabi said. "Do you always get a suite?"

"I always get down to work as soon as I meet anyone. That's what I always do."

"I know," Gabi said. "I checked you out."

The director wanted certain colours but he could easily change his mind, she told Gabi, as the film was being shot. Some of his ideas, she was sure, would not work. And what she needed to do now was to make clear to Gabi how quickly they would have to move were the director to want something else, and to find out how hard this might be in a small country where films of this scope and ambition were seldom made.

"The studio will have most things," Gabi said. "It's not bad."

"Not bad is no use. We'll have to go there as soon as I have spoken to a few more people and find out for ourselves. Can you drive?"

"No."

"The studio must have a driver it uses. Tell him to call for me tomorrow at ten. And phone the people at the studio in advance and tell them I'm coming. I'll need the person who actually controls the place, I have his name somewhere, for about two hours. You be there before me. And tell them no reception committee."

"Just down to work?" Gabi smiled at her almost mockingly.

"No tea, for example," she replied. "Or coffee or anything like that."

"And toilet breaks?"

"I hate people going to the toilet," Frances replied. They both laughed.

What worried her most was the scene in the pub that the director wanted. The director used to be young—she smiled at the thought as she opened the set of drawings she had carried with her—but now he was no longer young. But he was not old enough to know that you got nothing extra from using a real pub, no matter how quaint and full of atmosphere, instead of a studio-built pub. A set, she knew, just needed a few spare props that suggested something; with a real pub you would have to spend hours removing objects that suggested too much, and painting over colours that seemed faded to the eye but would jar once bright lights and a camera were shone on them.

She had never once argued with a director, and would not argue now. She would listen, take notes, think carefully and arrange as much as she could in advance, then she would get down to work, and when it was ready she would stand out of the way to allow the real work to happen. By the time the film was made, most people would have almost forgotten who she was; she could linger in the shadows at the final party, having made one or two friends, and maybe three or four enemies.

Besides her career, nothing interested her now except her own house and her own mind. She had no interest in cities; even Dublin, where she had been brought up, seemed a miasma of disconnected shapes and figures with which she had no involvement. She would see her niece Betty, now already a middle-aged woman, in Killiney on one of her last days here, and maybe her niece's grandchildren, and this would be a sweet time because they had no emotional pull on her and had enough money and would want nothing from her.

She had, in any case, told her niece years before what would happen to her money and her house in Los Angeles when she died. Betty had seemed almost relieved. She had appeared genuine in her approval of the plan.

Frances called them her neighbours now, but they were not her neighbours, they were the family who looked after her and lived in a cottage in her garden that had been, at her expense, extended many times.

Ito had been the driver she had used when she worked for one of the studios. She had liked his manner, his ability to be silent and never complain about late hours or time kept waiting, but also his intelligence, his good looks and his kindness. A few times, when he found that she was living on junk food, he had stopped the car at the places that he thought were best but had never once offered to take her to the apartment he shared with his wife, his mother and his daughters, for the suppers that his wife cooked. She had appreciated that. She knew that he came from Guatemala, but beyond that and his immediate circumstances she learned nothing. She never asked, and they often spent hours in the car together without speaking. He never once asked her a single question about herself and she appreciated that too.

It was when her tenant was leaving the cottage and she knew that she would soon be working in England that she had asked Ito one evening to come with her and look at the small property. It had only two bedrooms but she guessed that it was bigger and better equipped than the apartment where he lived with his family. He walked around the rooms and came into the living room and smiled at her and shrugged.

"Nice," he said.

"Is it better than where you live?" she asked.

He did not reply, and she took this to mean that it was much better indeed.

"You can have it for nothing," she said.

"Why?"

"Because I need someone to cut the grass and paint the fence and maybe grow some flowers, and check my house is not broken into while I'm away."

"Nothing else?"

"Nothing else."

Slowly, however, when she discovered that Ito's wife, Rosario, was as reticent and quietly smart as her husband, she found more things for them to do. They had gradually taken on the role of part-time housekeeper and part-time driver while Frances paid for their daughters' school and made the cottage as comfortable as they wanted it, adding on two small rooms. She had also managed to get them documents and then finally paid what it cost to get them citizenship.

They liked it, she believed, when she gave parties in the house, or when she had visitors to stay. It allowed them a glimpse of her when she was not working, an involvement in her real life that was otherwise denied them, just as they denied her any part in their domestic and intimate lives. Over years, she learned little more about them than she already knew, but she grew used to their tactful friendship and found evidence, sometimes at the most unlikely moments, that they trusted her and felt affection for her, and maybe, she thought, as she grew older, they came to worry about her.

Their daughters were grown up now, and on Sundays the

house and the garden were full of the sounds of their grandchildren, and, as these sounds made her happy and did not disturb her at all, she made clear to them that on such occasions
the garden belonged to them and she would not need anything
at all, and she was careful to refuse any invitation to eat with
them. It was their day with their family and she did not think
they needed an outsider with them, no matter how long they
had all been living in close proximity. In any case, she always
had things to do, even on hot Sundays when she was at home.

When she was away working as she was now, and then came
home, she found the refrigerator full and the bed aired, her
clothes washed and fresh and the garden full of flowers. Ito,
unless he was working for the studio, collected her at the airport. Now that she had more money she paid them more, and
when she made her will she asked Ito and Rosario to come with
her to the lawyer's office along with witnesses to see that she
had left them the entire property, which had grown more valu-
able with the years, and whatever money she had. By that time
there was no one more important in her life and she knew that
there would not be again.

She walked out of the hotel and along Merrion Row and then
down Merrion Street to the National Gallery. She wondered if
looking at the colours of the Irish paintings might give her ideas
for some scenes in the film. As she was checking her bag for her
purse to find the entrance charge she realized that it was free,
that she could walk in, that no one even wanted to inspect her
bag. She remembered from years back that there had been a long
room with two staircases leading out of it and in her mind this
room was straight in front of the entrance hall, but what she
found instead was a set of smaller rooms leading into each other.

The pictures seemed to go from the eighteenth century to the nineteenth and were full of stock scenes of bucolic happiness and figures standing near waterfalls. No wonder these rooms were empty of people, she thought; most of the pictures were not worth a second glance. It was only when she came to the last two rooms that the paintings began to interest her; they were by men with Irish names trying to paint like French painters. All of these artists, she thought, must have left here to get away from the dreary low skies, the dingy city, the bleak landscape, faces locked in northern misery. Her director, the man for whom she was working now, had got away too, she surmised. He was interested in Ireland only as a subject, but the colours he wanted, the backgrounds, his customary way of turning the camera and editing film, were pure Italian when they were not French.

She moved from painting to painting, especially the ones that depicted Irish scenes, studying the composition and the colour, which were French in style, and it made her remember her meetings in Los Angeles and New York with the director and caused her to wonder if she should not rethink the background colours she had chosen for certain scenes, have them bolder, wash any sense of Ireland out of them, so that the film might look more beautiful and much stronger. If she did it once, she would have to do it all the time, she realized. And then she thought no, it could be done using colours directly from some of these pictures, in a few key scenes, leaving the rest of the film starker. It would be a risk, but the director had told her that he wanted something stylish, and that his budget was high enough to pay for it and low enough not to need to make something for a mass audience.

She would come back later with a notebook, and now, as she began to examine French scenes painted by Irish painters, she took in the happy tone of some of the compositions and the sheer beauty of the colours and she smiled to herself at the idea of how relieved they must have been on spring mornings and summer days when there was no drizzle or dark clouds approaching, or shifts in the light every two seconds. It made her wish to be back now in her own house in California, but glad she had been brought up in this country for long enough to appreciate being so far away from it.

In one of the earlier rooms as she stopped in front of one of the paintings she had glanced at a uniformed porter sitting on a chair. When he had greeted her, she had returned the greeting briefly. He was a man in his early sixties, thin-faced, grey-haired, with bright eyes; he seemed happy in his job. Now, as she prepared to leave the gallery, she noticed him bustling by her, finding a colleague who was in the room adjoining the room where the Irish paintings done in France were hanging.

She took in through the doorway the encounter between the two porters while pretending to study a painting closely. She was not able to hear what they were saying, but she could watch as the porter who had greeted her told the other porter something and the man listened with an absolute curiosity and a sort of glee. At times both men laughed even though the story, whatever it was, had still not ended. Some of it seemed unbearably funny to both of them, but then they became serious again as the man who was talking whispered the last part even though there was no one nearby. Finally, they stared at each other in mock wonder and surprise.

They were too wrapped up in their exchange to notice that she had been watching them, and as the porter walked past her to return to his post, she averted her eyes and looked at the painting once more. What had come back to her suddenly was the single time in her life when she had been in love. The first porter's face did not in any way resemble Luke Freaney's face, which was much narrower. Luke was also a few inches smaller. His features were more irregular. But it was the lightness in the walk, and the way of speaking as though the slightest remark were a way of taking you into his confidence, the constant laughter and then the face, so vivid to her now as she remembered it, slowly becoming serious. All of it belonged to Luke. Perhaps, she thought, it was Irish, but he had brought it to a fine art and used it as a mask and made it into pure charm, something warm and loving, at the same time.

And now she had seen it again, enacted by a porter in the National Gallery, not having seen it for thirty years, having believed it was something that had belonged to Luke alone. He was dead for more than a decade. She had trained herself in the early years of losing him not to miss him or give him a thought. On this and other visits to Dublin since his death, she had kept him out of her mind. But she had not bargained for what she had just seen, the core of his personality, what she remembered most about him, appearing again as a part of life.

She was busy for the rest of the day with meetings and then, since she was too tired to go downstairs, she had her supper in her room and read for a while before falling asleep. In the morning, as arranged, the car took her to the studio; on the way she marked the scenes in the script where she thought she might heighten the colour, but she would make no final decisions on this until she spoke to the director again. She would need, in case he was against the idea, to make sure that the studio could quickly change the previous plans, but she believed that if she saw the director on his own and was absolutely clear about what she had in mind, then he would not be opposed to what she would suggest.

She had not dreamed in the night and had woken fresh, ready for work, so it was only now in the car as a drizzle settled over south Dublin and the strong coffee she had taken over breakfast started to kick in that the scene in the National Gallery came into her thoughts again. She had been with Luke for twelve years, but she had never lived with him. They had mostly met in New York, or London, or Paris. And his way of greeting her, or of seeing her to a taxi, almost tearful in the amount of tenderness he could offer, stood in for the domestic life they never had together.

When he was not talking about his work—and she had loved these discussions with him, had loved his earnestness about the roles he played and how he prepared for them—then he was busy making her laugh. When they met, they drank and stayed up late, but she knew there was another side to him, that he was disciplined, a rigid timekeeper, that he was deeply committed to his life in the theatre, but oddly tolerant of directors and writers and other actors, as long as they had something he could work with, even if it was something that irritated him, or that he found difficult. He was, she knew, the best comic actor of his generation, and if he had been luckier, and maybe if he had not been Irish, she thought, he could have been better again, he could have played more serious parts. Somehow, the gap between the two—his immense talent and his sense that it would come to nothing except playing clowns and fools—had eaten away at him, and at her too, as the years went on, no matter how much he tried to play the hero for her in their time together, the time they snatched between jobs.

A few times he came to Hollywood to act in Irish films and in a small part as an Irish-American barman, and these visits might have appeared to other people, she thought, like the happiest times for her and for Luke. But they were not the happiest times, despite the parties and all the hours they could be with each other. How he worked affected Luke, as though work were a season and bit parts were a harsh winter, just as anything by Eugene O'Neill or Sean O'Casey would always belong to high glorious summer. She saw how easily he could become despondent and how hard it was for him not to show contempt when he felt it.

Their happiest times, she thought, were spent alone in the dark with each other. His body was much stronger than it seemed. Sex excited him, or maybe it was she who excited him. There were nights in hotel rooms, nights when he had had a few drinks after a performance, nights when his own deep confidence in himself and a tender strength, things he kept mostly hidden, things he folded away wrapped in cynicism and self-mockery, were not afraid to appear. This was when she had loved him most.

He was the sort of man, she thought, that women might wish to reform or mother. But she had wanted none of this. She had her own needs; she never once, for example, let him get in the way of her work. This made their meetings all the more intense, but chaotic too, and there were years when her phone bill was almost higher than her tax bill and certainly higher than the money she spent on food. As Luke approached each new performance, he needed to talk to her, to tell her about it in detail, and she loved his voice and his seriousness and then the jokes he told. She never minded that it was often the middle of the night when she put the phone down. At the end of these long calls he left her smiling.

She was smiling now at the memory of this as the car pulled up outside the studio.

"How long will you be?" the driver asked her.

"I don't know," she replied as she gathered her papers.

"I mean, will I come back for you, or will I wait?"

"You will wait," she said.

As always, she needed to identify someone among the team with whom she could work. It could be someone young or old, who spoke early in the meeting or who remained silent throughout, who nodded when she emphasized a point or who seemed to resist every idea she had. She would know him—it was usually a male—by an aura of pure, calm competence he gave off. She would watch for the person who appeared to be concentrating most, the one least open to distraction.

She did not speak as she was introduced to the staff.

"Is everyone here?" she asked.

"You mean . . . ?" the studio manager asked.

"I mean everyone who will be working with me. The painters, the builders, the props manager."

"No, some of them are . . ."

"Get them all here. I need to see all of them."

Gabi had made large and more detailed drawings from the outlines she had given her and mounted these on cardboard so that they looked like paintings.

"Can these be copied?" she asked.

"Yes, I have made copies," Gabi replied. "And can make more."

She tapped the table with the index finger of her left hand as Gabi looked on.

"Well?" Gabi asked.

"Well what?"

"Are you not going to say thank you? I was up all night. Did you lose your manners in America?"

The manager and the props manager, who had just arrived, looked at them both, alarmed.

"Yes, I did," she replied. "That's where I lost my manners.

Now, young girl, get me a jug of iced water with plenty of lemon in it."

Gabi stood up and pushed her chair back. She glared at her briefly and then laughed.

"I'll pour iced water over your fucking head," she said and grinned defiantly.

"OK, do that, darling," Frances said, looking down at the drawings as though nothing special had been said. "Now hurry. Your drawings are wonderful and you are a national treasure. Is that enough? Now get the water. And don't forget the lemon. Did you hear? Lemon!"

The morning was easier than she had expected. She liked the woman who was in charge of props and was happy that nobody was too visibly disturbed when she explained to them that she had two different looks in mind for some scenes of the film and they would have to be ready to go with whichever one the director wanted.

On the way back into the city with Gabi she could sense the driver's resentment, which now bordered on rudeness. In the back of the car, she pointed her finger towards his back and indicated to Gabi by running her finger across her throat that he would have to go. Gabi shook her head in mock rebuke.

"What are we going to do about you?" Gabi asked.

In the days that followed she often had time to spare. When she went back to the National Gallery, she found the high-ceilinged room with the two staircases she remembered, and wandered around in the upper rooms before looking again at the colours in the Irish paintings in the room on the ground floor. She did not see the porter whom she had watched on her first visit. She phoned her niece and they arranged to spend a day together when her work on the film was finished.

The director, with whom she had a progress meeting one day in the lounge of the hotel, looked more like an actor, she thought, oddly baby-faced but with a strange brutality about him. He seemed even more distracted this time than when she had seen him in Los Angeles and New York, but distracted by his own dreams rather than the film he was about to shoot. It was only when she told him about the colours that she had in mind, emphasizing that some of them would be almost garish, that he grew attentive. He looked at her and nodded, but said nothing; suddenly, she saw, he had become interested in her.

"But you're really Irish, aren't you?" he asked.

"Yes," she said. "I worked in the Abbey before you were born."

"Do you like being back here?"

His smile was almost cruel.

"No," she said and looked at him steadily.

Luke lost interest in her and that at the time was a shock. He still needed to talk to her, tell her what he was doing, or what work he was turning down, but when they met it was clear to her, once they were in the dark, that he did not want to make love any more. She sighed now at the thought that it had never occurred to her that as she grew older he would be happier to sleep close to her on the nights when they managed to be together, embrace her and sleep beside but not make love with her. And that he would also, on the nights when he was tense from working, be happier to stay in the bar with anyone at all rather than come to bed with her.

*   *   *

She had not asked the director if he really wanted the pub in Wicklow used in the film; if he had changed his mind about it someone would have told her. But when she went to see it with Gabi she realized how hard it was going to be, so much would have to be removed, and there was so little space, and the owner, although he was being well paid, was grumpy and appeared uneasy in the presence of two women walking around discussing which pictures would have to be taken down, and how an entire wall would have to be painted.

"It would be so simple to build this," Gabi said in a loud voice. "Wouldn't it?"

"Why don't you then?" the owner asked. He seemed wounded and then belligerent.

"It's a lovely place," Gabi said as Frances went to the window, ignoring both of them. "I've always heard about it but never been here. I just hope we're not going to get in your way too much."

He did not reply at first and then asked if they would like a drink.

"Not today," Gabi said.

"On the house," he said as Frances turned around.

They agreed to have a glass of beer each and sat near the window away from the owner until Gabi had to make a phone call and Frances was left with him as he moved up and down behind the bar like an animal long used to its cage. They did not speak. She was happy somehow when she had established for herself that there was nothing in him that reminded her in any way of Luke, that she was not going to go through Ireland finding middle-aged men who had something of Luke in them.

But the end of their time together, how they both behaved, came to her now in this dimly lit space full of dust and old picture frames and faded paintwork; her feelings about what happened were tinged with regret, but not too much, more the sadness that it was all so long ago and that he was dead more than ten years and that she never saw him again after one night when he had not come back to the hotel room with her, but had stayed in the bar.

She remembered that when she woke in the morning all those years before, she had realized that he had slept elsewhere, or not at all. And they had not made love for the first two nights of her visit, and this was her third night and there were two more left. She decided that if he had not returned by eleven o'clock that morning, she would check out and go back home and that she would not see him again.

She remembered that she calmly watched the clock moving and began packing at ten and preparing to go, leaving his clothes strewn on the floor and his things in the bathroom. The room was booked in his name; he could, she thought, also pay the bill. It was a decision that, in its clarity and resolution, almost gave her pleasure, or perhaps it was pain, but she did not allow herself to feel pain, then or afterwards. She carried her bags to the lift at five past eleven and handed the key in at the desk, saying that her husband would be back soon but she must leave. And then she got a taxi to the airport and waited until there was a free seat on a plane home to the West Coast.

"Why are you smiling?" Gabi asked. "You look like someone in love."

Frances sighed.

"Dressing this pub for the film is going to be tough work," she said.

When the phone rang night after night, she knew it was Luke but she did not answer. Each time she thought it might be him, she let the phone ring out and then took the receiver off the hook. She knew that he also rang Ito and Rosario but they were careful to say very little. And then she was busy with a film in Brazil and then had work in the studios. She did not go to New York or London or Dublin for a long time. He never wrote, but if he had written, she would not have opened a letter from him.

She could not help following his career, however, because his Con in *A Touch of the Poet* won him a Tony nomination and his one-man show based on Eugene O'Neill's father won him all the awards in both New York and London. She could not have avoided either the news of his wedding to a woman who had been an actress, Rachael Swift. They looked happy in the wedding photograph published in the gossip magazines. She was blonde, it was hard to tell what age she was. She told a reporter that now that she and Luke were married, she hoped never to leave his side.

The only time in all the years when Frances felt regret over what had happened and wished she had kept in touch with him was when she heard the news that he had died. She would have liked to have been with him when he was sick, she thought. She knew that, no matter how happily married he had been, with her he had something he would not have forgotten, especially if he had had time to think about things at the end of his life. He would have thought of her, as she would of him. She would have liked to have touched his dead body, or maybe been at his funeral, but she was not sure.

But it might have been easier, she thought, to have regretted nothing at all, except that certain things are inevitable, including the fact that he grew tired of her. It was all a long time ago, she thought, brought back into her mind by two porters in the National Gallery and the shifting clouds in the Irish sky.

* * *

She did not have much time in the days that followed to think about anything except the film. She got up with the dawn and left nothing to chance; she worried about the lighting camera-man, who was too ambitious, too ready to establish his own style. Maybe she had made some of the sets look too ordinary, she thought, taken no risks with them. This man was all risk and brilliance, and she admired his daring but wished she had worked with him before so that she could know whether he got results only from sets that were as interesting in themselves as the sort of light he cast on them. He avoided her and she wondered if this was because of her reputation for being difficult or if he simply had no interest at all in consulting with her or asking her to make changes in what she was doing.

Slowly, she became anxious to leave. The lowness of the buildings in Dublin, shops that were cheap imitations of larger and better stores in bigger cities, ways of dressing that were either shabby or pretentious, and ways of moving in the street that lacked alertness or any style, all began to irritate her. At the weekend, especially on Fridays, the hotel lobby and the bars filled up with drinkers, and once or twice, having pushed her way through a crowd of half-drunken men and women, she was proud of having lived most of her life away from such people and glad that the staff of the hotel, unfailingly polite and self-effacing, came from elsewhere.

It struck her that she really would not come back, that she would work in future anywhere but here. Even Gabi's efficiency and sweetness seemed complacent to her, and some of the men moving sets were too slow, almost openly lazy. She found it difficult, especially in the third and fourth weeks of filming, not to show her impatience. She loved intelligent, decisive people who did things briskly, and on a few occasions when she had to phone home and found herself speaking down the line to Rosario, she realized how much she missed Rosario's intelligence, almost exquisite at times in its depth of perception, and her way of moving, so elegant and careful and poised.

They had learned over time to read each other's mind. Rosario was better, she thought, at reading hers, but Frances, too, was able to catch in a gesture, or a moment's hesitation, something that Rosario wished to communicate. In all the years, she had been ill only once, and that was two years earlier. It was a virus of some kind and, at its most severe, it had lasted a day and a night and a day. When she was feverish and helpless, Rosario seemed to be always in the room with her. She felt that she was watched over. The sheets and pillowcases were changed every few hours.

Frances remembered vigorously resisting the idea of going to a hospital. But even when she could sit up, she was too weak to do much and had no appetite. Rosario fed her and stayed with her and then left her alone to sleep when she thought that she could.

Once in those days Rosario had asked her if there was someone in Ireland she wished to contact. Frances shook her head; there was nobody. Rosario smiled and continued putting sheets into the laundry basket as though none of this mattered. Frances had not wanted her niece to be alarmed about her, or to hint in any way that her niece should travel to Los Angeles and oversee her care. It was best, she thought, not to get in touch with her at all unless she became much worse, or if it was clear that she was dying.

In those days she realized what was on Rosario's mind. Since Ito and Rosario had seen the will, they knew that she had not mentioned anything about a grave, or what should happen to her body after her death. This was partly why she loved America, its lack of interest in death; no one she worked with ever bothered about where they would be buried; so many of her friends and colleagues would be happy, she knew, to have their ashes scattered somewhere, or have their body buried in whatever cemetery was closest. But Ito and Rosario cared deeply for the dead; they had been grateful when she had paid for Ito's mother's coffin to be flown back to Guatemala, but had she not done so they would have raised the money themselves. When they went home every few years they made sure to visit the graves.

As she recovered from her illness Frances knew that Rosario wanted her to say where she wished to be buried. She realized that she would have to be fair to them, she was not their family and no matter how much money she was bequeathing them she could not leave them with no one in Ireland to contact and all the responsibility for disposing of her corpse.

She knew, from the conversations with Rosario in the immediate aftermath of Ito's mother's death, that Ito and Rosario did not believe in cremation, they believed that the dead should be beautifully dressed, laid out in an open coffin for a day or two and then buried in sacred ground. And for them sacred ground was Guatemala, just as she knew they presumed, without them ever saying so, that for her sacred ground was Ireland.

The pub in Wicklow remained a problem and, as the filming progressed, she worried about it a great deal. There was an intensity in the way the lighting cameraman was working that she admired; he was framing shots in which every detail had to be right, and thus she was careful to use detail sparingly but make it stand for a lot. Slowly, she saw that the film was acquiring a look, a coherence not only in how the story was unfolding and the actors performing, but something more subtle and unusual and remarkable that could be punctured easily and flattened; one scene badly shot or just competently filmed could make all the rest seem artificial, striving for effect rather than achieving it. How the film was being lit surprised her and she had to work fast and make changes in all her plans to match the lighting cameraman's interest in finding a sort of purity in his shots. The director watched this, she thought, with an air of detachment that only barely masked a concern that they were pushing the style too far but also a real satisfaction at how beautiful his film might look.

A few times she thought to approach him to suggest that they might scrap the idea of using a real pub and assemble a much more manageable space in the studio. She watched the director looking through the camera at each frame and then moving away, talking to no one, brooding over what he had seen, appearing like someone who had not slept, or washed, or combed his hair, or spoken a civil word to anyone for a very long time. The lighting cameraman was working almost in competition with her; each day was a war of nerves between them as she tried to anticipate how he might frame and light. She had no intention of allowing him to find out that she had gone to the director with a problem she could not solve.

She found that the manager of the studio knew the publican, the owner of the bar where they would film. He lived near the bar and was a regular customer. When she asked the manager if he thought she could have one extra day preparing the bar, clearing it of almost everything and then re-creating it so that it could be filmed, he said that he did not think so. The director really wanted it as it was and the owner was proud of how it had been preserved. Because he liked his regular customers and had not much time for outsiders, the owner had agreed to allow the bar to be used in the film only because he knew both the manager and the director. But it was against his better judgement. In the way the manager spoke to her, she felt that the owner of the bar had reported on her visit and had not liked her.

It was clear to her that the pub could not be repainted; the modern beer taps could be hidden or temporarily removed, the pictures taken down and unnecessary bottles and glasses put out of sight, but nothing else. When she returned for one last viewing of the pub before they would dress it for filming, she did not try to ingratiate herself with the owner, who recognized Gabi and herself immediately and then pretended that he did not see them. When they finally got his attention and ordered glasses of beer, he gruffly served them and charged them and handed Frances the change without speaking.

The following day the studio manager told her that she could have the pub from four o'clock on Sunday but filming would begin at eight. When she protested, insisting that she needed more time, he shrugged and told her that he could do anything else she wanted, he could build her a life-size model of the Eiffel Tower or the General Post Office, but four hours' preparation in the pub was as much as she would get. Even then, he said, it had taken persuasion to acquire. She arranged that the studio manager would be present in case there was any difficulty while she dressed the place and that four of his best workers could be at her disposal.

"Lighten up," he said.

"I want everyone there on time," she replied.

"It's just a three-minute sequence," he said.

"Tell them to make sure to bring all their tools. I don't want them driving all over the country because they have forgotten something."

"I'll make sure they have their Kango hammers and everything," he said.

"Yes, you do that."

The director had left this pub sequence until the last week of shooting; some of the less important actors had already departed. The crew, aware that something interesting and special was being made, were ready to do anything to make sure that nothing was spoiled. That Sunday, she had lunch in her hotel room with Gabi as they went through the plans. The director had not been consulted about making the space so sparingly furnished, but it would, Frances thought, take only an hour to change it if he should wish it to be changed. She hoped, however, that he would see the sense of it. As they drove to Wicklow, Frances realized that she had become used to the driver and grown almost to like him, although they had not spoken a civil word to each other in all the time. She realized that Gabi's natural tendency was to speak to everyone but she, nonetheless, refrained from speaking to the driver out of a mixture of loyalty to Frances and fear.

As they arrived early, they waited until the customers began to drink up and go, all of them having been alerted by the owner, using a dry tone, that a film was going to be made in his pub. The props manager and the studio manager appeared and then two assistants, who slowly and meticulously, with the owner's help, began to dismantle the taps and the connections for the draught beer and then carry the parts into a store at the side of the pub. Frances asked the manager if he would take the owner out of the way for a while as she was not sure how he would respond as every single item was removed from two of the walls and every single glass and bottle from behind the bar.

As both men went out, she noticed that there were two drinkers left sitting at a table close to the door, an older woman and a young man, and that they had full drinks, having just been served by the owner before he left in what had seemed like a parting act of defiance. She and the props manager began to unpack boxes. After a while, when she looked over, she saw that Gabi was sitting down talking to this couple and that they looked like a relaxed group of friends in a quiet country pub on a Sunday afternoon. She almost shouted across the room to Gabi to come and help immediately, but waited instead until Gabi came towards her.

"Could you help, please? Or is that too much to ask you?"

"I was saying hello, just saying hello."

For the next while Frances moved between the props and the bar, standing back all the time to study the scene as it changed.

A few times as she walked around the small space she noticed that the couple still had not left, instead were nursing their drinks and observing the scene with interest and amusement as though they were tourists who had hit on a fascinating way to spend an afternoon. When she found Gabi talking to them a second time, she watched from the shadows. The older woman was glamorous, did not look Irish; the young man had an agile face and seemed to be doing most of the talking as the two women laughed at what he said. Since she needed to summon up a fierce concentration for the next two hours, replace some pictures with others, perhaps rethink some ideas, she believed that the scene Gabi was involved in was precisely one that she did not need and would not tolerate. She waited until Gabi stood up and made her way nonchalantly back to her work, unpacking the bottles of Guinness, before she approached her.

"Can I talk to you?" she asked.

Gabi looked at her darkly.

"I'm working. I'm back working."

"Could you ask those people to go? They're a distraction."

"They'll go in a minute. They're friends of mine. Shane is an actor, he knows everyone in the film."

"Could you ask them to go?"

"Don't push this, Frances. They'll go in their own time. They're not in our way."

"Did you ask them here?"

"No, they just happened to be here. Rachael used to come here years ago. She hasn't been here for years."

"Rachael? Who's Rachael?"

"Rachael Swift. She's Luke Freaney's widow."

Frances looked over at the couple; the woman was busy listening to her companion.

"She's his widow," Gabi repeated. "She used to be an actress."

"Did you tell her who I was?" Frances asked.

"She isn't that interested in the film," Gabi said. "She's just finishing her drink."

"Did you tell her my name?"

"No, I didn't. For God's sake, why are you asking?"

Frances went out to the car, where she had left her handbag. She sat on the back seat without speaking to the driver and took out her make-up bag. Slowly, she began to work on her face, putting on some light mascara and some eye-shadow and eye-liner. She had learned years before from one of the greatest make-up artists in Hollywood that the area around the mouth for someone of her age was the most important, to keep the line of the lips defined and to cover wrinkles around the mouth and on the chin. She brushed her hair, and when she was finished she checked herself carefully once more in the hand-mirror. She sighed. There was nothing else she could do. She walked back into the bar and straight over to the table where the couple were sitting.

"Rachael," she said, "I'm Francie."

What she saw when the woman looked up at her was veiled sorrow and then a smile with even more sadness in it than her first look.

"Oh God! I didn't have any idea."

"I know. We never met before, did we?"

"He talked about you," Rachael said and stood up awkwardly to shake her hand. Her accent was English.

"He talked about you," Rachael repeated.

"I didn't know it was you," Frances said, "until Gabi told me just now."

"I thought you lived . . ."

"I do, Rachael. I'm just working here."

"I hope we're not getting in the way."

"Don't worry at all."

"Can you sit down and talk with us for a moment?" Rachael asked.

"I can, of course, Rachael."

Rachael introduced Frances to her companion.

"She was with Luke before me," she said, and once again her smile had a terrible sadness in it, but there was something elegant about her too, almost beautiful.

"This woman was the love of his life," Rachael said to her companion and then smiled again at Frances.

"He was lucky with both of us, wasn't he?" Frances asked.

"He was the love of my life," Rachael said. "I can say that."

In her voice and in her face Frances could see how kind she was, and how good she must have been with him.

"He loved this pub," Rachael continued. "He knew Miley, the owner, for years."

"I never knew that," Frances said. "You know, we were never in Ireland together, never once."

"I did know that. He talked a lot about you, especially when he got sick, but other times too. He was happy out of Ireland. It was just a few funny places he missed."

They looked at each other, but neither spoke now as the noise of the work went on all around them. Frances could say nothing. She knew there was nothing Rachael could say either that would make any difference. The years had passed; it was as simple as that. Luke had been loved and cared for; this woman would have watched over him as he was dying like no one else.

"I'm so glad to have met you," Frances said.

"I was going to write to you when he died, but I wrote to no one, and then it was too late."

"Yes, it's always hard."

"He talked about you. He said that there was no one like you."

"I'm sure, I'm sure."

In the way she glanced down to check where her handbag was, Frances realized that Rachael wanted to go now. She stood up to make it easy for her.

"There's always work to do, isn't there?"

"Yes," Rachael said, "and we must leave you to do it."

As Rachael and her companion were ready to leave, Frances shook hands with her.

"It was wonderful to meet you," Rachael said as they made their way towards the door.

"Yes, it was. It was a big surprise."

When they had gone, she stood with her back to the door for a moment as though guarding the place from intruders.

"What was that about?" Gabi asked her.

"Let's get on with things," she said.

"Have they gone?"

"They have," Frances replied and then moved to the middle of the room to inspect the shelves and the bottles of Guinness in a row.

"Behind the bar needs one more thing," she said to Gabi. "One more thing. Let's think and see if we can work out what it is."

Gabi nodded.

"Why did you put on make-up?" she asked.

"I needed to talk to your friends for a minute, that was all."

"Did you know Rachael?"

"No. I never knew her."

"You seemed all talk, the two of you."

"That's the way it might have seemed all right," Frances said. "That's the way it might have seemed."

One Minus One

The moon hangs low over Texas. The moon is my mother. She is full tonight, and brighter than the brightest neon; there are folds of red in her vast amber. Maybe she is a harvest moon, a Comanche moon. I have never seen a moon so low and so full of her own deep brightness. My mother is six years dead tonight, and Ireland is six hours away and you are asleep.

I am walking. No one else is walking. It is hard to cross Guadalupe; the cars come fast. In the Community Whole Foods Store, where all are welcome, the girl at the checkout asks me if I would like to join the store's club. If I pay seventy dollars, my membership, she says, will never expire, and I will get a 7 per cent discount on my purchases.

Six years. Six hours. Seventy dollars. Seven per cent. I tell her I am here for a few months only, and she smiles and says that I am welcome. I smile back. The atmosphere is easy, casual, gracious.

If I called you now, it would be half two in the morning; I could wake you up. If I called, I could go over everything that happened six years ago. Because that is what is on my mind tonight, as though no time had elapsed, as though the strength of the moonlight had by some fierce magic chosen tonight to carry me back to the last real thing that happened to me. On the phone to you across the Atlantic, I could go over the days surrounding my mother's funeral. I could go over the details

69

as though I were in danger of forgetting them. I could remind you, for example, that you wore a suit and a tie at the funeral. I remember that I could see you when I spoke about her from the altar, that you were over in the side aisle, on the right. I remember that you, or someone, said that you had to get a taxi from Dublin because you missed the train or the bus. I know that I looked for you among the crowd and could not see you as the hearse came after Mass to take my mother's coffin to the graveyard, as all of us began to walk behind it. You came to the hotel once she was in the ground, and you stayed for a meal with me and Sinead, my sister. Jim, her husband, must have been near, and Cathal, my brother, but I don't remember what they did when the meal had finished and the crowd had dispersed. I know that as the meal came to an end a friend of my mother's, who noticed everything, came over and looked at you and whispered to me that it was nice that my friend had come. She used the word "friend" with a sweet, insinuating emphasis. I did not tell her that what she had noticed was no longer there, was part of the past. I just said yes, it was nice that you had come.

You know that you are the only person who shakes his head in exasperation when I insist on making jokes and small talk, when I refuse to be direct. No one else has ever minded this as you do. You are alone in wanting me always to say something that is true. I know now, as I walk towards the house I have rented here, that if I called and told you that the bitter past has come back to me tonight in these alien streets with a force that feels like violence, you would say that you are not surprised. You would wonder only why it has taken six years.

I was living in New York then, the city about to enter its last year of innocence. I had a rented apartment there, just as I had a rented apartment everywhere I went. It was on 90th and

Columbus. You never saw it. It was a mistake. I think it was a mistake. I didn't stay there long—six or seven months—but it was the longest I stayed anywhere in those years or the years that followed. The apartment needed to be furnished, and I spent two or three days taking pleasure in the sharp bite of buying things: two easy chairs that I later sent back to Ireland; a leather sofa from Bloomingdale's, which I eventually gave to one of my students; a big bed from 1-800-Mattress; a table and some chairs from a place downtown; a cheap desk from the thrift shop.

And all those days—a Friday, a Saturday and a Sunday at the beginning of September—as I was busy with delivery times, credit cards and the whiz of taxis from store to store, my mother was dying and no one could find me. I had no mobile phone, and the phone line in the apartment had not been connected. I used the pay phone on the corner if I needed to make calls. I gave the delivery companies a friend's phone number, in case they had to let me know when they would come with my furniture. I phoned my friend a few times a day, and she came shopping with me sometimes and she was fun and I enjoyed those days. The days when no one in Ireland could find me to tell me that my mother was dying.

Eventually, late on the Sunday night, I slipped into a Kinko's and went online and found that Sinead had sent me email after email, starting three days before, marked "Urgent" or "Are you there" or "Please reply" or "Please acknowledge receipt" and then just "Please!!!" I read one of them, and I replied to say that I would call as soon as I could find a phone, and then I read the rest of them one by one. My mother was in the hospital. She might have to have an operation. Sinead wanted to talk to me. She was staying at my mother's house. There was nothing more in any of them, the urgency being not so much in their tone as in their frequency and the different titles she gave to each email that she sent.

I woke her in the night in Ireland. I imagined her standing in the hall at the bottom of the stairs. I would love to say that Sinead told me my mother was asking for me, but she said nothing like that. She spoke instead about the medical details and how she herself had been told the news that our mother was in the hospital and how she had despaired of ever finding me. I told her that I would call again in the morning, and she said that she would know more then. My mother was not in pain now, she said, although she had been. I did not tell her that my classes would begin in three days, because I did not need to. That night, it sounded as though she wanted just to talk to me, to tell me. Nothing more.

But in the morning when I called I realized that she had put quick thought into it as soon as she heard my voice on the phone, that she had known I could not make arrangements to leave for Dublin late on a Sunday night, that there would be no flights until the next evening. She had decided to say nothing until the morning; she had wanted me to have an easy night's sleep. And I did, and in the morning when I phoned she said simply that there would come a moment very soon when the family would have to decide. She spoke about the family as though it were as distant as the urban district council or the government or the United Nations, but she knew and I knew that there were just the three of us. We were the family, and there is only one thing that a family is ever asked to decide in a hospital. I told her that I would come home; I would get the next flight. I would not be in my new apartment for some of the furniture deliverers, and I would not be at the university for my first classes. Instead, I would find a flight to Dublin, and I would see her as soon as

I could. My friend phoned Aer Lingus and discovered that a few seats were kept free for eventualities like this. I could fly out that evening.

You know that I do not believe in God. I do not care much about the mysteries of the universe, unless they come to me in words, or in music maybe, or in a set of colours, and then I entertain them merely for their beauty and only briefly. I do not even believe in Ireland. But you know, too, that in these years of being away there are times when Ireland comes to me in a sudden guise, when I see a hint of something familiar that I want and need. I see someone coming towards me with a soft way of smiling, or a stubborn uneasy face, or a way of moving warily through a public place, or a raw, almost resentful stare into the middle distance. In any case, I went to JFK that evening and I saw them as soon as I got out of the taxi: a middle-aged couple pushing a trolley that had too much luggage on it, the man looking fearful and mild, as though he might be questioned by someone at any moment and not know how to defend himself, and the woman harassed and weary, her clothes too colourful, her heels too high, her mouth set in pure, blind determination, but her eyes humbly watchful, undefiant.

I could without any difficulty have spoken to them and told them why I was going home and they both would have stopped and asked me where I was from, and they would have nodded with understanding when I spoke. Even the young men in the queue to check in, going home for a quick respite—just looking at their tentative stance and standing in their company saying nothing, that brought ease with it. I could breathe for a while without worry, without having to think. I, too, could look like them, as though I owned nothing, or nothing much, and were

73

ready to smile softly or keep my distance without any arrogance if someone said, "Excuse me," or if an official approached.

When I picked up my ticket and went to the check-in desk, I was told to go to the other desk, which looked after business class. It occurred to me, as I took my bag over, that it might be airline policy to comfort those who were going home for reasons such as mine with an upgrade, to cosset them through the night with quiet sympathy and an extra blanket or something. But when I got to the desk I knew why I had been sent there, and I wondered about God and Ireland, because the woman at the desk had seen my name being added to the list and had told the others that she knew me and would like to help me now that I needed help.

Her name was Joan Carey, and she had lived next door to my aunt's house, where myself and Cathal were left when my father got sick. I was eight years old then. Joan must have been ten years older, but I remember her well, as I do her sister and her two brothers, one of whom was close to me in age. Their family owned the house that my aunt lived in, the aunt who took us in. They were grander than she was and much richer, but she had become friendly with them. Since the houses shared a large back garden and some outhouses, there was a lot of traffic between the two establishments.

Cathal was four then, but in his mind he was older. He was learning to read already, he was clever and had a prodigious memory, and was treated as a young boy in our house rather than as a baby; he could decide which clothes to wear each day and what television he wanted to watch and which room he would sit in and what food he would eat. When his friends called at the house, he could freely ask them in, or go out with them.

In all the years that followed, Cathal and I never once spoke

74

about our time in this new house with this new family. And my memory, usually so good, is not always clear. I cannot recall, for example, how we got to the house, who drove us there, or what this person said. I know that I was eight years old only because I remember what class I was in at school when I left and who the teacher was. It is possible that this period lasted just two or three months. Maybe it was more. It was not summer, I am sure of that, because Sinead, who remained unscathed by all of this (or so she said when once, years ago, I asked her about it), was back at boarding school. I have no memory of cold weather in that house in which we were deposited, although I do think that the evenings were dark early. Maybe it was from September to December. Or the first months after Christmas. I am not sure.

What I remember clearly is the rooms themselves, the parlour and dining room almost never used and the kitchen, larger than ours at home, and the smell and taste of fried bread. I hated the hot thick slices, fresh from the pan, soaked in lard or dripping. I remember that our cousins were younger than we were and had to sleep during the day, or at least one of them did, and we had to be quiet for hours on end, even though we had nothing to do; we had none of our toys or books. I remember that nobody listened to us or smiled when they saw us, either of us, not even Cathal, who, before and after this event, was greatly loved and wanted by people who came across him.

We slept in my aunt's house and ate her food as best we could, and we must have played or done something, although we never went to school. Nobody did us any harm in that house; nobody came near us in the night, or hit either of us, or threatened us, or made us afraid. The time we were left by our mother in our aunt's house has no drama attached to it. It was all greyness, strangeness. Our aunt dealt with us in her own distracted

75

way. Her husband was often away or busy; when he was in the house he was mild-mannered, almost good-humoured.

And all I know is that our mother did not get in touch with us once, not once, during this time. There was no letter or phone call or visit. Our father was in the hospital. We did not know how long we were going to be left there. In the years that followed, our mother never explained her absence, and we never asked her if she had wondered how we were, or how we felt, during those months.

This should be nothing, because it resembled nothing, just as one minus one resembles zero. It should be barely worth recounting to you as I walk the empty streets of this city in the desert so far away from where I belong. It seems as though Cathal and I spent that time in the shadow world, as though we were quietly lowered into the dark, everything familiar missing, and nothing we did or said could change this. Because no one harmed us or made us afraid, it did not strike us that we were in a world where no one loved us, or that such a thing might be of any significance. We did not complain. We were emptied of everything, and in the vacuum came something like silence—almost no sound at all, just some sad echoes and dim feelings.

I promise you that I will not call. I have called you enough, and woken you enough times, in the years when we were together and in the years since then. But there are nights now in this strange, flat and forsaken place when those sad echoes and dim feelings come to me slightly more intensely than before. They are like whispers, or trapped whimpering sounds. And I wish that I had you here, and I wish that I had not called you all those other times when I did not need to as much as I do now.

My brother and I learned not to trust anyone. We learned then not to talk about things that mattered to us, and we stuck to this as much as we could with a sort of grim stubborn pride all of our lives, as though it were a skill. But you know that, don't you? I don't need to call you to tell you that.

At JFK that night, Joan Carey smiled warmly and asked me how bad things were. When I told her that my mother was dying, she said that she was shocked. She remembered my mother so well, she said. She said she was sorry. She explained that I could use the first-class lounge, making it clear, however, in the most pleasant way, that I would be crossing the Atlantic in coach, which was what I had paid for. If I needed her, she said, she could come up in a while and talk, but she had told the people in the lounge and on the plane that she knew me, and they would look after me.

As we spoke and she tagged my luggage and gave me my boarding pass, I guessed that I had not met her for more than thirty years. But in her face I could see the person I had known, as well as traces of her mother and one of her brothers. In her presence I could feel that this going home to my mother's bed-side would not be simple, that some of our loves and attach-ments are elemental and beyond our choosing, and for that very reason they come spiced with pain and regret and need and hollowness and a feeling as close to anger as I will ever be able to manage.

Sometime during the night in that plane, as we crossed part of the western hemisphere, quietly and, I hope, unnoticed, I began to cry. I was back then in the simple world before I had seen Joan Carey, a world in which someone whose heartbeat had once been mine, and whose blood became my blood, and inside whose body I once lay curled, herself lay stricken in a hospital bed. The idea of losing her made me desperately sad. And then I tried to sleep. I pushed back my seat as the night wore on and kept my eyes averted from the film being shown, whatever it was, and let the terrible business of what I was flying towards hit me.

I hired a car at the airport, and I drove across Dublin in the washed light of that early September morning. I drove through Drumcondra, Dorset Street, by Mountjoy Square, down Gardiner Street and through the streets across the river that led south, as though they were a skin that I had shed. I did not stop for two hours or more, until I reached the house, fearing that if I pulled up somewhere to have breakfast the numbness that the driving with no sleep had brought might lift.

Sinead was just out of bed when I arrived but Jim was still asleep. Cathal had gone back to Dublin the night before, she said, but would be down later. She sighed and looked at me. The hospital had phoned, she went on, and things were worse. Your mother, she said, had a stroke during the night, on top of everything else. It was an old joke between us: never "our mother" or "my mother" or "Mammy" or "Mummy," but "your mother."

The doctors did not know how bad the stroke had been, she said, and they were still ready to operate if they thought they could. But they needed to talk to us. It was a pity, she added, that your mother's specialist, the man who looked after her heart, and whom she saw regularly and liked, was away. I realized then why Cathal had gone back to Dublin—he did not want to be a part of the conversation that we would have with the doctors. Two of us would be enough. He had told Sinead to tell me that whatever we decided would be fine with him.

Neither of us blamed him. He was the one who had become

close to her. He was the one she loved most. Or maybe he was the only one she loved. In those years, anyway. Or maybe that is unfair. Maybe she loved us all, just as we loved her as she lay dying.

And I moved, in those days—that Tuesday morning to the Friday night when she died—from feeling at times a great remoteness from her to wanting, almost in the same moment, my mother back where she had always been, in witty command of her world, full of odd dreams and perspectives, difficult, ready for life. She loved, as I did, books and music and hot weather. As she grew older she had managed, with her friends and with us, a pure charm, a lightness of tone and touch. But I knew not to trust it, not to come close, and I never did. I managed, in turn, to exude my own lightness and charm, but you know that too. You don't need me to tell you that either, do you?

I regretted nonetheless, as I sat by her bed or left so that others might see her, I regretted how far I had moved away from her, how far away from her I had stayed. I regretted how much I had let those months apart from her in the limbo of my aunt's house, and the years afterwards back in our own house, as my father slowly died, eat away at my soul. I regretted how little she knew about me, as she, too, must have regretted that, although she never complained or mentioned it, except perhaps to Cathal, and he told no one anything. Maybe she regretted nothing. But nights are long in winter, when darkness comes down at four o'clock and people have time to think of everything.

Maybe that is why I am here now, away from Irish darkness, away from the long, deep winter that settles so menacingly on the place where I was born. I am away from the east wind. I am in a place where so much is empty because it was never full, where things are forgotten and swept away, if there ever were things. I am in a place where there is nothing. Flatness, a blue sky, a soft, unhaunted night. A place where no one walks. Maybe I am happier here than I would be anywhere else, and it is only the poisonous innocence of the moon tonight that has made me want to dial your number and see if you are awake.

As we drove to see my mother that morning, I could not ask Sinead a question that was on my mind. My mother had been sick for four days now and was lying there maybe frightened, and I wondered if she had reached out her hand to Cathal and if they had held hands in the hospital, if they had actually grown close enough for that. Or if she had made some gesture to Sinead. And if she might do the same to me. It was a stupid, selfish thing I wondered about, and, like everything else that came into my mind in those days, it allowed me to avoid the fact that there would be no time any more for anything to be explained or said. We had used up all our time. And I wondered if that made any difference to my mother then, as she lay awake in the hospital those last few nights of her life: we had used up all our time.

She was in intensive care. We had to ring the bell and wait to be admitted. There was a hush over the place. We had discussed what I would say to her so as not to alarm her, how I would explain why I had come back. I told Sinead I would say that I'd heard she was in the hospital and I'd had a few days free before classes began and had decided to come back to make sure that she was OK.

"Are you feeling better?" I asked her.

She could not speak. Nonetheless, she let us know that she was thirsty and they would not allow her to drink anything. She had a drip in her arm. We told the nurses that her mouth was dry, and they said that there was nothing much we could do, except perhaps take tiny drops of cold water and put them on her lips using those special little sticks with sponge tips that women use to put on eye make-up.

I sat by her bed and spent a while wetting her lips. I was at home with her now. I knew how much she hated physical discomfort; her appetite for these drops of water was so overwhelming and so desperate that nothing else mattered.

And then word came that the doctors would see us. When we stood up and told her that we would be back, she hardly responded. We were ushered by a nurse with an English accent down some corridors to a room. There were two doctors there; the nurse stayed in the room with us. The doctor who seemed to be in charge, who said that he would have been the one to perform the operation, told us that he had just spoken to the anaesthetist, who had insisted that my mother's heart would not survive an operation. Her having had a stroke, he said, did not help.

"I could have a go," he said, and then immediately apologized for speaking like that. He corrected himself. "I could operate, but she could die on the operating table."

There was a blockage somewhere, he said. There was no blood getting to her kidneys and maybe elsewhere as well— the operation would tell us for certain, but it might end by being exploratory, it might do nothing to solve the problem. It was her circulation, he said. The heart was not beating strongly enough to send blood into every part of her body.

He knew to leave silence then, and the other doctor did too. The nurse looked at the floor.

"There's nothing you can do then, is there?" I said.

"We can make her comfortable," he replied.

"How long can she survive like this?" I asked.

"Not long," he said.

"I mean, hours or days?"

"Days. Some days."

"We can make her very comfortable," the nurse said.

There was nothing more to say. Afterwards, I wondered if we should have spoken to the anaesthetist personally, or tried to contact our mother's specialist, or asked that she be moved to a bigger hospital for another opinion. But I don't think any of this would have made a difference. For years, we had been given warnings that this moment would come, as she fainted in public places and lost her balance and declined. It had been clear that her heart was giving out, but not clear enough for me to have come to see her more than once or twice in the summer—and then when I did come I was protected from what might have been said, or not said, by the presence of Sinead and Jim and Cathal. Maybe I should have phoned a few times a week, or written her letters like a good son. But despite all the warning signals, or perhaps even because of them, I had kept my distance. And as soon as I entertained this thought, with all the regret that it carried, I imagined how coldly or nonchalantly a decision to spend the summer close by, seeing her often, might have been greeted by her, and how difficult and enervating for her, as much as for me, some of those visits or phone calls might have been. And how curtly efficient and brief her letters in reply to mine would have seemed.

And, as we walked back down to see her, the nurse coming with us, there was this double regret—the simple one that I had kept away, and the other one, much harder to fathom, that I had been given no choice, that she had never wanted me very much, and that she was not going to be able to rectify that in the few days she had left in the world. She would be distracted by her own pain and discomfort, and by the great effort she was making to be dignified and calm. She was wonderful, as she always had been. I touched her hand a few times in case she might open it and seek my hand, but she never did this. She did not respond to being touched.

Some of her friends came. Cathal came and stayed with her. Sinead and I remained close by. On Friday morning, when the nurse asked me if I thought she was in distress, I said that I did. I was sure that, if I insisted now, I could get her morphine and a private room. I did not consult the others; I presumed that they would agree. I did not mention morphine to the nurse, but I knew that she was wise, and I saw by the way she looked at me as I spoke that she knew that I knew what morphine would do. It would ease my mother into sleep and ease her out of the world. Her breathing would come and go, shallow and deep, her pulse would become faint, her breathing would stop, and then come and go again.

It would come and go until, in that private room late in the evening, it seemed to stop altogether, as, horrified and helpless, we sat and watched her, then sat up straight as the breathing started again, but not for long. Not for long at all. It stopped one last time, and it stayed stopped. It did not start again.

She lay still. She was gone. We sat with her until a nurse came in and quietly checked her pulse and shook her head sadly and left the room.

We stayed with her for a while more; then, when they asked us to leave, we touched her on the forehead one by one, and we left the room, closing the door. We walked down the corridor as though for the rest of our lives our own breathing would bear traces of the end of hers, of her final struggle, as though our own way of being in the world had just been halved or quartered by what we had seen.

We buried her beside my father, who had been in the grave

waiting for her for thirty-three years. The next morning I flew back to New York, to my half-furnished apartment on 90th and Columbus, and I began my teaching a day later. I understood that I had over all the years postponed too much. As I settled down to sleep in that new bed in the dark city, I saw that it was too late now, too late for everything. I would not be given a second chance. In the hours when I woke, I have to tell you that this struck me almost with relief.

The Pearl Fishers

In the late 1980s Gráinne Roche and her husband Donnacha moved to Dublin, where Gráinne became a fierce believer in the truth. When she argued, in her weekly newspaper column or on the radio, about the state of the Church and the soul of the nation, her tone made some people dislike her intensely. Nonetheless, her country accent and her insistence that she and other like-minded lay people represented the true Catholic Church more than the bishops and priests gave her a role in most debates about the changing Ireland; she insisted always that she stood for some middle ground, dismissing the attitudes of the country's liberal smart class. The few times I saw her in the city I enjoyed reminding her that when I had known her in Wexford she was young and walked around the town in her school uniform chewing gum. But in general I kept away from her. I had long before lost interest in arguments about the changing Ireland. But that is not the only reason I kept away from her.

I live alone now and I work hard. And when I am not working I am away. I do not see anyone I have no desire to see. It is easy to screen calls and avoid answering emails, and then they peter out. I love a long day when the night promises nothing more than silence, solitude, music, lamplight, the time broken by maybe half an hour on Gaydar to see if there is anyone new, or even anyone familiar, in the city centre who might stop by for what they call sex with no strings attached.

Viewed in the morning, it often seems a perfect life; once darkness falls it is sometimes sad, but only mildly so. It is easy being middle-aged, needs and appetites reduced to a level where they can be satisfied without much effort or pain or hardship. I make enough money from the grim, almost plot-less thrillers with gay sub-plots I produce, which are popular in Germany and in Japan, and from overwrought and graphically violent screenplays, one of which paid for the top-floor apart-ment where I spend my days, to live as I please. I let no one irritate me unless I can expect in return some compensation such as sex or serious amusement, or unless there are old and intimate attachments involved.

Thus when Gráinne left a message on my answering machine one day when I was out, I did not reply. I had no idea why she might want to speak to me. I pressed 9, which meant her mes-sage would be preserved on the machine for a week and then would have to be erased. When the week was up I erased it without a thought. She called again, and said into the voicemail that I was hard to get hold of. I might have smiled at the idea that this was as it should be, but I still did not reply.

Not long afterwards, however, I carelessly answered a call from someone with no caller ID and it was Gráinne. She had me now. She moaned at first about the number of calls she had had to make to find me.

"I have to see you," she said eventually, "and soon, and so does Donnacha. It's important."

"Can you tell me what it's about?" I asked. "Just a clue will help. Talk slowly. I'm not as bright as you."

"Don't start," she said. "I'll tell you when I see you. It might be best over dinner somewhere during the week. Somewhere quiet or where the tables are far apart."

"Somewhere quiet," I repeated. "Will you be there?"

"Don't start. Do you hear me? Don't start. We both need to see you."

I thought of saying that I was writing a book and was not seeing many people. I knew how pompous that would sound to her and almost relished the idea, but I also knew how ineffective it would be as a way of deterring her. The way she said "We both need to see you" made me stop for a moment longer. She seemed to be suggesting that this was not about her and her work, the two subjects that interested Gráinne Roche more than anything else in the world, and it was not to be a social occasion either. It was about her and Donnacha, whom I had known better than I had ever known her.

There was a time, indeed, when I had loved him, but that was something that had not bothered me for years. I knew he now worked in administration in one of the main Dublin hospitals. I had heard him once or twice on the radio sounding rational and competent and in full possession of a large set of complex facts. His voice, I remember noting, had not changed. Nor indeed had hers. She made me agree to see them in the Tea Room at eight o'clock the following Wednesday.

"Are you still in daily touch with the Virgin Mary?" I asked before we rang off.

"I am," she said, "and she is taking a very dim view of you."

I laughed. She had a lovely way of making herself sound as though she meant everything she said. Even when she tried to be ironic or sarcastic or funny, she sounded earnest. I could imagine Donnacha liking that too, finding it even more amusing and refreshing than I did.

I almost looked forward to seeing them until the time came close. But as I walked slowly towards the Clarence Hotel I actually dreaded the prospect of meeting them and I wished I had not answered the phone to her that day. There was something dull about Gráinne and her urgent needs and her strong and half-baked opinions. And there was something about Donnacha that I had never been able to fathom, some deep laziness or contentment, an ease in the world, a way of letting nothing bother him too much, a way of never allowing anything to happen to him that would require close analysis on his part. This beautiful nonchalance of his had made me want him at a certain time in my life more than I have ever wanted anyone, and it had made him tolerate me and enjoy things while they lasted until something more normal and simple moved into his ambit.

Such as a woman who did all of the talking.

Most of us are gay or straight; Donnacha simply made no effort, he took whatever came his way. In the past I had found that exciting, but I had not thought about him seriously for a long time. As I walked into the Tea Room, however, and saw that they were waiting for me, I was surprised that I still felt jealous. Of Donnacha's self-containment, of his ability to make people want him, or trust him, or like him. And maybe jealous too of the idea that he and Gráinne had now been together for almost twenty-five years, that she had him all the time, every night. I hoped to get away from them as soon as I could.

"We thought you'd be late," she said.

"Yes, I planned to be late, but it didn't work out."

Donnacha was wearing a suit and a tie. I wondered if he had come straight from work. He stood up and shook my hand as though he did not know me well.

"You're still married to her?" I asked.

He smiled almost shyly and looked at Gráinne.

"What God hath put together," she said.

"Well," I said. "I don't often meet a divinely inspired couple."

I wondered if my question had been unfortunate, if they

were in fact meeting to let me be the first to know that they were separating, but I did not think so.

Gráinne seemed to have arranged the table so that there were two places set opposite her, one for Donnacha and one for me. I had imagined that they would sit beside each other opposite me. She obviously wanted us both to look at her, or wanted to make sure that we were both listening to her when she spoke.

She handed me the wine list.

"We've ordered gin and tonics," she said, "but that might be too strong for you."

"It's nice to see country people back in the Clarence," I replied. "I'm sure the band are delighted."

"Bono was in the lobby when we came in," Donnacha said.

"Give me Larry any day," I replied.

"Order the wine," Gráinne said.

Donnacha had not changed. His hair was grey now, but the grey did not make much difference. His face had thickened but not very much. His teeth were still perfect. He was as slim as ever. But none of his physical attributes added up to much—he was not beautiful, or physically striking—and it was something else that made me glad I was not sitting opposite him and would not have to look at him all evening. His aura had not been affected by the years. He was lazily there, easygoing, comfortable, as their drinks came and we ordered our food and our wine.

"I see you are still keeping the old-age pensioners on trolleys in the hospital corridors," I said.

He smiled almost impatiently and slowly began to explain how things in his hospital were improving, mentioning in passing several meetings he had had with the minister and what she had said, and one meeting with the Taoiseach. I had forgotten how much he loved an argument and how rational he was and unwilling to deal with insult and half-thought-out invective. Nonetheless, it was not hard to tell him that the problem began and ended with the doctors and their greed and their arrogance, and that nothing would change until their salaries were halved and they had to clock in like everyone else.

"It's not as simple as that."

I almost said that it was precisely as simple as that when my mother was dying in a public ward over long months in one of the Dublin hospitals, but I did not want to talk about anything personal. I knew that Donnacha's parents had died, as had Gráinne's mother. I had not gone to the funerals, nor had they come to my mother's.

I noticed that Gráinne, who was facing the main door into the restaurant, paid absolutely no attention to this discussion, instead looked around her like a petulant child. She was behaving like herself, only more so. It comes with age, I thought. Donnacha was thus becoming all reason, all good sense. I was becoming all bored, or maybe all regret. I wished I could tell Donnacha that I had no interest in hospitals or health systems or ministers or meetings with the Taoiseach, that I was interested in his face and his voice, in the darkness of his eyes, in the growing intensity in his tone as he made his argument.

In St. Aidan's we had been distantly friendly for the first three years, although Donnacha was always in a different dormitory and was not involved in hurling, as I was then. Thus I never spoke to him much or grew close to him. He had friends from home and he spent time with them. I remember him as part of a group on semi-permanent watch for opportunities to cadge cigarettes, asking for a pull of yours, or a drag, or the butt. I remember that he could be trusted not to horse a cigarette if you gave him a drag, and, if he had borrowed a cigarette, he could be depended on to return it the next day.

In our fourth year we became friends because we both worked to get on the school debating team. Donnacha started out as a useless speaker but over time the logical, calm way he made points began to have an effect, especially if he was part of a team with other boys who had greater skills at delivery and drama or humour. I could do dramatic openings and endings as long as I could keep my stammer under control. Sean Kelly could do imitations and make jokes and barbed comments about the opposition. We left Donnacha to do the quiet summing up. By the end of January we had won the internal competition in the school, and this meant we could now represent the school in debates all over the county, mainly against girls' schools. Sometimes we got the topic a week in advance and were allowed time together to prepare, but there were some debates in which the subject was not released until an hour or two before and these were the hardest and the most exciting.

This was how we met Gráinne Roche, who at sixteen was the most fiery debater in the county, with a skill at insulting her opponents that thrilled the audience. Donnacha never rose to her bait. Nothing she said or did made the slightest difference to his style, and he could take a sentence of hers, or a point she had made, and dissect it coldly to make her seem like a fool.

Later, everybody who took part in those debates must have read the evidence against Father O'Neill, the science teacher who organized them within the school, and presumed that we, who travelled with him so many times, must have known about him or even suffered because of him. I suppose we knew that he took an interest in us that was more intense than normal, and that he was often very nosy. And of course he liked Donnacha and loved quizzing him about the smallest details of his life, almost blushing with pleasure the more diffident and remote Donnacha grew. I watched this and it meant that I knew about Father O'Neill. According to the evidence given, it was only after our time at St. Aidan's that he brought boys to his room and fucked them. But maybe there was other evidence that would have implicated him much earlier, and maybe it all happened in front of our noses. The idea of a priest wanting to get naked with one of the boys at St. Aidan's and stuff his penis up the boy's bottom was so unimaginable that it might have happened while I was in the next room and I might have mistaken the grunts and yelps they made for a sound coming from the television. Or I might have mistaken the silence they maintained for real silence.

On a night driving back to the school from Bunclody, where Donnacha's incisive and quiet arguments had seemed oddly powerless and flat, Sean Kelly sat in the front passenger seat while Father O'Neill drove and Donnacha and I sat in the back. I don't remember how we began to move closer to each other than we needed to be. It might have been because one of us wanted to be heard and thus sat over towards the middle to be within earshot of Father O'Neill and Sean Kelly. We did nothing obvious. But we moved close to each other so that our legs were touching and maybe, in the heat of the car, we had our jackets off and our shoulders were touching too and our arms. I eased off, I remember, in case this was a mistake, but it soon became obvious that Donnacha was deliberately moving towards me and that a few times, as though by accident, he touched my thigh with his hand. We continued talking as normal but by the time we arrived back to the school Donnacha and I were on fire. It was a question of what we could do now. It was late and all the dormitory lights were off. No one would miss us, as everyone knew that we were in Bunclody at the debate.

Donnacha and I were on fire, but as I was to learn, there was a great deal of difference between us. If I did not make a plan, or insist in some way, Donnacha's fire would happily go out. It would not cost him a thought to go to his bed on his own on a night like this. But if I said nothing, merely led him to a place that was not too risky, then he would follow, and in the dark especially and with no words being spoken or whispered between us he would be passionate in a way that I could never manage. It would be clear that he wanted this all along, planned it maybe, but always with the proviso that he could, if he were not openly encouraged, walk away.

Years later, when we lay in beds together, I learned more about him. But here in the dark, in this old school, with many nooks and shadowy spaces and unused rooms, I learned first how slowly I would have to move, how, for example, he would not let me touch him or kiss him until he had abandoned all modesty. This would take time. At first he would touch the light stubble on my face, or the hair on my chest. He would do this as though it were leading nowhere. I could touch his back and open his pants and pull him in against me, and slowly I could put my hands where I liked but only when I sensed from his breathing that he was ready for this.

That night we went silently to a place off the rehearsal room that was once used for storing musical instruments. It had two doors—one connecting it to the rehearsal room, the other giving on to a dark corridor, both of which could be locked. There was no light inside. At first, as we stood facing each other, I moved too fast and Donnacha almost pushed me away. I thought then that he just wanted to play a bit before going to bed. I did not know that he was building up to something and that soon he would be ready for anything.

I wondered that night, as I sneaked across the school to my

dormitory and then lay in bed, what Donnacha would do in the morning. I wondered if he would avoid me, if he would pretend that nothing had happened between us, if he would pretend that he had not left marks on my back with his fingernails and made muffled sounds that went on and on as he came all over my chest and stomach, if he would try to make me forget that I had fed his sweet, thick, pungent, lemony sperm into my mouth with my fingers as if it were jam, desperately trying to make sure that none was wasted.

As soon as I caught his eye at breakfast the next morning, however, he smiled at me, the smile cheeky and warm and affectionate. He told me later that I had glanced up at him in wonder, almost in fear, and immediately looked away. As soon as breakfast was over he made his way across and stood behind my chair, waiting for me to finish my cup of tea. He had never done this before. We walked out of the refectory as best friends.

It seems ludicrous now, and it is certainly embarrassing, but it was more or less at the time I began to have sex with Donnacha that I became deeply religious. I still believe that it had nothing to do with him. I believe that I became interested in religion because of a number of poems on the school course that I read and reread with considerable intensity. These were the sonnets of Hopkins and two poems by T. S. Eliot, "A Song for Simeon" and "The Love Song of J. Alfred Prufrock." If I ever happen to read "Prufrock" now, it is as a comic poem, but then, at the age of sixteen, I took seriously the idea of the "overwhelming question" that Prufrock wished to ask. I believed that there was such a question and that it was up to us, students of the poem, to formulate it. I believed that the question was existential, almost religious, and it concerned how we should live in the world, and how we should relate to God and to each other, and I grew so solemn and earnest on the subject that Mr.

Mulhern, the English teacher, suggested I go and see a priest who had come back from America and who worked only with the seminarians. He was a theologian. His name was Patrick Moorehouse.

The first day I knocked on his door he was busy, but I was struck by how polite he was. When I told him why I had come to see him, he nodded and said that Mr. Mulhern had mentioned me to him, and that he too was an admirer of Hopkins and Eliot. He suggested that I come back another time. I remember that I went up to his room every evening after tea for some weeks but he was never there. One day I saw him on the corridor but he did not notice me.

And then one Sunday, when I had presumed that I was travelling to New Ross for a hurling match, I was told that I had been dropped from the subs bench and the bus would be full. I knew it was my own fault for not togging out on the appointed afternoons, for disappearing into the library when I should have been on the playing field, but I was not alone in believing that I had been singled out by not being allowed to travel on the bus as a supporter. Even Donnacha had managed to get on the bus and he had never held a hurley in his life. This meant that I had a whole afternoon empty, from one o'clock, when the bus left, to five, when those still in the school would be expected to turn up for Rosary.

When I went up to Father Moorehouse's room that afternoon I did so merely as a way of passing ten minutes; I did not expect him to be there. He opened the door brusquely. He seemed preoccupied but once he remembered who I was and how long ago he had promised to see me he invited me into the room. I had been in other priests' quarters, but these were different from the rest. The main room was smaller. It was full of books and papers and LPs piled on desks. I could see no television but there was a record player and there were two speakers resting against the wall. Father Moorehouse had been working at a desk. He moved some books and pamphlets from the short sofa and made space for me to sit and then he began to talk. I had no idea what I had expected him to say, or why, in fact, I had been sent to see him, but I need not have worried. His voice was soft; he smiled when he stopped to think, looking for the right phrase, and a few times he would take a note of something he had said so that he would not forget it. I wish I had taken notes too, but I remember clearly some of the things he said that day because I wrote them down as soon as I left his presence. He said: "We must turn our bewilderment in the world into a gift from God." He said: "We must merge the language of our prayer with the terms of our predicament." He said: "We must humbly understand that consciousness belongs to each of us alone, it is part of us as much as it is part of God."

He asked me about prayer and when I said nothing interesting he found me books and warned that some of them were not Catholic books but they might help me understand Hopkins and Eliot. He asked me if I had read John Donne and I said that I had not. He told me I must and he quoted some lines. By the time I left his room, I had books by Lancelot Andrewes, Jonathan Edwards, Simone Weil and Fulton Sheen. He suggested that I come back even before I had read these books because he would like to talk to me more about faith and about prayer. I thanked him and I left.

I suppose it must be said that my interest in Patrick Moorehouse's mind, and my fascination at the points he made and the terms he used and the writers he quoted from, were entirely sexual. But maybe it should be said only once, and perhaps whispered or put into parentheses, or consigned to the realm of the obvious. At that time, no one knew that a sixteen-year-old boy and a priest twice his age could or would have sex, and so it never awoke as a thought in my conscious mind. Now, I have to say, even now, the idea of it—of Father Moorehouse naked, for example, or Father Moorehouse with an erection, or Father Moorehouse's tongue—is exciting. I regret that I did not put more thought into it then.

Instead, I tried to read the books he gave me. They were difficult, and I was glad that he had given me permission to go back to his room before I had finished any of them. I had found some essays by Eliot in the library and a book about his religious belief and his poetry and thought that this might be an excuse to go to Father Moorehouse's room again, maybe with passages marked that had puzzled me, to see what he thought.

The next time I found him in his room I was surprised to see Gráinne Roche and a friend of hers. They were both sitting on the sofa. Father Moorehouse got a chair for me from what I supposed must be the bedroom. I knew Gráinne, of course, from the debates. Now Father Moorehouse informed me that she was asking the same questions as I was and he was glad both of us had met in his room to discuss matters of faith rather than in the false world of the debating chamber. Gráinne was very quiet and appeared almost embarrassed. Father Moorehouse completely ignored her friend, who seemed not to notice, or not to mind. When he stood up, he made it clear that he had to go. All three of us left before him, the girls to walk back downtown, me to return to the study hall.

For the rest of the term, then, and for some of the following year, I had permission maybe once a week or once a fortnight to take time from the study hall and go to Father Moorehouse's room. It was presumed, I suppose, that I was being groomed for the seminary, although Father Moorehouse never mentioned that possibility. Most times when we met by arrangement

Colm Tóibín

Gráinne was there too, often with a friend or two friends but sometimes alone. A few times another guy from my class, who later did spend time in the seminary, came. He was clever and asked intelligent questions.

Donnacha, on the other hand, had no interest in poetry or theology. I must have talked to him about what I was reading but perhaps not much because I have no memory of us ever discussing what went on in Father Moorehouse's room.

It is hard not to squirm when I think of some of the things I said in that room. Father Moorehouse sometimes spoke about complex matters, about God's role in chance and choice, in accidents and in decisions made on the basis of free will, about faith and its paradoxes. He loved words like "paradox" and "ambiguity," he loved speculating and he often turned to poems or books to help him as he went along. At the end, and sometimes at the beginning, he asked us to pray out loud, to follow him in finding words to match our feelings. I have no memory of any of Gráinne's friends ever doing this, but she did it and so did I. Father Moorehouse disliked cosy platitudes, as he called them, and simple stories. He pushed us all the time towards working our doubts and fears into sentences, towards using only the most precise metaphors. Sometimes we would kneel, sometimes face each other directly. Only one of us would speak. Occasionally he would ask us to address God personally, sometimes as though God were in the room with us, other times as though he were far away, a distant presence with whom we needed to communicate urgently.

It was awful, some of it, like Teilhard de Chardin crossed with Donovan or bad Bob Dylan. I know that Gráinne must remember how involved I became in it, how profoundly I talked to God! One of my greatest worries when she came to Dublin was that I would meet her somewhere and she would

100

remind me, or start telling others, all about it. Or even that she might remember phrases or moments. Instead, strangely, her silence on the subject made me wish to avoid her even more, and made me uneasy now as I sat opposite her in the Tea Room as the wine was poured and the starter served.

"We got one of your things out on DVD and watched it one night when the boys were out," Gráinne said. She sounded for a second as though she and Donnacha were meeting me in order to discuss the screenplay.

"The boys go to dances," Donnacha said. "I have to wait around the corner in the car for them so as not to make a show of them."

"I hope you found the film true to life," I said.

"We thought *The Silence of the Lambs* was bad. I mean it gave Donnacha nightmares. But yours was worse."

"It didn't give me nightmares," Donnacha said.

"It did. It gave you nightmares. You don't remember because you were fast asleep for them, but I do because I had to listen to you."

Donnacha looked at me and smiled.

"I have never had a nightmare in my life. It would take more than a film to give me a nightmare."

"What was your film called?" Gráinne interrupted.

"*A Raw Deal*," I said.

"It was raw all right. I mean—the dentist's chair! How did you think of it?"

"The director added it. I didn't think of it."

"I thought you wrote it."

"Originally I had something much worse."

"I don't want to hear," she said.

"I hope you didn't ever let the boys see it."

"God knows what they're looking at. Except in our house

the computer is in the kitchen, so at least we know what they're looking at there."

"Ruins all the fun," I said. "The smell of cooking is bad for a computer as well."

She sipped her wine and ignored me and looked all around the restaurant. I wondered when she would get to the point. In her company there was never exactly silence, even when nothing was being said. The way her eyes took in the room made a sort of noise. I noticed a red patch, almost a rash, becoming more obvious on her neck. Suddenly she seemed nervous.

I had never worked out what to do if she asked me straight out if Donnacha and I had ever been together. One night—and it must have been the night I spent most time in their company since they came to Dublin—we were in a bar in Donnybrook and I was almost drunk and had probably made one joke too many at the expense of decency. I sobered up quickly, however, when, once Gráinne had gone to the bathroom, Donnacha turned and spoke to me with lines that sounded like something from a bad play.

"Gráinne doesn't know anything about us," he said.

I shrugged.

"I'd like to keep it that way," he said. He had been drinking as well and there was a hint of accusation.

"Well, you'd better not tell her then," I said. "Wouldn't that be the best thing?"

"You know what I mean."

"You mean—I shouldn't tell her?"

"I mean you should never say it to anyone. Anyone at all."

"I never have."

"I'm glad to hear that."

I remembered, during that scene, how soft and biddable alcohol used to make him when he discovered it first, when he was nineteen or twenty, how funny he could become, and how uninhibited, once the light was turned off in my flat in Harcourt Terrace. I remembered that nothing made him happier when he had had a few drinks than to have me lie on my back while he knelt with his back to me and his knees on either side of my torso. He would bend as I pushed my tongue hard up into his arsehole while he sucked my cock and licked my balls.

What was strange about him later, when he would come to stay for a weekend, was that he remained part of the culture that produced him. In that culture no one ever appeared naked. In the school, there were doors with locks on each shower, and a hook to hang your clothes within each shower cubicle. Only one guy, who was from Dublin, would strip off after a game of hurling and then move bravely towards the shower. Everyone else, even in the dormitory, moved gingerly. And Donnacha, including when he was very drunk, wore his underpants to bed. A few times I enjoyed tossing his underpants across the room when he was not paying attention so that in the morning he would have no choice but to wander naked in search of them. I knew he was burning with embarrassment at the idea that I was lying in bed watching him.

Observing him now, I could sense that nothing was different. He probably slept in pyjamas, sitting each night at the side of the bed and edging them on without standing up. He was someone who never saw any reason why he should change, who lived as he was meant to live, who could be trusted, who never in his life had wanted anything more than what he had.

When the main course was served and we had ordered a second bottle of wine, Gráinne began to speak.

"I don't know if you have been reading my pieces on the Hierarchy," she said.

"I look at the pictures."

"Seriously," she said. "I thought it was time. There has been a great change and I wanted to write about that."

"You mean that Mass is on Saturday night as well?"

"Stop making fun of me! I mean that there is a new humility among the Hierarchy. All of them know the Church has made mistakes."

"You mean they've decided to stop fucking altar boys."

"Hey, here now," Donnacha said. "You're in a posh hotel."

"I mean," Gráinne said, her face becoming redder, "that they know they are servants of the people, and servants of the truth."

"You sound as if you're on *Saturday View*," I said.

"I've seen the archbishop a number of times. I was involved in an advisory group to his predecessor."

"For all the good that did," I said.

"He did his best. No one anywhere else did any better. But what I am saying is there has been a change, a real change."

"Lovely," I said.

"But it was something the archbishop said that stopped me in my tracks," Gráinne said. She had put her knife and fork down and I thought I saw tears in her eyes. This, I said to myself, is unbearable.

"He said that it was important not only for the Church now that the truth be known, but it was something that the Church of the future would demand from us. The Church of the future would, he said, stand for truth."

"I see."

"I came home and I spoke to Donnacha, and then with his support I spoke to the boys and then all four of us knelt down and prayed and we asked our Saviour to guide us, and then we decided that the truth should be known. And I want nothing to do with tribunals of inquiry and I want no compensation but I can no longer hide the truth."

"What is the truth?" I asked.

"And I need you to know before I speak out," she said. "The priest in question is no longer in the Church and there have already been other allegations against him."

"Which priest?"

"You know which one," she said.

"I don't."

"Which one do you think?" Donnacha asked.

"You tell me."

"Patrick Moorehouse."

"Are you saying you had sex with Patrick Moorehouse?" I asked. I quickly wiped the beginning of a smile from my face.

"Keep your voice down, for God's sake," she said.

"Hold on. Did you?"

"Yes, I did."

"Sex? Actual sex?"

"Yes, actual sex."

"When?"

"Sometimes before those little prayer meetings we had, and sometimes after."

"You were often there with one of your friends."

"On those days I doubled back and went to his room later."

"And on the other days?"

"I got there early."

I tried to think, to remember evenings when I had come from the study hall to find Gráinne and Father Moorehouse alone in that room. I realized that there was nothing, not a single detail, not a blush, for example, on either of their faces, not a thing unusually out of place, that I had noticed or could now recall.

"What has this got to do with me?"

"I need a witness."

"To what?"

"That we were in that room, that we knew him and we were vulnerable."

"Speak for yourself."

"I was vulnerable. That is me speaking for myself. And you were vulnerable too, just in case you don't remember."

"You were vulnerable enough to arrive early and double back?"

"He had us in his thrall."

"Speak for yourself."

"I repeat—he had us in his thrall. Are you denying that?"

"I didn't have sex with him."

"That is hardly the point."

"What is the point?"

"Keep your voice down. The point is that I was taken full advantage of, aged sixteen."

"And you want to talk to Joe Duffy on his radio show about it? Is that right? Talk to Joe!"

"I've written a book."

"And you want my imprimatur and the archbishop's *nihil obstat*?"

"She already has the archbishop's *nihil obstat*," Donnacha said drily.

"Is it a long book?" I asked.

"It's as long as it needs to be."

I realized that I wanted to ask her how much was in the book about me, how much about that room where we said prayers, and then it struck me that I did not actually care what she put in her book.

"I am going to tell the story of my life," she said. "And it is going to be the truth."

"I thought you said you'd already written it."

"I have."

"When does it start?"

"It opens on the night I met Donnacha."

"When was that?"

"You were there too. Do you remember that awful opera they let us go to in Wexford one year? I checked back the year and then we both remembered. It was called *The Pearl Fishers.* My book starts that night."

She smiled at Donnacha. I put my knife and fork down and poured another glass of wine for each of us.

"I vaguely remember it," I said.

"That was the first night for us," she said. "I mean the first time I knew I fancied him. And vice versa."

As she went on I pretended for some time more that I barely remembered the night, and then I excused myself to go to the bathroom. I hoped that neither of them had noticed I had been telling lies and trying to change the subject. I hoped I could soon get away from the high drama of Gráinne's life, which was now on display for me and Donnacha as a sort of preparatory gesture to the world, a piece of recitative for a great diva who would go on to sing many great arias. This supper was merely a way of warming up her voice, letting her know how wonderful she herself sounded, especially in the upper register.

In those first months when Donnacha and I began to have sex whenever we could in the school, it was announced that any pupil in the senior years could attend a dress rehearsal of *The Pearl Fishers,* which was running as part of the opera festival, as long as he came to the rehearsal room every afternoon and listened to the opera on record and attended a lecture on its form and its meaning from one of the priests who was also a music teacher. Since I was still sulking about being turfed off the bus to the hurling match and refusing even to tog out between class and Rosary in the afternoon, this seemed an opportunity for revenge on the hurling coach and the captain of our team. I could tell them that I was busy in the rehearsal room listening to an opera. I convinced Donnacha to come too. We were informed on the first day that anyone who missed one of the five sessions could not attend the dress rehearsal. By the last day, because the music and the explanation of the plot and the motifs in the opera had bored the majority so badly, there were only seven or eight of us left.

I stayed because the music took me over, especially one of the duets by the baritone and the tenor. I was also interested in the idea of a motif, a set of notes that played, say, on a harp could remind you of the same set of notes as sung by the soprano, or by the baritone and the tenor in the duet. The men's duet was about eternal friendship sworn between them as they knew they were in love with the same woman. By the end of the opera that same melody would be sung as a duet by the tenor and the woman, who had found love, thus leaving the baritone alone and miserable.

I found this beautiful and compelling. Donnacha liked it too, or maybe he just tolerated it; he was never very enthusiastic about anything much. He came along perhaps because I did. It might have mattered to us both that the room, where the music teacher's personal stereo had been specially set up for us, was just beside the smaller room where we had gone that first night. I never for a second thought anything as banal as that I was the tenor or the baritone and Donnacha was the other singer in the duet. But the music lifted me, and the aria they sang haunted me. It made me feel happy that I was close to Donnacha while I listened to it, and afterwards back in the study hall I composed some poems in response to it, and, I am almost ashamed to say, some prayers that I later showed to Father Moorehouse.

Students from St. Aidan's and from the convent in the town filled two rows of seats at the dress rehearsal. Because there were only eight of us, we had been allowed to walk down to the opera house without supervision but with instructions to come straight back to the school once the opera was over. Walking to the opera house that evening was like being an adult. I had never been to an opera before; I think I may have heard a live orchestra once or twice, but only a chamber orchestra. I was surprised by the lighting and the costumes and the set, how yellow and stylized everything was, and how rich the sound coming from the orchestra and the chorus. But I was overwhelmed when the two men began to sing. When we were told about the difference between a baritone and a tenor I had understood it but it had not meant much to me. Now the tenor's voice seemed vulnerable and plaintive, and the other voice masculine and strong. I was surprised too at the real difference between the voices, much greater here than on the recording. You could hear each voice clearly when it came to the duet and when the voices finally merged in harmony I was almost in tears. I could not take my eyes off the two men. What they had done together in that aria was the beginning of a new life for me, not only because I would follow music and singing from then on, but because it had given me a glittering hint of something beyond the life I knew or had been told about. That made all the difference to me, and I presumed that it had made a difference to those around me as well, who applauded warmly when the aria was over.

When the interval came and we got outside, however, I found Gráinne Roche laughing and gathering her friends around, delighted that she would not be going back into the

cond half. Instead, she was going to lead a posse, she said,
wn to Cafolla's for a hamburger and chips. No one would
notice our departure, she said, and we would even be able to
smoke there in freedom. I stood apart and remained silent. I
watched other people standing outside who appeared, like me,
to have loved the first half. I waited for Donnacha to come over
and join me, but he was busy talking to Gráinne and her friends
so I left him there.

It was a strange feeling, looking up at the tall buildings in
the narrow street, and at the night sky, knowing that back-
stage here the singers were in dressing rooms preparing for the
second half. And that over the next two or three weeks people
would come from all over the world to see *The Pearl Fishers,*
people who lived their lives in a way which seemed to me that
night glamorous and exotic. People rich enough or free enough
to travel a distance to be beguiled by music. I wondered what
it would be like to be among such people.

Donnacha walked over to me looking happy.

"Are you coming?" he asked.

"Where?"

"To Cafolla's. We're all going."

"Are you going to miss the second half?"

"I'm starving."

He was, I could tell, utterly impervious to how I felt and
that came as a shock. I thought he surely must have realized
from my response to the music as I sat beside him that the idea
of going to Cafolla's to eat chips and hamburgers instead of
going back into the opera would be pure dull madness. I saw
that that did not occur to him. I saw that the music had meant
nothing to him. I saw that he did not notice how much it had
meant to me.

"No, I'm going back in."

By that time Gráinne was standing beside us. She had a packet of cigarettes in her hand. She was chewing gum.

"Listen to Goody Two-shoes," she said.

"It won't be noticed," Donnacha said.

"I'm going back in," I repeated.

When his eyes caught mine I knew that he sensed there was something wrong.

"I'll be waiting outside when it's over," he said.

"Let us know if there's any more screeching," Gráinne added. "God, that woman did more screeching! My nerves are in bits from her."

Gráinne did a loud, jarring imitation of a soprano hitting a high note until a few people turned around to glare at her.

"We're off," she said. "See you."

"I'll be waiting outside when it's over," Donnacha said again. I did not reply but turned and walked back into the opera house.

Afterwards he was lurking in the shadows and slowly we walked back to the school together.

"How was the second half?" he asked.

"It was great. How were the chips?"

"They were great."

I enjoyed the idea of us walking together through the empty streets of the town. Neither of us spoke much; we had different things to think about. Donnacha could not have known or even suspected that ten years ahead, when he was working as an accountant in one of the midland towns, Gráinne Roche would be the star journalist on one of the regional papers, covering sport and local court cases, and they would meet again and within a year they would marry. I could not have suspected that the music which had lifted me out of myself that night, which had seemed like a great new beginning, would within a decade seem sweet and silly to me, not Germanic or hard enough. The future is a foreign country: they do things differently there.

Once we got in the back gate to the school that night and were in the dark we held hands as we walked across the playing fields. It was cold. We made our way silently to the room beside the rehearsal room and started to make love. It was only when Donnacha began to ejaculate that I noticed the line of light under the door and knew that if there was anyone in the next room they would hear him now. His orgasm took time, the slow moan he made grew louder and, while he did everything to control it, it was accompanied by a set of gasps. As I felt his hot jets of sperm hitting the skin of my belly I heard footsteps and then a voice in the other room, something like "What the hell?" In that second Donnacha, who had not finished coming, unlocked the door leading to the corridor and ran out. I moved quickly to the door between our room and the rehearsal room. I put my foot against the door, preventing whoever was there from entering. I was desperate to stop him moving out into the corridor where he would have me trapped. I needed to keep him here. It became a battle between the force of my foot and my shoulder and his force. I knew I had one second before he began to push harder, one second to let the door free and dart across the small room and out the same door through which Donnacha had departed. The voice I heard as I ran was the voice of the music teacher. I raced down the dark corridor and then along another, illuminated corridor, and then through the narrow doorway that led to the dormitory. I knew that the music teacher could easily have seen me from behind in the second of these corridors if he was following closely enough. The trick now was to take my shoes off and get straight into bed, cover myself with blankets and pretend to be asleep.

It was not long before I heard footsteps in the dormitory. All he had to do was use his sense of smell and he would smell semen or stand silently watching me until I turned to check that he was gone. I was careful to lie still, to do a perfect imitation of someone sleeping for at least half an hour, before quietly undressing, tasting what sperm was still caked on my skin and then getting into my pyjamas and going to sleep.

In the morning I felt drained and guilty—the sounds Donnacha made would have been unmistakable—but I knew there was nothing the music teacher could do. After breakfast when I looked over I saw that Donnacha must have slipped out of the refectory. It was a few days before he began to speak to me again, and when he did he was guarded and I knew he did not want to talk about how close we had come to being discovered.

I took my time drying my hands in the toilets of the Clarence before returning to the table. When I got there I found that Seamus Fox was sitting in my chair having an animated discussion with Gráinne Roche. I knew Seamus because we had served together a number of years earlier on a jury at a film festival in Galway. I found him friendly and funny, which was surprising since the columns he wrote were notable for their sourness and a level of support for rural and traditional values that at times made Gráinne Roche seem radical and cosmopolitan. I tapped him on the shoulder.

"Get up," I said.

He turned and grinned.

"I now declare this meeting of the Catholic cranks of Ireland suspended," I said. "Go back to your own table."

"What are you doing together?" he asked. "How do you know each other?"

"We are the only two people who have read your book *Reading the Bible with Bono,* and we often meet to discuss it," I replied.

"OK," he said. "Wexford. I get it. The Wexford mafia."

"Our aim," Donnacha said, "is to rule all Ireland."

"Wash your hair," I said to Seamus Fox. "It's too long and too greasy."

"Fuck off."

"Here now," Donnacha interrupted.

"If the bishops heard that," I said.

"You can take them out of Wexford," he said, "but you can't take Wexford out of them."

"Tell me something," I asked.

"What is it now?"

"Is the Church still against fornication? Or has that gone the way of Limbo and the burning of heretics?"

"Fuck off."

"What is the current thinking on wankers?" I asked.

Seamus Fox stood up and grinned and then sullenly turned and walked back to his table.

"How to make friends and influence people," Donnacha said.

"Hey, it worked," I said. "He's gone."

"You're worse than ever," Gráinne said. She then caught the eye of one of the waiters and did mock handwriting in the air as a way of calling for the bill.

"Are you paying?" I asked.

"Yes, I'm paying," she replied.

"Are you going to send me the book?"

"When it's published."

"What do you want me to do with it?"

"Read it."

"Is that all?"

"There are things about you in the book. I used your name. I thought it was polite to tell you."

"What about me?"

"About the prayer meetings we had."

"I don't remember much about them," I said. "And I don't care much about them either."

"What do you care about?"

"Don't try that stuff on me. Save your sincerity for Seamus over there. He needs it more than I do."

"I just want you to say something that you really mean, that's all."

"Do you? Do you really?"

"Yes, I do."

The bill came and she paid by credit card.

"It was nice to meet the two of you," I said, pushing my chair back and standing up.

"Do you remember the poem you wrote," Gráinne asked, "called 'There's Blood Flowing Out from the Rose-Bowl'? I still have the copy you gave me in your handwriting. I've quoted from it in the book. The publishers will be writing to you asking for permission."

"Blood flowing out from what?" I said.

"The rose-bowl," Donnacha said. "I thought it was a bit strange myself." He laughed.

"Tell the publishers no," I said.

"I told them you'd be fine with it, that you're actually a big softie," Gráinne said. "So when they write to you, just reply and say yes. There's no reason to be ashamed."

"No reason to be what?"

"Ashamed. It's a good poem for a sixteen-year-old."

I sighed and stood up. The three of us walked out of the

restaurant together. As we passed Seamus Fox's table, Gráinne and Donnacha waved goodbye to him. I ignored him.

"Can we give you a lift? We're parked over on Lord Edward Street."

"No. I'll walk."

We stood and looked at each other. Donnacha grinned.

"Good to see you anyway. Thanks for the dinner," I said.

"You're a nice guy," Gráinne replied.

"I wouldn't bet on that," Donnacha said and grinned more. I looked at him for a second but he did not give me even the smallest hint of recognition.

They turned and walked towards Parliament Street as I walked towards Temple Bar.

When I came to Dublin first you could walk home alone on nights like this, alert mainly to the dampness and the shabby poverty of the city. You would pass lone drinkers who had been ejected from public houses at closing time. There would be almost no traffic. It was too sad to be dangerous; no one had the energy to commit crimes. The route I took now varied only slightly from the old route. Meeting House Square and Curved Street were new, but the streets that led to Dame Street had always been there. But Dublin, no matter what remained, was new with gay men in twos or threes or hungry ones alone on their way to the Front Lounge or GUBU or some new joint that I have yet to hear about. If I know them, we nod or smile.

I have always liked corners and side-streets and thus I made my way quickly across Dame Street and turned left at the sign saying "Why go Bald," walking by the side of the Stag's Head and then into Trinity Street and Andrew's Street and Wicklow Street, hitting Grafton Street at McDonald's. I love these turnings, and now, in these years of change and prosperity, I love the untidy crowds in the streets, the idea of a night not finished, the Garda car edging its way along the pedestrianized street with young Gardaí looking out at us suspiciously as though they were thinking of having furtive sex with us. I love seeing drunk people on their way elsewhere.

It is the last stretch I cannot bear, when I come to the top of Kildare Street and have no choice but to walk in a straight line along Merrion Row and Baggot Street towards Pembroke Road. This is the grim city with a few damp bars and creepy nightclubs and places to buy chips and hamburgers and kebabs. The street lights are dim and there is a sense in behind the house façades of murderous old spaces with half-rotting floorboards, with crumbling brick and rattling windows and creaking stairways and alarm systems in urgent need of repair. Front rooms tarted up or shiny signs outside for solicitors and auctioneers and public relations firms make me shiver even more as I pass them on my way to my nest of attic rooms, my wireless broadband, my stack of CDs, my new printer, the closets half full of clothes that soon won't fit me, the wall of books, the lamps that all turn on from a single switch. Each time I take this route I marvel at my foolishness for not finding another way home.

Across the city I imagined Gráinne and Donnacha driving to their home in Terenure; I imagined her going over the evening, indignant about some of the things said, satisfied at others. And Donnacha in the driver's seat nodding mildly, making the odd amused remark, or turning serious when a matter of fact was in dispute. I imagined the drive of their house where the car could be parked, the single tree, the flower beds, the mowed lawn, the PVC French windows leading from the dining room to the long back garden. Their sons up watching television. I imagined her in the kitchen, where they kept the computer, making tea and Donnacha sitting with the boys not saying much. I thought of the two of them going up to bed, wishing the boys goodnight, a biography of someone or other on the table at Donnacha's side of the bed, some new books about Ireland and its ways on the table on the other side where Gráinne slept. I imagined lamplight, shadows, soft voices, clothes put away, the low sound of late news on the radio. And I thought as I crossed the bridge at Baggot Street to face the last stretch of my own journey home that no matter what I had done, I had not done that. No matter how grim the city I walked through was, how cavernous my attic rooms, how long and solitary the night to come, I would not exchange any of it for the easy rituals of mutuality and closeness that Gráinne and Donnacha were performing now. I checked my pocket to make sure I had my keys with me and almost smiled to myself at the bare thought that I had not forgotten them.

Barcelona, 1975

At first there were two. They watched me easily, nonchalantly. They were good-looking and, like actors, utterly
alert to themselves, dressed I remember now—and I may be
wrong about some of these details—in black and white, one
with a waistcoat, the other with a grandad shirt. One was taller;
both were thin and lithe. The taller one was braver, cheekier;
the other seemed content to wallow in his own skinny beauty.
They were watching me now and they wanted something from
me and I was not sure what that was.

I was twenty then. I had left Dublin just after my final
exams, taken the boat first to Holyhead and then the night
train to London and then the plane—my first plane journey—
to Barcelona. I was raw and unhappy and I missed home. Sometimes at the beginning I stayed in bed the entire day, listening
to the city sounds—metal blinds being pulled up and down,
motorbikes, voices—wishing I was back in my old bed in a
back room in Hatch Street with everything familiar and easy.

I dreamed one night that I found a great balloon to take
me over the Pyrenees and the Bay of Biscay to the comfort of
Dublin. I dreamed of watching the kingdoms of the world from
this height, all made golden by the prospect of abandoning the
daily ordeal and the constant excitement of being in a foreign
city alone for an indeterminate time without a word of the language.

Colm Tóibín

The two of them were watching me still. To make sure I was
not imagining that they were somehow in pursuit, I stood up
from the seat and moved slowly down the Ramblas towards the
port. They stood up from the seat opposite and, when I looked
behind, I saw that they were following. I sat down again on
another seat and they sat brazenly opposite me. When one of
them smiled, I returned the smile. They were not threatening
me; they were not frightening; and they were not going to go
away. By now I was not sure, in any case, that I wanted them to.

The taller one walked over and sat beside me. Soon we discovered we had a problem. I had no Spanish and he had no
English. When I spoke in faltering school French, he shook his
head and pointed to his friend and called him over. His friend
had no English either, but he spoke fluent French. Soon a number of facts became clear: they lived nearby in Plaza Real; one
was a painter; the other, the smaller one, was studying literature. They were not surprised when I said that I was alone in
the city and was living in a *pensión* nearby and looking for work
as a teacher. They spoke to me as if they would never let me go.

We must have had a drink, or spoken at greater length. But
it is also possible that, trusting and needy, we made our way
quickly to the apartment on the top floor of a corner building
on Plaza Real, an apartment that had within it, like a maze,
other smaller apartments and locked rooms, one of which was
owned by the painter. The student of literature's room, which
had its own bathroom as well, was across the badly lit and
dingy corridor.

I did not know what we were going to do when we went
back. Talk some more, I presumed. Have a drink, perhaps. But
I must have really known. I was not that innocent, even though
I had never done anything like this before. I suppose what I
really did not know is how or when or in what combination it

would be done. I know that I eventually spent time naked in a bed with each of them separately, but I am unclear now about the order or the precise circumstances.

I know that we were in the painter's room. I thought his paintings were bad, too literal and crude, but the room itself was wonderful, laden with strange objects, prints and posters and funny ornaments. There was a small stereo and one classical record, among the collection of jazz and rock and old Spanish songs. It was Beethoven's Triple Concerto. I asked them to put it on and it became the theme music for my visits to that room over the subsequent months, the only music I heard at that time. The lovely cello coming in first was more than an aspect of the pleasure I felt and the things I learned in that room, it stands in for them now; the concerto's chords and cadences and sudden gorgeous shifts are enough to conjure up the scene in all its newness and excitement and glory.

The painter's room comes to me now in two guises. It was a small, intimate, lamp-lit room, dominated by a large bed; it was also a large room where many people could happily sleep. I don't know how it could have been both. That first night it was a small room. There may have been a chair. The music was on. One of us was sitting on the bed. The painter was wandering in and out of the room as the other, the one interested in literature, came towards me and began to kiss me. There was a taste from his breath I had never encountered before. It was the taste of garlic. And even now, should I smell it from someone's breath, it carries an erotic charge with it, a sense of pure easy pleasure, beautiful lips and tongues and teeth, and the promise of soft warm skin and sex.

I was unhappy that the painter might return and find us kissing, and when he did, I moved away, as though we had been caught by a parent or a teacher. This amused them. Barcelona in 1975 was a foreign country, I soon learned. I tried to work out the rules. These two young men were friends, not lovers. They seemed to have followed me without discussing which of them might entertain me when we got home. They had no interest in being together with me, but they were not embarrassed at being watched by the other in this, the preliminary stage. So we kissed again, this time as though it did not matter who was watching.

That night, or some night soon afterwards, I fucked the literary guy on the painter's bed. He was by far the more beautiful of the two when he was naked; he was smoother, more feminine, with a much thinner waist and beautiful long legs. His arse was hairless, almost fleshy.

He kissed with slow passion and responded slowly, carefully and deliberately to every movement. His lips and his breath were what I loved most. In a drawer on the right-hand side of the bed he found the Vaseline and he rubbed it on his arsehole and on my dick and then he turned away from me, face down, his arms stretched out in front of him, his head to the side.

I had done this only once before. I presumed it was easy. I lay on top of him and shoved my dick in hard, with an aggression he might not have seen in me earlier. He screamed, yelling at me in French to take it out, take it out, I was hurting him. When he was free of me, he turned away, holding himself and moaning. The idea that I had hurt him made me excited, but I was also alarmed that he would not speak to me or turn back towards me. I did not think that I had done anything wrong.

Somehow, over the next few minutes, the French language ceased to work for us. He had to make sounds and gesture with his hands to emphasize that I had pushed in too suddenly, too fast and too hard, and I must go in more slowly, gradually and gently. All of these instructions took time. It did not occur to me that I could lose interest in finishing what I had begun. I remained ready to be educated, longing to fuck him some more. I was thus ready to start again and do as he said. He turned once more and put extra Vaseline on his arsehole. He wanted to be fucked again; I knew now that he did not want to be hurt. In seeking to oblige, I nonetheless made him wince as I put my dick inside him as fully as I could and began as slowly as possible to fuck him, trying to keep going and going until he seemed to be both hurt and happy at the same time.

I do not know if it was that same night I ended up in another room, a much smaller room, with the painter, and watched him growing bored with me, having begun with an immense and all-governing fervour, kissing me, holding me, running his hands all over me. I do not know if we ever came to orgasm with each other, but if we did it was the end of our sexual time together. The passion we had was a small game and it ended soon after it began.

As the old dictator began to die, we three tried to meet again. A few times I turned up at the apartment and rang the various bells and was let in by an electronic switch, only to find a stranger on the top floor. A few times I left a note. Once, the guy I had fucked came to my *pensión* and left a note for me. My landlady was curious about him, made nods and gestures as if to say that an interesting man had called for me. Once I met the painter on the Ramblas; he signalled that he was in a hurry but would see me at the apartment later.

I wonder if the next time I found my friends in residence was the first night of the orgy. In any case, in my memory now the painter's room expands and there are suddenly other beds and mattresses on the floor and maybe twenty young guys. No one that night was drunk and there was no alcohol in the flat, which surprised me. In Ireland, were an orgy to take place—and this was unimaginable in 1975—then everyone would have had to get drunk first and begin by pretending it was not happening. In this orgy, in the flat on the top floor of the building in Plaza Real, the twenty of us were very quickly and rampantly naked. There were no drugs; there was a great deal of easy laughter. In my innocence, I believed that there were no rules in an orgy. You took who you liked for as long as you liked and then discarded him when you got fed up with him and then you took someone else, or indeed several someone elses at the same time, if the occasion should arise.

I took the first guy who came towards me. He was friendly and large-framed, with brown eyes and soft skin. As soon as I touched him, his dick was erect. We found a bed to the side of the big bed and started to play. Bit by bit, a set of rules began to emerge. No one in the room fucked or sucked cock. Everyone kissed and fondled one another. It was as though a strange modesty had broken out. Everyone was in a couple; no one disturbed another couple, or moved from the guy of their choice to another guy of their newer or greater choice. After half an hour of pleasurable monogamy, I realized that I had misunderstood everything. I should have waited. I had made a big mistake.

That mistake was smiling at me now as we kissed. I smiled back. He was a nice guy. But across the room, alone, was another guy who was even nicer. He was watching the orgy with considerable engagement but he was still wearing his underpants. He noticed me watching him. He was not tall, but he was strong without being too muscular. He could have been a runner or a swimmer. He had shiny brown hair that hung around his head untidily, and dark eyes, but he did not look Spanish. He could easily have been Dutch or from Eastern Europe. I wished I had waited for him and slowly it became obvious that he wished I had too. The problem was how to get away from the guy I was with, who was increasingly passionate and eager.

If I made the guy come, I wondered, would I then be free? But he did not want to come, nor did anyone else in the room, it seemed. This was another of the secret rules. That loss of serenity, as the Pope once called it, was not part of this orgy. Coming would be a moment of self-exposure and no one wanted to do it in public. I would have to wait. It took time before my loss of interest became clear to my partner. He was good-humoured about it. He stood up and walked out of the room, signalling that he would be back soon. I realized that there were other rooms off the corridor with other beds. I followed him to find the toilet. As I passed the guy whose underpants were still on, I nodded to him and he nodded back. I soon found an empty room and an empty bed and I waited.

The new guy was shy and hesitant when he came into the room. He sat on the edge of the bed and looked at me. He already knew that I was Irish, someone had told him. He spoke very good English, but often waited between sentences and phrases to think. I noticed how smooth his body was, how tightly packed and coiled he seemed. I wondered what he wanted and I wondered what it would be like to kiss him. There was something almost remote about him. His sexuality was more hidden, more cared for than that of the other guys in the room. He held himself apart.

Suddenly, without warning or excuse, I put my hand on his chest. He looked at me gravely, remaining still. Before this, he had smiled as he spoke, and a few times as he grew silent we had smiled at each other. Now this was too serious for smiling. He sat and looked at me. It was as though his blood were changing its colour or its nature and it was going to take time.

He could do nothing until that was completed. For five minutes then we were like statues. But I knew that it would have to end in him coming towards me, and once I knew that I was happy to watch him as he prepared himself for it.

I stroked his back and his chest as he lay down. He touched me as though every touch would be remembered and would come to mean something. He left his underpants on. I judged that as a reticence that mattered to him, so I did not touch him there. He kissed with an astonishing seriousness. Soon we were joined in the room by the guy I had been with earlier and the painter, who was, I suppose, the host of this event. The painter was now dressed up with a mantilla on his head and a brassière on his chest and nothing below. He was wearing makeup. Both of them were brazenly discussing my brazenness, my nerve at having moved so quickly from one guy to another. My new friend translated for me, and we both laughed, but I realized that I had broken a rule and that this was a house of rules, even though it did not seem like one.

I don't know when I first let my new friend fuck me. I had been fucked for a few seconds the year before, but it was so painful I had made the guy take his dick out forthwith and keep it out. Another guy, the summer before I left Ireland, had tried more successfully, but it was better when I fucked him. So when my new friend asked me if I liked fucking or being fucked, I said I liked fucking. He said he did too, and in fact he hated being fucked and couldn't do it. He was shy about saying all of this, but still he left me in no doubt. We had a problem. So I gave in.

We would never have done it while others could come in and out of the room. I think we waited until the early hours, when there was peace in the apartment and most people had gone home and the rest were sleeping. I was nervous. He had a way of suggesting an immense inner life in which outward actions were considered first as theory and then gradually and deliberately put into action. His dick took time to harden and then it stayed hard. It was very beautiful. Long and lovely to hold and not too thick or unwieldy.

I began to wish to be fucked by him as he held me and kissed me, assuring me that there was no hurry, we could do it another time. But I knew he wanted to do it now and for me in those years there was never another time. I wanted everything now. So in the night in this strange room, I turned around, my face down, and he moved with his mysterious slowness, touching my shoulders, and then moving his hand down to my arse and testing my arsehole with his finger, probing it gently. I could hear him breathing hard, as though this action, more than any other, had made him very excited. I was excited too, but I was tense. The thought of being fucked was much sweeter than the awkward, fumbling and painful mechanics of really taking another guy's dick right up inside your arse.

At first it was panic. I thought I was going to shit and I wanted to warn him. He had put his hands under my shoulders and was gripping me tightly, not moving or thrusting, just letting his dick slide in farther. I could not hear his breathing. He was absolutely still, and holding me still too, calming my panic with a fierce and stable energy. Eventually, I began to relax and, having wanted to make him take it out, I now began to want it there. Slowly, he started to fuck me.

The poet Don Paterson, in *The Book of Shadows,* a collection of aphorisms, writes: "Anal sex has one serious advantage: there are few cinematic precedents that instruct either party how they should look." My friend looked, as far as I could imagine, as though the mysteries of the universe were close to being solved by him. I imagine he kept his eyes wide open. At times he would turn my head and we would kiss as passionately as we could, considering the angles. When he came, he held me for a long time without moving. Then he put all his energy into making me come. On a later occasion, when his dick slipped out five or ten minutes after he had come, he said "Goodbye," but I don't think that happened the first time.

The city was a vast distraction. I found a restaurant I liked; a few bars; a few English-speaking friends. I got some hours teaching. I signed up for Spanish classes. Like everyone else, I followed the news about the failing health of the old dictator. And now and then over those months, a crucial time in the history of Spain, I noticed how generally indifferent people were to anything except the private realm, which was inhabited by the young with great intensity. The books you read, the friends you met, the lovers you slept with, the music you listened to, the new identities you took on, these were the things that mattered in that autumn in Barcelona. The disintegration of the old man and his regime was like an invisible undertow. The surface of life was too exciting for anyone to do more than shrug at the possibility that this undertow would begin to pull us elsewhere.

I called around to Plaza Real whenever I felt horny. Sometimes, my friend was there and we would make love. We would arrange to meet and make love again, often in different bedrooms in buildings elsewhere in the city that were owned by friends of his. I never introduced him to anyone I knew. I never told anyone about this secret life. A few times, when I called and he was not there, I stayed if there was a party. The parties were good. I realized that the painter, with his elaborate mantillas and costumes and fans, was slowly becoming a personage in the city. He moved up and down the street, cheeky, full of mockery and wit, with one or two friends, dressed like a young Spanish girl at a fair or a religious ceremony, but wearing two or three days' stubble.

He was, I realized one night, very funny. I had stayed over in his room, sleeping with some others on a mattress on the floor. Early in the morning he began a monologue, imitating accents, putting on voices. I had no idea what he was talking about, but everyone in the room was howling with laughter. It might have been that morning, or maybe it was another, when a woman, who seemed to have a room in the warren of rooms on that floor, arrived with her child, a little boy less than a year old, who could crawl but not walk. She left him with us, twenty half-naked, half-sleeping men. Our friend the painter set about entertaining the child, and we all joined in. Everyone was jealous of whoever had the child's attention. The baby crawled on top of us all, laughing and making us laugh. We made faces, did voices, played in whatever way we could with the little boy, until his mother came back. The baby cried at being taken away from us.

I discovered that my lover could read English with astonishing ease and fluency. When he spoke he was hesitant, but then I realized that he was also hesitant in Spanish and in Catalan. A few times at night I lay beside him and watched him reading late Henry James novels, amazed at his sharp grasp of the most complex sentences. Once, when the painter was out, and my friend had a key to his door, or it had been left open, we made love on his bed. I knew where the Vaseline was kept. It was the first time that he fucked me from the front, my legs spread out, my ankles on his shoulders. At first, this was even more painful than before, but soon it was easy. I loved looking at his face as he fucked, his gaze so intense, as though he might eat me. When the painter came back and saw us on the bed and the Vaseline on the table beside us, he put his hands in the air and said: *"Por favor!"*

My lover was not there the evening the dictator died, nor was I. He later told me that he had heard the party that night was the best of all. Outrage after outrage was committed, and, I supposed, many new unwritten rules were devised. I was sorry I had missed it. I was drifting away. The painter had got tired of me sitting on his bed listening to the Triple Concerto. I was very interested in those years in taking my clothes off; putting more of them on, dressing up as a señorita, was not my style.

So I did not go to the opening of Ventura Pons's film about the painter in the Cine Maldà. I read about it in the newspaper. By this time, the painter's name was a byword for the new freedom and all the youthful happiness that came in its wake.

I stopped seeing my lover. Six months later, however, when I got a flat around the corner from Plaza Real, I discovered that he had moved to another flat on the same floor of the building where we had met. If he was home, the lights were visible from one of the streets between Escudellers and the Plaza Real. Sometimes when I walked home I would check the light and if I was feeling in the right mood I would call in to him. He would play his old game of talking and listening as though there were no sexual charge between us. And then I would move towards him and touch him, and, just like the first time, he would remain still, in his lovely old trance. This transformation from the social to the sexual, which I could do in a split second, took him time. And then he was ready.

All these years later, I can still take pleasure in the tight, hard shape of him, his tongue, the knob of his dick, the glitter in his eyes, his shy smile. I always knew that if I did not keep him, he would go. Someone else would claim him.

One night, towards the end of my time in the city, he hesitated for even longer than usual when I touched him and then he told me that he could not make love with me. Someone else had come along and wanted him, he said, and he could not fuck anyone else. He was sorry. I nodded. It was my own fault. I should not have wandered off as I did, coming to him only when I felt too horny to keep away. I walked down the stairs of that flat in the Plaza Real for the last time and into the shining city. I was ready, once more, for anything.

The New Spain

When the bus left the passengers from the airport at Plaza España, Carme Giralt wondered what she should do. It was almost midnight. The heaviness, the murkiness in the air, the fetid smell from the drains and the absence of any wind, made her understand that, whether she liked it or not, she was home. She had spent two frenzied days in London throwing out clothes and papers and giving away furniture and books, and then making the basement in Islington tidy so she could get her deposit back. She had put no thought into this part, what she would do on her immediate arrival in Barcelona with her family nearby, her parents maybe getting ready for bed in the old apartment, her sister somewhere in the city with a husband and two children whom Carme had never seen, and her grandmother newly buried in the cemetery in Montjuïc not far from where Carme now stood.

It was eight years since she had left the city, since her father had silently taken her to the airport; his rage against her then was palpable and elemental as he stood watching to make sure that she made her way through the departure gates. To spite him, she remembered, she had waved and flashed a smile. She had imagined that she might never see him again but, she thought, as she prepared to cross the desolate street, she had been wrong. She would be seeing him soon.

First she decided that she would find a small hotel or a *pen-*

sión and stay the night there. In the morning, when the air was fresh in the city, and she had slept, she would consider how long she might wait before she called to tell them that she had come back.

Somewhere in the police station in Via Laietana there was a file on her. Or maybe, she thought, with the arrival of democracy they had removed the files and even destroyed some of them. But not that much had changed. They had legalized the Communist Party—Carrillo was back in Madrid and so were La Pasionaria and Rafael Alberti—but there still must be, she thought, a need to know who the Communists had been. She imagined an underground space, a bare bulb and a long row of tightly packed folders. One of these would have photographs of her and an account of her interrogation. They might even have noted her deep revulsion for the southern accents of the two policemen who asked the questions, a revulsion she made no secret of during those two days. And they might have snaps of her, she thought, in the year or two after her arrival in London, demonstrating outside the Spanish embassy for the end of the dictatorship and the return of democracy, or someone might have written an account for them of the party she organized in London to celebrate on the night after Carrero Blanco was blown up.

Now the old regime had died and she had been away. She had not been here to toast the death of the dictator. When her grandmother had called to mark his death, she had announced jubilantly that the bottle of cava they had been saving all the years had just been opened. As Carme moved slowly along the Gran Via, her suitcase becoming a burden, she still did not regret that she had missed that night, or that she had missed voting in the referendum for a new constitution or in the first election; she had heard enough from her sister, who had come

138

to London alone just a year earlier, and from her grandmother once or twice on the phone, about old friends and former comrades who had joined the Socialists, or others who were now talking about Euro-communism and jockeying for position. All of them had avoided the demonstrations unless they saw a need to be photographed. They were, she knew, filled with the sly knowledge that they would soon be taking power in Barcelona and Madrid, serving under a king who had happily served under the dictator.

The lobby of the hotel she found was opulent and bright but the room was grim, the furniture dark and too big, the curtains depressing, heavy with dust. There was something dingy about everything including the bedclothes and the bedside lamp, which gave off a light too faint to read by. She would stay here just tonight, she thought, and then she would move. She had never stayed in a hotel in the city before. In the silence as the night wore on, a silence broken intermittently by gurgling pipes and noises in the corridor, she did not know if the gloom that came over her arose from the dismal atmosphere or from the fact that she felt no desire to make contact with anyone, no one she had left behind in London, and no one here among her family or former friends.

In the morning, once she had showered and put on fresh clothes, she felt more courageous, more prepared to deal with them, but when she phoned her sister's apartment there was no answer. On an impulse then she phoned her parents, holding the receiver out as though it were in danger of exploding, but there was no reply there either. It was strange, she thought, how easily the two phones ringing without response came to seem like large defeats, made her feel powerless, depressed and unable to decide whether she should check out of the hotel now and leave her bags at reception or go for a walk, buy a newspaper, have breakfast somewhere, and return later and phone them again.

She walked towards Rambla de Catalunya, allowing herself at first to feel that this was aimless, that she was merely straying, but then becoming determined that she would actually go towards her parents' apartment, and stand outside it and look at it, or have a coffee in one of the *granjas* nearby.

Democracy, she thought, had not affected the morning here—the men in dark suits, the buzz of traffic in the wide, ordered, grid-like streets, the shops where they always had been, the sense of an old, stable wealth. Slowly, as she began to notice the women and the clean, elegant, conservative cut of their clothes, she felt that what she was wearing was wrong, and that it would take her a long time to find out again what was right. She must appear to these women, she thought, like a tourist with cheap English clothes who had wandered into the city from the coast.

That impression of not belonging here made her feel braver than if she had dressed up. Thus she found herself in the hallway of the building confronting Gloria, the *portera,* who had been there for as long as she remembered.

"They are not here," Gloria said, even before she greeted her.

"Where are they?"

"They're not here."

Gloria seemed almost insolent. In the tense silence that lay between them, it struck Carme that Gloria must know that since her grandmother's death Carme owned a third of this entire building, that she was no longer the girl who had caused all the trouble, the Communist, the one who was arrested, that she was equal to her mother and her sister now. She stood to her full height and stared directly at Gloria, allowing her gaze to contain all the arrogance and effortless aura of entitlement that her mother and her grandmother had exuded all of their lives.

She made to speak and then thought better of it as she realized that Gloria was still not going to let her pass, or offer her the key to her parents' quarters.

"They're not here," Gloria said again, as though it were an excuse or an alibi.

"I think I heard you the first time."

She was aware how Catalan she sounded and how fully in possession of herself she appeared. She would not ask Gloria the question again. She had asked it once, that was enough. The power she had in this hallway, a power she had never felt, not even once, in all her time in England, gave her a surge of energy. She knew it would not be long before Gloria said something.

"They have gone to Menorca."

Carme did not smile or even acknowledge that Gloria had spoken.

"Your sister has gone too, and the children. They've all gone. They'll be there until Sunday. They'll be there for San Juan."

Carme nodded and turned back towards the street. She should, she thought, have realized what the date was and remembered where they would be.

"Do you want me to . . . ?" Gloria called after her, but she did not reply. As soon as she saw a taxi, she hailed it and asked the driver to stop at the hotel, where she collected her bags before telling the driver to go on to the airport.

There was a wind over the sea that day that she had not noticed in the city. It meant the plane was late departing and, once airborne, seemed almost too small and weak to make its way across to the island. It was normally a smooth, short journey. When they were children, she remembered, they had always gone by boat, and she could feel now the pure excitement of the car being driven by her father down through the city and then slowly into the belly of the boat and then herself and her sister being led by their parents to their berth, all neat and air-conditioned, and then on deck to watch the city gradually recede.

She tried to think now: the journey out at the beginning of the summer began at dusk and took all night, and then the journey home when the summer ended lasted all day, they docked in the port of Barcelona when it was almost dark. The city was alien to them each time they returned because the summer was long and had no rules, and her grandmother's presence had softened her mother's impatience, had eased her father's inability to settle or relax.

She and Nuria looked forward more than anything to those weeks in August when their parents went sailing with friends and the two girls were left alone with their grandmother and the guests who came and went. Everything in the house was shaded and cool and austere. There was a long table under the balcony at the back that was set perfectly three times a day for meals. The garden was scorched by the sun and the sea wind; the beach close by was empty in the mornings and sometimes even in the heat of the day. She remembered the smell of burning citronella to keep the mosquitoes away as they dined late; she remembered the salty heat as she fell asleep at the table while the adults talked and then was carried quietly to bed.

She had not left Ian, who was her last English boyfriend, because of what he said about Spain, but his remarks had not encouraged her to stay with him. It was an evening when she had too much wine in a Spanish restaurant in Camden Town. She had not meant to talk about the house and the summer and the sea; it was something she had never done before. But once she began, she found that she had summoned up too much emotion and she could not stop herself talking more, describing how the adults always took the rooms that did not have a sea view, how the view of the sea was for the children, how her parents and her grandmother each had a bedroom with its own terrace, a private boudoir, a bathroom and dressing room, and how much the women kept out of the sun and away from the beach.

And Ian had interrupted to say that he had been in Spain too, that he had gone to Lloret with his brother and his parents, and he said how much he had disliked the food; it was too oily, and how there was hardly any beach there at all and the apartment they had was dingy.

She looked across the table at him, remarking once more the fineness of his face, its paleness, the greyness of his eyes, the thinness of his lips. She desperately wanted to go on describing the house where she had spent every summer until she was twenty, the shutters and doors painted dark blue, the old tiles on the floor and the high ceilings with exposed wooden beams, and some of the furniture, including the rocking chairs and the piano that had come from Cuba, where her grandmother had been born. But she stopped herself and sipped her drink and hoped that Ian would stop too, and would have no further reason to mention the oily food and the dingy apartment and his time in Spain.

She knew during her time in England, especially on sweltering days in the London summer, that she was missing the best years of her life in the best place she had known, the years when she would have most relished the salt water, the calm waves in the early morning, and enjoyed the ceremony her grandmother had made of family meals at that long table in the shade. She imagined herself sitting on one of the rocking chairs with a cat on her lap and the sound of crickets and the smell of food cooking. That was all lost to her now, and it was hard not to feel as the plane landed and she waited for them to open the doors that she had made a mistake with a decade of her life, that she had started too many college courses in London and finished none, that she had been with men she did not love and lived in houses and in streets that she hoped now never to see again.

When she had rented a car and had her bags in the boot, she was tempted again to find a hotel, but she had postponed things once already, she felt, and she should be courageous now, she should drive across the island and find them in her grandmother's house, the house that she and her sister had inherited between them, which would, she supposed, always be theirs now. Her family would, she presumed, have been alerted by Gloria the *portera* with the news that Carme had arrived and that she knew they were in Menorca, but they would hardly expect her to arrive so soon.

She opened all the windows wide in the car and felt the heat in the air and the breeze from the sea and the smell of something almost spicy, something that she could not identify, mixed in with the smell of melting tar. This was all she wanted, she thought, the whitened light, the air blowing directly from the sea, the smell, whatever it was, and the straight road like a ribbon across the flat island. If she had realized fully how much she loved this place, she thought, she would have come back years before, she would have flown back to the island on the first day it was safe for her to do so.

As she turned left, she was surprised for a moment by the way the road had been paved when before it had been a road of dried mud and dust in the summer, almost a track, and further surprised by the sight of rows of new houses and then single houses with gates. But she was too light-headed to care about this, and too filled also with excitement about seeing the house again to care about having to face her parents after all this time.

Soon she came to a fork in the road that she did not recognize. She took the road that veered left and brought her closer to the beach. At first she believed that she had simply not remembered this fork, but it struck her then that the road was new. On the right-hand side were small bungalows with tiled roofs and gardens in front, each one planted with bougainvillaea. She presumed that if she drove beyond them there would be a turn to the right that would lead to her grandmother's house but soon she saw that the road led to a group of bars and restaurants facing the beach and there was no road to the right. As she turned the car, she saw people sitting at outside tables with bright umbrellas over them, having drinks or being served food. She studied them for a second as though she might recognize them, but by their skin colour and a sort of distant, strained look on their faces she saw that they were tourists.

The house could not be gone. It was just a few minutes' walk from the beach, so it must be, she was certain, at the end of the other road, which veered to the right. She turned and drove along it, noticing more bungalows on the left-hand side of the road that must back on to the ones facing the sea. These had bigger front gardens, all manicured, each one the same. After a while she saw her grandmother's house, which looked desolate and strange, almost ungainly after the pretty, perfect, minuscule bungalows.

When she parked the car under the shade of an awning beside two other cars, she saw that one of them seemed hired like hers; the other had all the dust of the island on it. She wondered if it had belonged to her grandmother.

As she moved into sunlight, she felt the hard, bright heat of the afternoon. She heard music coming from the beach and listened carefully now in case there were any sounds coming from the house itself, but there was nothing. It was difficult to work out what to do, whether she should fetch her luggage and walk around the corner to the entrance, which faced away from the sea, as though she belonged here and was casually returning, or whether she should appear around the corner timidly and call out their names to see where they were and return later to the car and get her bags.

Suddenly, she found that she was nervous; she would have loved it had the house been empty, the key hidden where it had always been, and the rooms inside closed up and shaded, waiting for her to enter so that she could open them and let in the summer light. These were rooms that she remembered now and longed for as no other rooms she had known in her life. But she wanted them emptied of the people who might be in them. She felt, as she moved towards the entrance to the house, with just the car key in her hand, an immense hostility towards anyone she might meet.

The first thing that struck her as she turned the corner was a long modern swimming pool where there had once been a grove of olive trees. Her mother and two children were swimming and splashing in the pool. Her father was lying in his bathing trunks on a long green plastic easy chair with a plastic table beside it. He was the first to see her. As he stood up she noticed that he had become much heavier; she tried as she approached to look him in the eye to avoid glancing at his bare bulging belly.

"We were expecting you," he said and moved as though to embrace her. "Gloria called."

She stood her ground.

"All of this?" She pointed at the pool as her mother, aware now of her presence, began to swim towards the edge. The two children were wearing inflated swimming supports; they did not pay any attention to her arrival.

"Yes, we were just saying that you would find changes."

Her mother climbed the ladder out of the pool.

"Don't come near me," she said. "I'm wet."

Carme looked at her and then back at her father.

"Nuria is inside somewhere," her mother said.

She wondered what she should say, if she should suggest going into the house in search of her sister, but she remained silent and did not move. Her mother turned away from her and went to the shower at the side of the pool as her father put on a sleeveless shirt. The children were still splashing in the water.

"How did you get here?" her father asked.

"I hired a car."

"We thought you might not come until tomorrow."

He attempted a smile but she did not respond.

"The olive trees?" she asked.

"Your grandmother wanted a pool for the children."

When her sister appeared, they embraced and kissed. Carme noticed how tanned and slim Nuria was, how elegant, even though she was wearing just a thin skirt and blouse and simple sandals. Something had changed in women's clothes in the years she had been away, she thought, and she wished that she knew what it was.

Her mother moved towards them and began to dry herself with a large beach towel.

"It's so much better now that we have the pool," she said. "You see, we don't know who's on the beach any more, it's all changed. It's so much nicer to be private. No tourists here."

She smiled at Carme.

"Would you like a drink, or a coffee?" her father asked.

"No," she said.

"But do sit down," her mother said. She moved a chair towards her as Carme looked around to see where the rocking chairs were but saw no sign of them.

"Gloria was amazed to see you. And then she called because she was worried that she hadn't invited you in," her mother said.

"I stayed in a hotel," she said. She remained standing.

"You should have let us know," Nuria said.

As the two children came out of the pool, they were introduced to their aunt. The older one, a boy, shook her hand but his sister glanced at her shyly before they both found towels and retreated into the house.

"They really do love it here," her mother said.

There was silence for a moment. Carme watched her mother trying to think of something else to say.

"We should organize a room for you," Nuria said.

"It's not like it used to be here," her mother said. "With the children, we're much less formal and we don't really have guests, at least not to stay."

Carme was about to point out that she was not a guest, that, according to her grandmother's will, she now owned half the house, but caught her sister's gaze, which appeared to warn her off saying anything. She presumed that Nuria was in one of the suites just above where they stood and that her parents were in the other. She almost smiled to herself at the thought that this would soon change. Her grandmother must have considered that, she thought, when she made her will and decided not to leave any part of the house to her only daughter, the girls' mother, who was now busy putting on a long summer dress. It must, she thought, have been her grandmother's revenge for something her mother had done or not done.

"Nuria, why don't you arrange everything," her mother said,

"and then we'll all meet for drinks before dinner down here. I need to have a shower and I might even have a rest."

Carme found it strange that no one had set the table properly for dinner and that no one told the children to sit up straight and be quiet during the meal. Neither of the children was wearing shoes. Everything seemed confused. She wondered if it was always like this as Nuria spent all her time trying to calm the children down, or encouraging them to eat their food. She waited for someone to ask her how long she was staying or what she intended to do, but noticed as the meal ended and Nuria brought the children to bed that her parents found ways of keeping themselves apart from her. Her father went into the sitting room and made phone calls while her mother moved into the kitchen and then emerged and began tidying around the pool.

Carme sat on her own at the table, listening to the noises of the crickets in the grass and snatches of her father's phone conversation through the open window. He was talking about flights and buses and timetables. She heard him calling the airport then and checking times of incoming flights. She was tired and thought she might soon disappear to the bedroom at the other side of the house that she and Nuria had prepared before dinner.

As she began to clear the last things from the table a man came around the corner looking for her father. He did not look like a friend and spoke to her in Spanish. She was surprised because it was now after eleven o'clock and the man's tone seemed casual, as though he often called at this time. When she told him that her father was on the phone, he walked past her and into the house. He obviously knew his way around.

She listened at the window again as her father spoke to the man about keys and numbers of cottages and which cottages were empty. She wondered what her father had to do with incoming flights and keys and cottages. Then she collected the few glasses that were left and brought them inside, putting them beside the sink in the kitchen. She went to the bedroom without saying goodnight to either of her parents. Once upstairs, she was tempted to find Nuria, but decided instead that she would wait until the morning and ask her questions then.

She woke early and pulled back the shutters and opened the windows fully. The sky was clear, and the blue of the sea was soft, almost whitened by the morning sun. In London, the sky could be like that as well, she remembered, but it would never mean that the day would remain fine. Even in high summer, she always found a hint of cold in the English wind, and no day passed when there were not some clouds in the sky. She knew that the day here on the island would be perfect, and the night would be warm.

As she looked over to the left she saw the tiled roofs of the new houses she had passed the previous day. She tried to recall what had been there before, and was sure that there had been nothing, that it had been windswept in the winter and too sandy for anything much to grow in any case except tough sparse grass. And then she realized that this land had belonged to her grandmother, that her grandmother had often complained about having to maintain it, but had liked it because there was nothing built on it to break the view of the sea from the house.

Over breakfast, she almost asked them how her grandmother had come to sell this land, but once more there was too much confusion with the children for her to be able to fix on one of them with a direct question. Soon, her father went into the village, Nuria disappeared upstairs and her mother and the children dived into the pool. It was still only ten o'clock in the morning. She wondered how she would spend the day. Despite her mother's invitation, she did not change into the bathing suit Nuria had found for her and join them in the pool. Instead, she walked around to the front of the house, noticing that the path down to the beach had been blocked off by a new wall. She walked down the drive and along the narrow dusty road until she came to the first group of bungalows, the ones that did not have a view of the sea. A few of them, she saw, were inhabited. The fact that they were joined to each other when none of the old traditional houses on this part of the island were joined like that, and that they had security bars on the windows, reminded her of how much she had hated the grubby tourist villages in Majorca when she had been there years before. She supposed that there were many places like this on Menorca too, but had never imagined that they would come so close to her grandmother's house.

Later, when Nuria appeared and said that she was going into the village to collect some cooked chickens she had ordered the day before, Carme said she would go with her in the dusty car, their father having taken the new one.

"What happened here?" Carme asked as they came to the bungalows.

"You'd better ask Father."

"What does it have to do with him?"

"He built them."

"Who let him do that?"

"Ask him."

"I'm asking you."

When she looked at Nuria, she saw that her sister was concentrating on the road as though there were something dangerous coming towards them.

"Granny worried about money a lot."

"She owned the entire building in Barcelona, and the shares."

"The building in Barcelona is rent-controlled, and she didn't want to sell the shares."

"Why not?"

"Because she was afraid to touch her savings or the capital. She wanted the income from them because she wanted to go on sending you money every month in London and she wanted to give me the same, and don't complain about that."

"She had plenty of money."

"She didn't think so."

"So she sold that old fool prime building land?"

"Yes, and he built the houses."

"What does he know about building?"

"Nothing. Which is why he has a problem."

Nuria parked the car but kept her eyes fixed on a point beyond the windscreen and did not move.

"And what is the problem?" Carme asked.

"She sold him the land, and there was a clause that he could build houses on it if he liked, and he could rent them and the money was all his, but he couldn't ever sell them without her permission. That's what the clause said. She insisted on it."

"She liked holding on to things, didn't she?"

"And now he wants to sell them because he owes the bank money and he's having problems with the repayments. Or at least he wants to sell some of them."

It took Carme a moment to understand the implications of what her sister was saying.

"Did we inherit that clause?"

"Yes, we did."

"So he needs our permission, our signature."

"Yes, he does."

Carme almost laughed out loud.

"Don't gloat," Nuria said.

"I think we should get the roast chickens before they grow cold," Carme said.

As they drove back to the house they did not speak for a while. Carme waited for Nuria to ask her something, but then realized that Nuria intended to say nothing.

"Have you seen a lawyer?" she asked eventually. "I mean your own lawyer."

"No," Nuria said.

"Why not?"

"I'll tell you why not, because the man I'm married to invested in some of the bungalows, and he wants them sold too. Both Jordi and Father think it is the best time to sell."

"Does Jordi have problems at the bank too?"

"No."

"Does he need the money?"

"No, but he likes selling when the time is right."

"Are you sure that Father needs our permission to sell?"

"Yes, I am. And so is he. No one will buy unless we sign."

Over lunch, her mother suggested that Carme move into the bigger room and leave her parents the room she was occupying, or they could move into one of the other, smaller rooms.

"We can move out now, can't we, Paco?" her mother said.

Her father nodded in assent.

"I mean, you've been away for so long."

Her mother smiled.

"I think Carme is happy where she is," Nuria said. "And we're only going to be here two more nights."

"She might like us to move now," her mother said. "And if she does, we can be out in a second."

"I'm fine where I am," Carme said.

"No, really . . ." her mother continued.

"That's enough about it, Mother," Nuria said.

The change in her mother's attitude was too deliberate; she saw that Nuria was embarrassed by it.

"Well, our room is lovely," her mother went on, "we always love it, but the two of you will have to decide if you want to redecorate. You know, the plumbing . . ."

"Yes, there'll be plenty of time for that," Nuria said.

Soon the children began to attract everyone's attention and the man who had come the previous evening returned and went into the house with Carme's father.

"I wish he didn't come during meals," her mother said.

"Don't offer him coffee, Mother," Nuria said. "We need a bit of peace today."

Carme asked her sister if there was a place on the island where she bought clothes and Nuria mentioned a shop in Ciutadella where she knew the owner.

"Oh, don't go there today," her mother said. "They have most of it closed off for the festival tonight. You'll never get parking."

"They'll open again at five," Nuria said. "But they'll be closed tomorrow. I can call her if you want."

"No, I'll drive in and have a walk around," Carme said.

She went upstairs, passing on the way her father and his visitor, who were going through a ledger with close attention. She had a shower and put on fresh clothes before setting out for Ciutadella. She would have a coffee while she waited for the shops to open.

Almost everything she saw in the small boutique on a shaded side-street in the old city to which her sister had directed her was simple and light. And yet the clothes were designed in a way so different from what she had bought in England that they all seemed strange to her. She tried on a number of outfits, but felt that she would need new skin and new hair and a new expression on her face before she could wear them. She was sorry that she had not asked Nuria to come with her; Nuria at least would have been able to keep the owner at bay. But she might also have given her advice about sandals, or suggested that she deal with her hair, her nails and her skin before she begin to buy skirts and tops, no matter how right they were.

The owner, who was alone in the shop, appeared offended when she handed her back the clothes she had tried on.

"I'll need to come with my sister," she said. The woman made no effort to disguise her irritation and looked at the clothes as though they had been soiled. She herself was dressed in a severely cut grey dress. She was wearing shoes that could have been slippers they were so light. She was also wearing too much jewellery, rings and earrings that were too big. Her suntan had to be fake, but Carme could not be sure. In London, her look would have stood out, been too elaborate, but here, even in this small city on the island, it seemed almost natural. Carme sighed and checked herself in the mirror and walked out of the shop.

As she made her way slowly along the street, she stopped to look into the window of an antiques shop. Her mother's remark about redecoration came into her mind and she wondered if she and Nuria should talk about buying some good old furniture. Suddenly, she noticed a piano that seemed familiar. When she pushed the door and went inside to check, she also found two rocking chairs, unmistakably the same as the ones her grandmother had owned, and realized that the piano on display was her grandmother's piano, which had come from Cuba and had been in the wide corridor leading to the staircase of the house. When she looked around she saw other furniture that also belonged to the house. As the owner approached, she knew that she would look to him like someone who had bought property on the island in the recent past, an outsider. She spoke to him in a deliberately hesitant Spanish.

"And these," she said, "where did they come from?"

She pointed to the piano and the chairs.

"They were from the house of an old lady who died," he said. "They would need restoration, but they are very good."

"How much?" she asked.

He gave her the price, which was high.

"Have you had them for long?"

"No, a month or so," he said.

"I'll take them," she said.

She probably, she thought, should have bargained. Now, as the owner watched her, she did not want to give her name or address, or even a cheque or a credit card in case he recognized her name.

"Can I come and pay you on Monday?" she asked. "When the festival is over?"

When he agreed, he asked for a name.

"I'll give you my husband's name," she said. "Ian Lee. Will that do?"

"Your Spanish is very good," he said.

"Thank you."

He wrote the name down using a large black marker and put it on the piano.

"I'll see you on Monday," she said.

"Enjoy San Juan," he replied. "Make sure you come in early tonight and see the festival before it gets rowdy."

"I will," she replied.

Over supper, while Nuria was upstairs, having taken the children to bed, and there was a strained silence at the table, Carme mentioned that she thought she might drive into Ciutadella later to see the festival.

"Oh, we never go to that any more," her mother said. "Not for years now. No one goes."

"No one?" Carme asked.

"No one we know. It's too full of outsiders and tourists now."

"It's been completely spoiled," her father said.

There was silence again, broken only by the sound of crickets and frogs beyond the swimming pool. Carme watched her parents and was tempted for a moment not to say anything, or to wait until Nuria came back. But there was something about the way her mother was eating, something so self-satisfied, that she could not contain herself.

"Completely spoiled," Carme said in a low voice, "like the view from this house."

Her father sipped a glass of water, her mother stared into the distance.

"Like the view from this house," she repeated, raising her voice.

Her parents pretended that she had not spoken.

"Did you hear what I said?" Carme asked. "Spoiled like the view from this house. Don't you agree?"

As Nuria returned to the table, her mother moved as though to say something.

"Excuse me," Carme said to her father, "don't you agree with what I said? Or have you grown deaf as well as fat?"

"Carme!" Nuria said.

"He has grown fat selling our property to tourists and now he has the nerve to complain about them spoiling things!"

"Keep calm, everybody," her father said.

"By the way, I bought the furniture back. I found it down a side-street. The old piano and the rocking chairs. And if you sell anything else"—she turned to her father—"I will call the police."

"Oh, listen to the Communist!" her mother said. "The police! Will that be the Russian police? Or the Chinese police?"

"The bungalows are ghastly," Carme said.

"Do you know why your grandmother sold the land?" her mother asked. "So she would have enough cash in the bank to send money to you every month. How we used to laugh as we went to the bank together! You know, even the manager used to laugh as your grandmother would announce that she wanted to send money to her little Communist in London."

"Montse, shut up!" her father said.

"Her lazy little Communist, too lazy and useless to work and too lazy and useless ever to finish a course."

"Montse, I asked you not to . . ."

"How we used to laugh when she said it! The little Communist living off her granny. And now the little Communist is eating our food. And complaining about the view."

"Montse, we are going to need . . ." Her father seemed angry and agitated.

Carme turned to her father.

"Need what?"

Her father stood up.

"Come on," Carme said, "finish it. Sit down and say what you were going to say."

"You know what we need you to do, Carme," her father said, sitting down again. His voice was calm. "Nuria has told you. I asked her to tell you."

Carme looked at Nuria, who kept her head down.

"Who sold the furniture?" Carme asked.

"It was rotten," her mother said.

"'Rotten,' that's a good word," Carme said. "Taking land from an old lady, that was rotten. And has your husband grown fat too, Nuria, has he grown fat too on the profits you made from her?"

Nuria got up silently and went into the house.

"Every stitch you're wearing was paid for by the poor old lady," her mother said. "And you phoned once a year, that is what she got in return. And you come back just in time to claim your inheritance!"

"Just in time, that's right," Carme said. "Just in time."

She stood up and left the table. Upstairs, as she fetched her keys and some money, she passed Nuria in the corridor without speaking to her. As she left the house again, she saw that her parents were still sitting at the table. She walked by them and went to the car and drove into Ciutadella.

There were lines of cars parked on both sides of the narrow road on the way into the city and there was a sound in the distance of firecrackers going off and people shouting. It was pitch-dark as she walked along, but she knew that the dawn was only three or four hours away. It was St. John's Eve. She would already have missed the early part when sacks of hazelnuts were left in the square for people to take and throw at anyone at all, a friend, a lover, a stranger, an enemy. She was amused at the idea that she could have thrown one each at her father, her mother and her sister, and they, in turn, she supposed, could have thrown one with even greater force back at her.

She was still disturbed by one thing her mother had said. She did not mind the part about being called "her little Communist in London." It was typical of her grandmother to make such jokes and to tell them to her bank manager if he would listen. But she was wounded by the statement that she had phoned only once a year. It was true. She had often thought of phoning more often, but she never did. She should have got in contact more often, there was no excuse. She had let too many years go by, it was as simple as that. The regret came to her sharply now as she walked into the city centre, the place her grandmother had loved most in the world.

Carme knew how much her grandmother would have loved now to come in alone with her like this for a few hours of the festival, watching the horses parading through the streets. As she turned a street corner and saw the yellow sand spread on the cobbles to keep the horses steady, Carme whispered a few words to her grandmother's ghost. She said she was sorry. She said it was too late now, she knew. But she was back here and she was sorry. Sorry that she had stayed away so long. And sorry too that she had not been in touch more.

From the doorway of a house a woman stopped her and offered her a *pomada* in a tiny plastic glass from a tray. She laughed as she took the drink and had her first sip. The taste brought her back years; the mixture of lemonade and local gin made her feel that she was in her teens and had come here with Nuria and her friends. At that time she was the youngest of all of them, she remembered, and had to beg her grandmother for permission. And then her grandmother had overseen every-thing, had ensured that Carme did not look either too young or too sophisticated, and made her promise that she would have just one or two *pomadas,* no more, and that she would stay close to Nuria, and that she would keep away from the boys who ran after the horses. When Carme had promised that they would be home early, she remembered her grandmother saying that that would be a mistake, that no girl on the island had ever come home on St. John's Eve until well after the dawn, and that Carme and Nuria were not to let the family down by breaking that tradition.

It was strange, she thought, to be alone like this in the streets of Ciutadella. In the busy parts of London, even at night, a young woman walking alone, or sitting alone, or going to the cinema alone, would not be unusual. Here no one was alone. There were even no couples. Young men walked around in large groups, or five or six girls wandered in the streets with five or six boys, or older women walked up and down in groups of three or four. She was, she saw, the only person on her own, and that, she supposed, made her look like a tourist more than anything else. Yet, despite what her parents had said, there appeared to be no real tourists. Maybe because it was after midnight the tourists had all gone to bed, whereas people from the island knew that midnight was the time when things began. And no one seemed like an outsider either; people greeted each other with familiarity and appeared fully at home as they lined the narrow streets now and waited for the horses and their riders to come galloping through.

The horses were bigger than she remembered and they came at speed and were greeted with shouts and cheering. The rid-ers were dressed in mediaeval costumes and were unflustered as groups of young men moved out into the middle of the street to block their progress; the men placed themselves under the bellies of the horses, using their shoulders as, almost gently, they began to lift the animals so they were standing on their hind legs. The horses had been trained, she knew, not to kick or panic, but still there was a sense of struggle and drama that came from the shouts of encouragement from everyone in the street and from crowds at the upper windows of the houses. The men were trying, as though it were a competition, to hold the horses in the air for as long as they could before lowering them to the ground to stand on all fours.

And now that the horses had been slowed down, women came to the doors of their houses and asked riders to take the horses through the narrow doors to their hallways and into their living rooms for a *botet.* They kept appealing for a *botet,* for the horse to lift its front legs for a second within the building and thus bring luck to the household for the rest of the year. Carme watched as some riders obliged, guiding the horses through the almost impossibly narrow spaces, and, once outside again, looking away as more requests came, and then beginning to move towards the next street.

As she watched them going, she noticed again what she remembered from years before when the horses, having performed their ritual, left the street on St. John's Eve. There was a melancholy that came over everyone, a sort of communal deflation as people realized that the excitement had come and gone. The summer was at its peak; from now on the days would get longer, the shadows would grow deeper. This feeling lasted only a few minutes, but it brought with it memories of those who had witnessed this night over the years and had died, those who would have loved this night and were gone for ever. As she looked around her, especially at the faces of the women, she saw it, the look of regret, a sudden stillness. And then it lifted just as quickly as it had come. People reached for drinks, which were handed free from the houses, or decided to move on and follow the horses, or turned back and made their way home.

She was planning to return to the car when she saw a group of men coming towards her and found that she recognized some of them from summers on the island in the past. A few of them were islanders, she knew, and a few from Barcelona. She wished she could have slipped by them until she realized, with relief, that none of them seemed to know she had been away. They spoke to her as though they saw her every day. They were surprised that she was alone as she told them Nuria was at home minding her children; and then they insisted that she come with them. She did not bother to ask them where they were going; she knew they were ready to walk the streets and then go to bars and later to the beach as the dawn broke and the jousting began. She loved their easy manners and was amused by their purposeful attitude as they pushed through the crowds at the first corner they came to as though they were organizing the entire festival and were urgently required to be elsewhere. And she loved too that none of them asked her a single question and that none of them tried to make a claim for her or flirt with her in any open way. They took it for granted that she was coming with them; their company and the heat of the night made her feel free to laugh and smile with them as they moved along.

In the first bar they ordered beers and included her without asking her; she had not tasted an Estrella beer in all her years away and the taste uncovered almost limitless sets of feelings and memories—of summers on the island, of drinks with friends and comrades in bars around Plaza Universidad in Barcelona after meetings in the university—all of them mixed in her mind now with pleasure. She closed her eyes and drank the beer down; one of her companions ordered her another before showing her a rolled joint and asking her if she wanted to come around the corner with him and his friend and smoke it. As she looked at the group she was with, she understood that their mixture of speedy determination and mellow humour came from the fact that they were all stoned. It was something, she thought, she should have noticed the second she saw them on the street.

Outside, she was shocked at the openness with which they smoked the joint, the nonchalant way it was passed from one to the other. Although many people went by, no one seemed to care. Her two companions were from Barcelona but she knew them both from the island rather than from the city. The taller one she had known as Nando, but he now was called Ferran, which she thought was funny; the other had always been Oriol. She understood that, by coming out now with them like this into the street, she had at least left it open to one of them to move closer to her and stick with her for the rest of the night. If she didn't want this, she knew she should move back into the bar soon and leave them there. They would know not to pursue her. She took a few more puffs on the joint and drank the cold beer; she thought about it as she looked at the two of them. They had a lovely way of pretending that this was all nothing, but she knew from the way they stood that they were waiting for her to stay with them or go back in. She shrugged and leaned against the wall and decided to let things happen, to linger here, to make no decisions, to let Ferran and Oriol work it out between them. But if one of them wanted to stay near her as they walked the streets, if one of them wanted to get drinks for her in bars and go to the beach with her when the sun came up, then that, she thought, would be fine.

Once they both seemed to know that she was going to stick with them, she almost laughed out loud at their different ways of being the one who might end up with her. She almost asked them if there was a shortage of women on the island. And she found herself giggling at the thought that every mother in Menorca was keeping her daughters indoors, away from the clutches of Ferran and Oriol. Ferran tried to talk to her, explaining something about the house they were all staying in, his Catalan filled with Spanish slang words and some local terms; she enjoyed how he was barely making any sense. Oriol simply stood by, looking cool. His hair was long, his jeans were tight, he was skinny like a rock star. He managed to be part of the conversation without saying anything; she was tempted for a moment to poke him in the stomach and ask him to rescue Ferran, who in mid-story had lost his way. When they finished the joint, they went back into the bar and found the others, who were ready to move on.

In the next bar they ordered gin and tonics; the music was too loud for anyone to speak much, so Ferran and Oriol just hovered, Ferran swaying and smiling, Oriol remaining more mellow and distant. For a second, when Oriol brushed his hair back, she noticed how beautiful his face was. He saw her looking at him and smiled with a look of recognition that was proud, almost self-regarding. And that made her turn towards Ferran and say something to him that she knew he would not be able to hear; they moved closer to each other. And once he let his arm linger around her waist, she brushed against him and then moved away. It was enough to signal that, unless something happened, she would stay with him for the rest of the night.

The next bar they went to had softer music. They found

places to sit and were joined by other friends of the group. She liked the way Ferran left her alone and Oriol admitted defeat by keeping away; Ferran did not try to impose himself on her, but talked to the others and went regularly to the bar, but he remained within her orbit and made sure she understood that he was not going anywhere without her. Eventually he came over to tell her that one of the group wanted to go up to the convent and wait outside, that the horses and riders before going to the beach for the jousting were going to visit the nuns, who would be awake before dawn. They were all going to go soon, he said, when they finished these drinks, or it might be a while more. There was no point in being there too early, he said, as the nuns might not be dressed yet.

She laughed and said that the nuns would, no doubt, be delighted to see them all. He sat beside her. For a moment she thought that he was going to kiss her, but he was distracted by something and instead merely looked at her closely several times, the expression on his face serious. As she sipped her drink, she felt tired and was almost sorry she had stayed out so late; she wondered if she might go. But then, when the music changed and became louder, she settled back in her seat and enjoyed being tired. When Ferran suggested that they go outside and smoke another joint, she stood up and followed him.

By the time they were on the beach the sun was almost hot and the crowds had gathered, some revellers from the night, others who had risen specially to witness the jousting, which had all the elements of a mediaeval pageant. Two large poles had been dug into the sand and between them a piece of wire had been hung with an opening in the centre. The riders carried a javelin in one hand; the horses began slowly way down the beach

and then moved at breakneck speed as the riders attempted
to pierce the hole with the javelin as they passed to the cheering of the crowd. While earlier at the convent, and then when
they had made their way lazily to a café to have coffee, Carme
had felt exhausted, almost irritated, and desperate to lie down
anywhere and get some sleep, now she was filled with energy
again and found herself shouting with the others as the horses
and riders approached.

The sea was soft and beautiful in the morning light, and
there were times over the next hours when she felt exhilarated
by the night that had passed and wanted to take Ferran home
with her and make love with him. But still she kept him at
arm's length, never once moved towards him, or touched him,
or let him find that she was looking at him. She knew, however,
that he would not go, and the feeling that they had made a tacit
arrangement added to her ease and happiness as it became clear
that it would soon be time to leave.

She waited for a while and then caught Ferran's eye and nodded to him. They walked into the city together as though all of
this had been set up in detail. She was glad that he did not try
to hold her hand or put his arm around her; instead he brushed
against her fondly and remained silent as they went towards
the car.

When she checked the time, she discovered it was only
six fifteen. They would be sleeping still at her grandmother's
house; she would not have to worry about introducing Ferran to
her family. Nonetheless, she put her finger to her lips when she
had parked the car; they moved gingerly around the corner like
teenagers coming home late. She almost panicked as Ferran let
out a shout when he saw the swimming pool, indicating to him
that he would have to be quiet. He looked around as though he
were a thief in a comedy as he made signs in return asking her

if she wanted him to roll another joint. She almost laughed out
loud as she let him know that she did.

As she sat back and smoked, Ferran quietly stripped to his
underpants and then, having taken a pull from the joint, turned
and dived into the pool. The noise of the splash filled the air
and caused some pigeons that had been nesting nearby to fly
away in an immense flutter. Ferran swam using a vigorous and
awkward breast-stroke and she realized that the sound of him
in the water would surely wake those sleeping in the rooms
above. Thus she was not surprised when one of the shutters
opened and her mother's head appeared. Her mother made a
dismissing signal with her hand to suggest that Carme and her
friend, whoever he was, should take themselves off the property. Carme responded by having a long relaxed pull on the
joint and then waving at her mother with the joint in her hand.
She began to laugh. As her mother closed the shutter, she found
that she could not stop laughing.

When Ferran came out of the pool and dressed himself,
they both discovered they were starving. In the kitchen, they
made sandwiches from cheese and meat they took from the
fridge; Ferran opened a cold bottle of cava to toast the morning and let the cork pop noisily against the ceiling of the
kitchen.

Later, when she woke to the sound of children's voices, she
looked at Ferran sleeping; one of his arms lay stretched out
away from him and the other was curled around her shoulder.
No Englishman could ever sleep like that, she thought, or none
she had ever known. Ferran's mouth was slightly open, she
could hear the rise and fall of his breath, which was almost gentle, and could sense how peacefully he was sleeping. Ian would

always snore if he slept lying on his back, she remembered, and he could never sleep in any case with an arm wrapped around her. He turned away from her in the night, and if in the morning he moved towards her it was a sign he wanted sex.

But maybe in the end there was not that much difference between these men, they had the same tender needs. They would spend a whole evening, as Ferran just had, as Ian once did too, tactfully watching and waiting, making sure they did nothing that would cause her to want to sleep on her own. They were alert at each moment to what was ahead. They were like children on their birthdays, she thought, and found herself having to stifle a giggle. Whatever Ferran had put into the joints, she thought, had lasted through the morning.

Ferran, when he woke, told her that he had arranged to meet his friends at five that afternoon. It was something they did every year, he said, on the twenty-fourth of June, they went to a restaurant that two of them owned and ate there in the hours between lunch and supper when it was closed to customers. They had all paid for the food, he said, and it would be good. She said yes when he suggested that she come with him. They used the bathroom down the corridor to shower. Carme agreed to stop by the house where Ferran was staying so he could get fresh clothes.

Downstairs, at the table outside, her parents and Nuria were having guests to lunch. Carme had warned Ferran not to stop, that she was not doing introductions, they were just going to walk by and say they were in a hurry if anyone spoke to them. Her mother, when she saw them appear, made as though to stand up. Carme looked at her bravely and showed the key of her car to everyone at the table and led Ferran past them without saying a word or waiting to be introduced to the guests. She was tempted to peer around the corner for a second once she had reached the car and see what her mother was now doing, but instead she drove away from the house towards Ciutadella.

The restaurant was more like a cabin; it was built at the edge of a cove, was close to a pier. Under the awning in front the owners had placed a long table, set perfectly for twenty or more people. When they arrived, one of Ferran's friends, whom Carme had met the previous evening, shouted to Ferran from the pier. He was going down the coast in his motorized dinghy, he said, to collect two or three people, and he invited Ferran and Carme to come with him.

She sat on the edge of the dinghy as it moved out of the harbour at speed. The water was clear and blue and the sun was hot in the cloudless sky. But there was also a wind that made the journey rocky at times and meant that the dinghy had to be steered with skill and deliberation. Within a few minutes she was covered in sea spray and had to sit right down in the boat. She closed her eyes and held on to a rope and laughed as the bottom of the dinghy filled up with water. Her clothes were now completely wet and her hair destroyed by the salt spray. At one point as the dinghy turned in towards a cove, she almost cried out to Ferran's friend to slow down and go more carefully, but he would not have heard her with the sound of the engine.

When they had collected the others and were about to make their way back, she was on the verge of suggesting to him that he should take it a bit easier on the return, but the look on his face and the way he dealt with the dinghy made her hesitate. She realized that she had failed to recognize how much his behaviour, which was gruff, masculine and utterly competent, belonged to the island. He would think she was silly and from

Barcelona if she asked him to go more slowly. In his flip-flops, his torn jeans, his faded T-shirt and his uncombed hair, he was in full command.

By the time they returned, bowls of salad were being put on the table, and one of the cooks, wearing a white apron, was bringing out bottles of white wine and jugs of water. She could smell the fresh prawns being grilled. When finally everyone was seated, the seafood came to the table as soon as it was cooked, with regular promises that there was more. The first prawns were small and sweet, but the ones that came later were larger, some of them closer to crayfish. They had been cooked perfectly, without garnish or any sauce; the texture was hard but not too hard or rubbery. They were full of flavour. She loved the idea that there was nothing else except the salad to accompany them, no rice or potatoes or vegetables. She wished Ian could see this table now as everyone feasted with constant good-humoured shouting and banter and passing of dishes and pouring of drinks. Big ceramic bowls were brought for them to throw the leftovers into, and dishes with water and lemon wedges to wipe their fingers clean when they were finished.

When the plates had been taken away, and the cooks had been allowed to sit down to eat the last of the prawns, and the cups for coffee were being put on the table, a woman whom Carme did not know, sitting at the other end of the table, called to her.

"Have you been on the island for long?" she asked.

"No," she said. "I mean I haven't been here for years."

Since this was the first time the table was listening to a single conversation, she wished it was about something else, or addressed to one of the others.

"You were in England?" the woman asked.

"Yes."

"Did you have to get a British passport?"

"No. I had a student visa."

"But did they not take your passport away?"

"They delayed it when it needed to be renewed, but I didn't . . ."

"They were such bastards!" the woman said.

"Who? Who are you talking about?" a man down the table asked.

"The police," the woman said. "They tortured her."

"No, they didn't," Carme interrupted.

"Your grandmother told me that they did."

"I was arrested."

"Your grandmother said that you had to be got out of the country very quickly."

"When was that?" someone asked.

"It was under Franco."

They all became silent. Carme looked at Ferran, who was studying her with a new attention. The way the last statement had been made seemed to suggest that Franco was a long time ago, part of a history that had passed. Even though he was dead for less than three years, his name had been spoken as though it came from a time as remote as the reign of Ferdinand and Isabella. Carme felt suddenly singled out as if her presence, or politics itself, had cast a brief shadow over the lives of these people, the meal, the festival. She was glad when the coffee came in two huge pots, a bottle of Mascaró cognac was handed down the table and everyone was distracted and no one paid her any more attention. When she caught Ferran's eye he shrugged and then gestured with his hands out flat towards her, signalling that she was someone he would not safely meddle with. When she pointed at him with her finger threateningly, he recoiled, and they both laughed. He rolled another joint.

* * *

It was after midnight when they came back to her grandmother's house, which was, once more, quiet. She was glad everyone had gone to bed. Since they were tired, they were going to go straight to her room until Ferran said that he wanted to get some cold water to take upstairs. When she turned on the light in the kitchen she gasped when she saw the fridge. Someone had wound a rusty chain around it and locked it so that it could be opened a chink but not any more than that. Once Ferran had examined the lock, they stood back in amazement.

"No sandwiches tonight," he said. "And no cold water either. Who did this?"

"My mother," Carme said.

She moved towards the door of the fridge and kicked it, thus knocking the fridge itself against the wall. Ferran kicked the door too, putting a dent in the front of it. The hum from the fridge grew louder as though it were in pain, and then it settled down to making a calmer noise. As they stood in the kitchen, Carme knew that the whole house must be awake now and she put her fingers to her lips and motioned to Ferran to follow her quietly up the stairs to her room. When he went to the bathroom, she could hear him urinating into the bowl and then washing his hands. She knew that the rest of the house could probably hear him too.

In the morning, as she crossed the room to go to the bathroom, she found a note under the door. It was from Nuria. "We're all leaving now," it said. "The keys are on the table in the kitchen for you to lock up when you're going. Can you leave them under the big stone, the usual place? I'm really sorry about the fridge.

It has nothing to do with me. And Papa is really angry about it as well. Mama is categorically refusing to hand over the key so we can open it for you. This was no way to welcome you home. Call me soon. Love, Nuria."

It was the word "categorically" that caused Carme to begin laughing, and by the time Ferran got out of bed to read the note, she was almost hysterical on the floor.

Later, once they had had coffee in a small café in a village, she drove him to collect his things and then to the airport to catch a flight to Barcelona. She wrote down his phone number and promised she would be in touch soon and then she left him there and drove back to her grandmother's house.

She was tired. She sat on one of the plastic chairs beside the swimming pool, which her family had covered before they left. She thought for a second that she would like something cold to drink and something light to eat and found she had forgotten that the fridge remained locked. She went in and looked at it again and wished she had a camera so she could take a photograph of it.

She wondered what to do now in this old empty house. She worried that if she took a nap she would wake in the middle of the night and not be able to sleep again; she resolved to stay awake for as long as she could. Upstairs, she changed into her bathing costume and put a light dress over it. She put on sandals and found a bag into which she placed her purse and a towel and the keys of the house. Years before, she could have been on the beach in a few minutes, she thought, but now that the path was blocked she would have to walk around by the bungalows.

The beach was almost empty and all the sand on it was tossed by people who had spent the day lying out under the sun or running down to the water's edge. In the old days when she came here, she thought, the place had been deserted at this time in June. The sand, as she remembered it, had always been smooth, unruffled. Now it was clear that there had been tourists here all day, and there were still tourists sitting at the outside tables in the bars and restaurants that overlooked the beach. She left her bag down on the sand and took off her dress and walked towards the shore. The water had that lovely feel of the end of the day; the soft waves had been rolling in and out under the full heat of the sun, even the sand below the waves felt warm on her feet. She swam out, with a skill that had never left her, breathing deeply and turning on her back once she was out of her depth so she could stare up at the sky. Then she floated, being nudged in by the pull of the waves; she faced the cove that had once been a place of great empty beauty and now had been filled by crowds. She saw the tourists sitting at the tables under garishly coloured umbrellas drinking beer and listening to some song by Julio Iglesias coming too loud from the speakers outside one of the bars.

When she had dried herself she found an empty table outside a bar and then noticed a small shop wedged between the bar and a restaurant that sold postcards and camera film and beach balls and children's toys. She went over when she saw a rack of foreign newspapers outside the shop; she checked the English papers, which, she found, were two days old. She bought a *Guardian* and went back to her table and ordered a beer and some *calamares*.

Soon, she thought, she would go to Barcelona and she would look up some of her friends from university, the ones who were still in politics, who were getting ready to take power in the new Spain. One of them, she was sure, would have a father, or an uncle, who was a lawyer. She thought of an office with high windows in one of the cross-streets of the Eixample, in Calle

Mallorca, or on Gran Via; she imagined an elderly man at his desk looking carefully at her grandmother's will and offering her good advice in correct, old-fashioned Catalan about how she should handle them all—her father, her mother, her sister Nuria. And the property she had inherited from her grandmother, and the shares.

All around her now were foreign voices, people calling to one another in English and German and Dutch. The first thing she would do, she thought, was find a contractor to knock down the new wall that cut her grandmother's house off from easy access to this beach. She would consult no one about that. She would begin the search in the morning when she had paid the antiques dealer for her grandmother's furniture. In the meantime, she would read in the newspaper about England, where she had been for eight years, and then she would have a good night's sleep, alone, in peace. As she raised the glass of cold beer to her lips, she felt a contentment that she had never expected to feel, an ease she had not believed would ever come her way.

The Colour of Shadows

Nancy Brophy, one of the neighbours in Enniscorthy, phoned Paul in Dublin to say that his aunt Josie, his father's sister, had been found that morning on the floor, having fallen out of bed in the house where she lived alone; they thought that she had been lying there most of the night. An ambulance had come, Nancy said, and taken Josie to Wexford Hospital.

When Paul contacted the hospital, the nurse in charge of the ward said that his aunt was stable. He explained that he was busy at work and wondered if he might postpone his visit until the weekend, and the nurse told him that his aunt was in no immediate danger and it would be fine if he came on Saturday. He left a number, in case they needed to reach him. Later, he was phoned by a social worker, who said that she did not think his aunt could return to living alone; nor could she stay in the hospital indefinitely. She gave him a list of residences for the elderly in the Enniscorthy area; she refused to recommend one over another.

When Paul phoned Nancy Brophy on the Friday of that week, she seemed unsurprised that the social worker wanted his aunt in a nursing home.

"She won't go easily, that's all I have to say."

"Has anyone mentioned it to her before?" Paul asked.

"We all have, but she likes her independence."

"Is there anywhere local that is good?" Paul asked.

"Noeleen Redmond and her husband have a place near Clo-hamon, and some people say that it's lovely. Noeleen was a friend of your mother's."

Paul almost replied that he did not believe his aunt would want help from someone who had been a friend of his mother's.

"Is there nobody else I could ask?"

Nancy hesitated before she replied.

"That's all long ago, Paul. It's all long ago."

"I know it is," he said, "and I'm grateful for your help, Nancy, so maybe I'll call Noeleen Redmond now."

"That would be the best, Paul."

He arranged, having phoned Noeleen Redmond and explained the situation, to come and visit the residence for senior citizens once he had seen his aunt. And then he drove the two-hour journey from Dublin down to the hospital.

"She won't eat," the nurse said to him as they both stood looking at his aunt, who was asleep.

"She eats well at home," Paul said.

"She spat out her toast this morning."

"That's very unlike her."

The nurse looked at him and shrugged.

"There's nothing actually wrong with her. We did X-rays and everything."

"She probably doesn't like being in hospital."

"Well, she's lucky someone found her."

He sat with her. After almost an hour, she turned and saw him.

"Oh, God," she said.

"You're all right."

"I hate those nurses."

"They're awful," he said.

"I hate those nurses," she repeated. It was clear to him that her hearing, which had improved after she had had the wax cleaned out of her ears, had now worsened again. "But they'd better not hear us or they'll starve me altogether."

"You were fast asleep when I came."

"You were good to come down, but don't say too much, now—they're all listening."

She tried to sit up.

"Tell them I want a private room."

"I'll do that."

"Tell them I want a private room in my own house."

Once he'd made sure that she was not too agitated, he drove to Enniscorthy, passed through the town, and turned off the Dublin Road to Bunclody. It was a crisp early winter day, and he was surprised, as he always was when he visited Enniscorthy, by the volume of traffic and the new roundabouts and the tiny scale of things that, when he was growing up, had seemed to him like monuments. This was what he still called home, he thought, but if his aunt were to go into a residence, then he might best begin thinking of his own house in Rathmines, in Dublin, as the only home he had.

He turned left, away from the Slaney, as he had been told to do, and then right again, and drove along a narrow road until he came to the nursing home, which had a large sign outside. Already he could see, from the gardens and the layout, that the place was well kept, with a clear view of woodland and the soft light over the river.

Noeleen Redmond was waiting for him on the porch. She

made him tea and said that she had a place free and he could move Josie in whenever he liked. When she told him the price per week, he thought for a moment that she meant per month. She spoke then about the cost of things, the amount of regulation there was, and how hard it was to keep staff. He tried to work out in his head how much Josie's pension was, wondering also how much money she had saved, and thinking then about what her house was worth.

"She was very good to you, wasn't she? And now she's lucky to have you."

Noeleen smiled at him warmly.

"She won't feel lucky leaving her own house," he said.

"She'll be treated very well, and she'll be well fed and warm here."

"I might tell her that it's just for a while."

"That might be best, all right."

It was almost dark a few days later when Paul arrived at the nursing home and waited in the hallway for the ambulance from Wexford to arrive. Once he saw it turning into the driveway he went into the office and alerted Noeleen; they stood at the front door as Josie was taken from the ambulance and put into a wheelchair.

"You go in and they'll make you a cup of tea," Noeleen said to him. "We'll come and find you when we have her comfortable."

As he made his way to the dining room, he passed a large room with chairs all around the walls and figures sitting in them, none of them speaking or reading, some of them asleep or staring at a television that was blaring in the corner. He stood and looked at them, but then felt as if he were intruding on something strangely private and he moved on.

Directly outside the door to the dining room, there was a woman sitting in an armchair. He felt for a moment that he recognized her, knew her from childhood, but she was so old now and frail that it was hard to think who she was, or had been. Her gaze as he passed her was defiant, almost challenging. Whoever she was, he thought, she knew how to be difficult.

As he sat in the darkened dining room and drank his tea, he asked himself how long it would be before Josie would demand to be released from here. He wondered if there was another solution, if there was someone who could spend nights with her and call in to check on her throughout the day, and he thought that he would ask Nancy Brophy when he next came down. There were a lot of new people in the town, Poles, Lithuanians, Latvians, Nigerians, and maybe there would be some woman whom he could pay to look after his aunt in her own house.

When Noeleen came to find him, she suggested that he merely tiptoe into the bedroom where his aunt was but not disturb her.

"We'll find out what she likes," Noeleen said, "and we'll feed her. She needs to put on weight. And she'll be asleep in no time. She's not sure where she is."

When Paul drove down from Dublin the following Saturday, he found his aunt in the large room with all the others. She was asleep, her head slumped. One of the nurses on duty carried in a chair for him, and he sat down in front of Josie and waited for her to wake up. Although there was a low sound coming from the television, there was a hush in the room, of which he became acutely conscious as he sat there.

When he looked behind him, he found that five or six old ladies were watching him, some suspiciously, others in a way that was too dulled to be menacing but was nonetheless unfriendly. It occurred to him that he could go and check Josie's house, light a fire in the living room, maybe, and return later. But he resisted this impulse; he knew that it was really an urge to flee from this place and not have to deal with whatever his aunt had to say.

She smiled when she woke and saw him, and nodded her head.

"They said you'd be down," she said. "You're great to come down."

"How are you?"

"Did you bring the car?"

"I drove down."

She did not seem to hear him.

"Is the car outside?"

"I drove down." He raised his voice.

"We'll go, so," she said. "I knew you'd come. They all said you'd come. Do I have a bag or anything, or a case?"

"It's very cold outside," he said.

She looked at him, puzzled.

"What?"

"It's a freezing day."

"I'd say that." She smiled.

"You're very warm in here."

"Will you get me my coat?" She made to stand up.

Later, when she had been calmed by one of the nurses, he left her, promising to return the next day and saying nothing when she asked him if she would be leaving then, if he was coming back in the car then, to take her to her own house. He was aware as he turned and carried his chair back to where it had been that the roomful of inmates had heard every word that had passed between him and his aunt.

Noeleen was waiting for him in the hallway. As he sat in the dining room with her, she suggested that he get a set of forms from his aunt's bank and her solicitor that would give him power of attorney, or at least the power to deal with her financial affairs.

The house had a smell of damp and old cooking. He was amazed at how small everything was, not only the rooms themselves but the objects in them—the armchairs and the television in the corner of the front room, the dining-room table and chairs in the back room. Somehow, the place had shrunk in Josie's absence. He remembered spending each Christmas here in recent years and loving the coal fires lighting in both rooms, the Christmas tree, the warmth of the place as he helped her wrap presents for neighbours and friends and later watched the television with her or gave her a hand in the kitchen.

When he went upstairs and looked at his old bedroom, he noticed how worn the carpet was and how the colour on the wallpaper had faded. He must, he thought, have noticed this before, but now the room seemed shabby and strange, almost unfamiliar, and not the room he had slept in every night throughout his childhood, with the small desk in the corner where he did his homework.

Suddenly, he realized that he was dreading the night ahead in this house; he did not think he would sleep. When he went to look for sheets to put on his bed, he found a musty smell in the hot press. He turned away and walked down the stairs and made up his mind that he would search for Josie's papers and bank statements and then he would go.

He made a call to the Riverside Hotel, and when they told him they had rooms free he said he would be there in an hour.

Josie would hate the waste of money, and the thought that he might not want to spend the night in her house, but the idea of having to make up a bed for himself and try to sleep in his old room made him shiver. That's all over now, he thought. He suppressed any urge to feel sorry for himself for losing it.

As he rummaged through papers on the shelf near the chair where Josie usually sat in the front room, a knock came at the door. He knew that it would be Nancy Brophy, who would have seen the light on. He invited her into the front room and told her that Josie was unhappy and wanted to come home.

"It's the same for all of them," she said. "But they get used to it, or maybe they just stop complaining. But it's a good place, although it isn't cheap."

"And her hearing seems to have gone," Paul said, "and her sight maybe a bit. I don't know."

"Her sight is fine since she had her eyes done," Nancy said. "Before that she wouldn't recognize me some days."

"It was the same with me," Paul said. "One day she thought I was Tom Furlong."

"I know," Nancy said. "She told me. She was mortified. She thought she had offended you."

Paul asked her if there was another solution, if there was anyone who could look after Josie at home, but she replied that she did not think so.

"There's work for everyone now, so no one wants to look after old people," she said. "No one wants to do real work. I hope it lasts, that's all I have to say."

"But if you hear of anyone?"

"I'll let you know. But maybe she'll settle, Paul. That would be the best."

When Nancy had left, he located Josie's post office book among her papers and was shocked at the amount of money she had saved. He had thought at first that he would have to sell the house to pay for her care, but now he realized that she would have enough for some years, especially when her pension was added to the savings. As he looked for her pension book, her missal fell to the floor and out of it five or six memorial cards, all bordered in black. He picked them up and looked at them: one for his grandmother and one for an uncle, and one for Rose Lacey, an old friend of Josie's with whom she had worked in the office of Davis's Mills before she had moved to Whyte's Insurance off the Market Square. And then among them he found one for his father, who had died when he was a baby. He looked at the date of his father's death and his age and realized that he would be in his eighties if he had lived. He would likely be too frail to help, Paul thought, or advise him on what to do about Josie. There was no point any more in regretting that he had not lived.

Once he'd put his aunt's missal back where it belonged, he decided that it was best not to keep looking through her private things. He took the post office book, found his coat, turned off the lights in the house and locked the door before making his way to the hotel.

As he sat alone in the dining room having his supper, he smiled to himself at the thought of someone mixing him up with Tom Furlong, a local elderly member of the Knights of Columbanus. He knew how much Tom Furlong would disapprove of him. In all the years, Josie had never once referred to Paul's sexuality; it was not something that could be mentioned. And he had never found out when she'd known for certain that he was gay. He had made a point of bringing friends to the house to visit; they were always male, and some of them were boyfriends or lovers,

Colm Tóibín

and thus they appeared in Aunt Josie's front room a number of times over a year or two and then never again. Somehow, it seemed, she had understood, or maybe, he thought, someone had told her.

She had not mentioned, either, that at Mass on Christmas mornings he did not go with her to Communion but sat in his seat. He remembered her face as she walked back down the aisle towards him, her expression a mixture of reverence and strain. He knew that others would have noticed his not going to the rail, and he supposed she might have minded that, too.

Only once, as the AIDS crisis was daily in the news, had she made any oblique reference to his being gay. One day when he was leaving her house, having stayed over on a Saturday night, she turned to him gently as he stood up to go.

"Are you all right?" she asked, narrowing her eyes.

"What do you mean?"

"I was just worried about you, that's all. I read the paper and I watch the television and I worry."

"There's no need to worry."

"Are you sure, Paul?"

"I am," he said. "But thanks for asking."

He almost moved towards her then to touch her arm or hold her hand for a moment, but instead he tried to smile to show that he loved and appreciated her tact. And then he left and drove back to Dublin.

The evening when she mistook him for Tom Furlong he had entered the house with his own key, as Tom must also have done regularly. With the light going, Josie was in the front room listening to the radio. It was the time when both her eyes and ears were failing her, and she had not even heard him enter. He did not want to turn on the light without asking her, in case he frightened her.

188

Slowly, however, his aunt became alert to his presence. But he had to shout his name several times, even though he was standing in front of her.

"Oh, sit down, Tom," she said. "And it's always lovely to see you."

"No, it's Paul. Paul."

She said nothing for a while, and he wondered if he should turn on the light. But he waited and then sat down on the small sofa at the window.

"Tom," she said warmly.

"No, Paul, Paul."

"Oh, Paul," she said sadly. "Paul got involved with a rotten crowd up in Dublin, Tom. A rotten crowd! I don't know whether I was right or wrong when I decided I wouldn't even pretend I knew about it. I made the decision all on my own not to get on to him about it. Oh, I don't know."

"Aunt Josie, it's Paul. This is Paul."

In the shadowy light, she stopped talking and peered towards him.

"What?" she asked.

He wondered if it would be possible to run out of the room and behave as if this scene had never taken place, make her feel that she might have dreamed a visitor, so that she could put it out of her mind, as he would, too.

"Aunt Josie, it's Paul."

"Oh, Paul," she said, and then mumbled something. "Is it you, Paul?"

"Yes, it's me. How are you?"

"Paul," she said, and then stopped. "Paul, you won't . . . I thought . . . Will you turn on the light?"

Once he had switched on the light they talked for some time about the roads and all the traffic and the work being done and the length of time it took now to get through the town of Gorey. When he stood up to leave, she looked at him imploringly.

"You will come again, won't you, Paul?"

"Of course I will, Josie, of course."

He almost laughed to himself now at the memory of this scene, the one moment in all the years when her tact and sense of decorum had failed her.

When he came down to the nursing home the following Saturday, she was ready to leave once more, insisting that she knew where her coat was and that she had nothing of any value in her room, so they both could slip out—he could help her, and no one would be any the wiser. He sat patiently with her, noticing that her hearing had improved, explaining how fiercely cold it was outside, and asking her about the food and how she had slept, and smiling each time she pressed him to take her home and slowly explaining again that her house was freezing and that she was warm here.

"Did you not bring the car?"

"Aunt Josie, it's the coldest day of the winter."

"What day is it?"

"Saturday."

"Will you go and get the car?"

He tried to change the subject and spoke about all the new houses being built on the edge of the town and all the new people who had been taken on at his office, including two accountants from England. As he spoke, he became more determined to ask her to sign the form he had received from the solicitor that would give him power of attorney. Observing her, he realized that she must know where she was, and he believed that she must have some inkling that she was not going back to her own house. She seemed to alternate between an almost childish helplessness and a weary resignation.

He took the form out of his jacket pocket.

"I need this form signed for the bank," he said. "I have a pen here."

"What are they for?"

"They mean that I can lodge your pension for you, and get you money when you need it without you having to bother."

She pretended that she did not hear. He knew that every word was being taken in by the others around them. He decided not to repeat what he had said. He merely handed her the sheet of paper and held out a pen and pointed to the spot where she should sign.

"Just your name. I'll put the date in."

She looked at him, her expression cold and hard and wounded. He knew that if he flinched now, or changed the subject, or offered any further explanation or even apology, he would lose this chance.

"Here," he said, and pointed again to the line where she should sign.

"I never thought . . ." she began.

Paul did not move. He held the paper steady and offered her the pen again. Slowly, Josie signed her name and then she pushed the sheet of paper away from her.

As the year went on, and spring gave way to summer, she began to complain less, agreeing that she liked the food at the nursing home, and that she found being put to bed at six each evening very restful; it was something she looked forward to, she said. Paul grew to recognize some of the other old people and learned to smile at them and greet them when he came to visit. Some of them, he saw, were always keen and on the look-out for news; others seemed dazed. As the year went on he became used to coming to the nursing home and Josie became almost used to the idea that she would not be leaving with him in his car.

When Christmas approached, he spoke to Noeleen, who said that many of the patients went to their families on Christmas Day, but she would be happy to look after Josie if Paul wished. He had friends in Dublin who usually had their Christmas dinner at four in the afternoon, so he could drive to the nursing home on Christmas morning and spend an hour or two with Josie and then return to Dublin.

When he came in at about eleven that morning, Josie was asleep and Noeleen was in the office. She was the one on duty all day, she said as she sat with him in the hallway, but she didn't mind. She would have her Christmas dinner in the evening and be able to relax then.

"She talks about you a lot," Noeleen said. "When you're coming next, and what you're doing. That's her big subject."

Paul smiled.

"She's great most of the time," he said. "And she's put on weight."

"I was thinking about you and her just this morning," Noeleen said. "It was awful what happened, of course, and I knew your mother well. Josie was marvellous the way she took you in and reared you. I used to see the two of you walking back to her house together after her day's work was over. And she was very proud of you."

She looked at him and nodded cheerfully. He could think of nothing to say in reply.

"And, of course, your mother always got news of you and she must have been glad that you were being looked after. There were people in the town who kept in touch with her. She always asked about you, Paul. I heard that, now."

Paul glanced over at his aunt. He hoped that she would wake up soon, so that this conversation could end.

"And she was wise to come home to Enniscorthy after all the years, to be among her own in the town," Noeleen continued. "There's a friend of mine is a neighbour of hers on the Ross Road, and she says that she's in right form."

Paul saw that Noeleen was watching him carefully. He did not know that his mother had come home to Enniscorthy and was living on the Ross Road. He wondered how long ago this had happened.

"There's no love lost, of course, between her and Josie," Noeleen said. "But that's the way. That's the way the good Lord made them, and they're too old to change now. It would take a miracle."

He had, he thought, no real memory of his mother, just a sense of being somewhere in a car with her and the memory of a smell of something that had made him sick. But he was not even sure about the memory. It was too vague. He had been aware, because he had heard someone say it, that she drank, but it wasn't until he was a teenager that he understood what this meant. He knew that his mother had come to Josie's house once when he was seven or eight and created a fuss in the street when Josie would not let her see him, because his friend Liam Colfer had told him the next day. He had been in the front room that night watching television and had no idea what all the shouting was about. Josie had merely said that it was a woman who delivered kindling and she would be coming back on Saturday, thank God, with that delivery, which was long overdue. She had refused to pay the woman, she said, until she delivered the kindling.

His mother, he supposed, had gone back to England then. He had never asked about her. Her name had never been mentioned. Every day after school until he was twelve he would go and sit in Whyte's Insurance, at his own special desk close to Josie's, and do his homework, or make drawings, or read comic books. And then, at half past five, he would go home with her.

Josie made sure that he was happy and that he studied hard. As soon as it became obvious that he was good at maths and science, she learned everything she could about careers for him and what points he would need. She paid for grinds so that he would have honours in maths and thus gain entrance to University College, Dublin, to study engineering.

He was always sure that his mother was alive, because he believed that someone, even Josie herself, would have to tell him if she died. She had sisters in the town whom he knew by sight, and a few times he had met cousins of his in one of the bars there, but he had not spoken much to them. Someone, he was certain, would tell him if anything happened to his mother. But no one had told him that she had come home.

Over the next year he saw Josie whenever he could. He always stopped and talked to Noeleen if he had time, and there was another woman, who seemed the most sprightly and alert among the patients and, he thought, the most lonely, to whom he spoke as well if he found her on the porch. The talk was always easy, of the weather, or the traffic, or the news of the day. He began to think of the nursing home as a place of comfort, the best refuge for Josie to be in now, and felt that the food and the routines of the place were keeping her alive, just as the other patients were keeping her stimulated.

Halfway through the year, Josie changed and became even

brighter. Not only did she put on more weight but she was happier and smiled if one of the nurses came towards her. She was also more forgetful, however, and could ramble when she spoke. Nonetheless, she recognized him and thanked him for visiting. Noeleen told him that the woman who had recently begun to sit beside Josie, Brigid, looked out for her, and they often talked to each other in whispers.

Paul noticed that the two women used the same rug to keep warm, and when tea came Brigid made sure that Josie did not spill hers and took the cup from her when she had finished drinking. On some visits, having driven for two hours, Paul felt guilty for staying only a short time, but it was hard to think of anything to say, and it was, he reassured himself, more important that he simply made the visit each time he promised he would. Despite the fact that her mind was gradually fading, Josie had a way of making him feel loved while he sat with her, and something close to proud that he had driven all that way.

She never mentioned the past, never spoke about her own childhood, or the years working in the insurance office, when she took care of him. Most of this appeared to have been forgotten or erased now that her world had narrowed.

He noticed new arrivals at the home more than he noticed who was missing, but slowly it became clear to him that the line of old ladies who had watched him when he first appeared in the large room had gone and that some of them must have died or were now confined to their rooms. Josie seemed not to register new arrivals or to miss those who were no longer there. She merely viewed the people in the room and the staff, Paul thought, as she viewed the television, with vague puzzlement.

Once, when he had supper with an old boyfriend who asked about Josie and seemed to want to hear about the nursing home and the empty house in the town, Paul came close to confiding that his mother, as far as he knew, after an absence of many years, was now living in Enniscorthy as well. Instead, he decided to say nothing. He knew that his friend would argue that he should try to make contact with her. He did not want to hear that argument.

When Josie's second Christmas in the nursing home approached, Noeleen took Paul into her office one Saturday after he had finished his visit.

"She's worried about Christmas," she said.

"Why?"

"She's been talking about it to Brigid. She brings it up all the time, according to Brigid. She thinks, well, she thinks . . ."

"What?"

"That you spent last Christmas with your mother and left her out here."

"But I didn't."

"I know, Paul."

"I drove down to see her specially, and I went straight back to Dublin."

"I know, Paul. I remember you saying, but I'm telling you, just in case."

"What should I do?"

"Maybe try to reassure her. Say something, if you can."

"But I told her last Christmas that I was going back to Dublin."

"Well, that's all you can do again."

The following Saturday, he raised the subject, telling Josie that he was lucky his friends Denis and David always had their Christmas dinner at four or five on Christmas Day, reminding her that she had met Denis a few years earlier and mentioning that his friends lived in Rathgar, not far from him. He had gone to their house last year, he said, and he was going to go again this year, once he had seen her. It would take him two hours, or even less, to get back to Dublin.

Josie did not respond.

Normally, Brigid greeted him warmly as he arrived and then pretended not to listen to any of the conversation he had with his aunt, but now she did not disguise her interest in what they were saying. She turned and nudged Josie, nodding at Paul.

"That's right, now," she said. "Isn't that what I said?"

Josie looked at the floor and smiled distantly, as though nothing being said were getting through to her fully.

"Did you hear him?" Brigid asked her.

Josie looked up at Paul, her expression absent-minded.

Brigid caught his eye.

"She heard you, all right. Don't mind her, now."

On Christmas Day, she seemed cheerful as she tried on the cashmere cardigan he had brought her; he told her again that he had driven down that morning and that he was going back soon to have Christmas dinner with his friends in Dublin.

"I'd say the road was quiet coming down," she said. "Years ago there'd be no traffic at all on Christmas Day, but I suppose that's changing too, like everything else."

She looked at him directly, as though she were checking now if he really had meant it when he said he was returning to Dublin. He held her gaze, trying to make it clear to her that he was not lying. She grew silent and appeared locked in some reflections of her own for a while until she noticed the buttons of the new cardigan, which she began to admire.

In the New Year, she started to weaken. Paul began to drive down one evening each week, as well as Saturday. He often found her asleep when he came on Saturdays, Brigid nudging her to wake up when she saw him coming. In the evenings when he visited, she was always in bed and usually did not wake. He would move a chair close to the bed and sit there for a while watching her. She seemed tiny in the bed; he could see the veins on her hands almost breaking through the skin. Noeleen assured him that if there was an emergency she would call him immediately.

When Noeleen finally did call, in the late morning one Wednesday in the spring, he was not surprised.

"Should I come now?" he asked.

"You should, Paul."

"How long does she have?"

"It could be a matter of hours," she said. "She's weakening. The pulse is slow."

"Is she awake?"

"No, Paul, she's asleep, and we have her very comfortable."

"Does she know she's dying?"

"Ah, who can say?"

When he arrived at the nursing home, he did not go into the large room where Josie normally was but waited by the office for Noeleen to finish a phone call.

"The doctor saw her earlier," she said when she put the receiver down. "And he'll come back if we need him. And I phoned the manse and told them. There's no priest there now, but they'll phone back as soon as someone comes in. She woke a while back and took a drink of milk, but she's asleep again now. She's in the room on her own. I wanted her to be private."

They left him alone with her. A few times when she struggled for breath he thought to go into the corridor and find one of the nurses, but he presumed that they knew what was happening. A priest came and performed the last rites.

Every time he walked down the corridor to go to the bathroom or get some air, Paul had the sense that he was being watched with a sort of grim silence by the old people who saw him. He was the messenger of death, he realized. He was the one waiting. They must have seen it before. None of them even acknowledged his presence.

Later, when it was dark, the doctor came and said that Josie could not last much longer. They left food for Paul in the dining room and put an armchair in Josie's room, in case he wanted to sleep.

"You can never tell. She could last longer than any of us think," Noeleen said as she prepared to retire for the night. "That's God's decision—it's not ours."

One of the women working all night was from Lithuania; the other was local. He was not sure if they were nurses or orderlies; he did not know their names. Slowly, however, as the night wore on, he realized, by the way the local woman came and took Josie's pulse and by her skill at making his aunt more comfortable in bed, that she was a nurse. A few times when she came into the room he went out into the corridor with her afterwards.

"I've seen it before," she said. "She's holding on. It's impossible to know for how long. You learn things in this job. And one of them is that sometimes it's the hardest thing to die, almost harder than to live. For some people, it's the hardest thing of all."

A while later, when Paul was alone having a cup of tea in the kitchen, she came and told him that he should return immediately to his aunt's room. "She's awake now. I didn't think she would wake again."

Josie, he saw, was lying on her back with her eyes open. There was a bedside lamp on, but he kept the door open as well so that light from the corridor came into the room.

"It's Paul," he said. "You're having a great sleep."

She mumbled something and then made as if to turn.

"I'm here now," he said. "If you need me for anything. I'm sitting here. And I'll get you anything you want."

She seemed to grow more agitated, and her right hand began to shake. She was trying to say something, but he could not make out even a single word.

"Don't make yourself tired," he said. "You can rest now, and we'll talk later."

She turned her head and looked at him and tried again to speak.

"Her," she said. "Her."

"Who?"

He could not understand the next thing she said.

"We can talk later, when you are up and dressed," he said.

Josie's hand started to shake again, and her breathing sounded like a set of sighs.

"Josie," he said. "Can you hear me?"

She fixed her eyes on him.

"Can you hear me?"

She mumbled, and he thought she might be saying that she could hear him, but he was not sure.

"I won't see her. Do you understand?"

Her gaze was sharp now, almost accusing. She made an effort to move.

"No, don't move. I'll get the nurse in a minute. I just want you to know that I won't see my mother. I didn't visit her. I didn't. I don't even know where her house is. I haven't seen her. And I won't. I promise I won't."

She nodded, but he was not certain that it was a direct response to what he had said. He leaned in towards her and held her hand.

"I promise you now that I won't see her. I don't want to see her."

He was still not sure that she had understood. When she closed her eyes, her face changed. For a moment it could have been a smile, but it was hard for him to tell. Her breathing grew shallow. He thought that she was going to die then and touched her arm tenderly for a moment and went to find the nurse. When he came back to the room, Josie's face had changed once more, he thought, the expression softer, calmer. The nurse checked her pulse and looked at her watch.

"No, she has a while to go," she said. "She'll go in her own time. The doctor prescribed something for pain if she needs it, and I have the keys to the press where it's kept. But she won't need it now. She's slipping away without any pain, that's what she's doing. But she's not ready yet."

As dawn broke and the morning light crept in through a chink in the curtains, new nurses came on duty, and the early routines and noises in the nursing home, which he had never witnessed before, began. When Noeleen appeared and said that it must have been a long night for him, he realized that the whole night had felt like an hour or two, nothing more. What was strange now, when he went back to the room and sat with Josie again, was how much she changed every few minutes. He wondered if it was a trick of the light, or maybe his eyes were tired. Her face, for a while in the morning shadows, seemed to him like the face of someone young. He had not known her when she was young. He remembered her always as a middle-aged woman with grey hair, someone content as long as nothing new or unusual was happening, someone always happier in her own house when the day was over and everything was in its place. He sat and watched her.

In the middle of the morning, they asked him to leave for a short time as they shifted her position in the bed again.

"It won't be long now," the nurse whispered to him when

she came to tell him that he could return to the room. He stayed with Josie for the next hour or so until the nurse appeared once more and took her pulse and then returned with Noeleen and another nurse and they said a decade of the Rosary as Josie faded into death.

The day was warm. Paul stood out in front of the nursing home and phoned work to say that he would not be there until the following Monday and then texted some friends in Dublin to say that his aunt had died. As he came back in, he found that Brigid had been taken by Noeleen down to the room to see Josie and say goodbye to her. He waited in the doorway as Brigid stood beside the bed. She smiled at him as she turned.

"Paul, I'd say you'll miss her now," Brigid whispered to him as she moved towards the door. "We'll all miss her."

"We will, all right," he said.

Brigid sighed as she passed him.

"Well, that's the way it is," she said.

He stood in the doorway and watched her walking down the hallway back to her place in the large room, with Noeleen behind her to make sure that she did not fall. He turned then and closed the door and sat on his own with Josie. He thought for a moment of pulling the curtains back and letting the room fill with light so that he could look at her clearly for the last time, but he knew that it was better to leave the room as it was. Her arm, when he touched it, was already getting cold.

He did not touch her again, but stayed there silently with her. He was tired, but he did not have even the smallest urge to sleep. He checked his mobile phone as a text came through from a friend. He thought that later he would go to Dublin and get a suit and some clean clothes and then come back and maybe stay at the hotel. In the meantime, he would wait until the undertaker arrived and then think about the death notice to be put in the newspaper and the arrangements for the funeral. There was, he thought, nothing else to be done.

As he sat there, he realized that he should go to Josie's house, that staying at the hotel would do nothing for him. He could, he thought, leave the door ajar in her bedroom and her sitting room, or open a window, do something in the house to mark the fact that she had gone. He was surprised at how much that thought seemed to satisfy him, almost console him, and how quickly that thought led to another, one he had been keeping at bay.

Somewhere not far from here, he knew, his mother was living in the same day as he was, under the same sky, in the same watery light that came from the sea and the Slaney, and someone would surely tell her before evening that Josie, her sister-in-law, had died. The knowledge that he had promised not to see his mother merged in his thoughts with an image of her being told the news of Josie's death. Her life and the one that he had lived apart from her filled his mind now, as though a space had been freed for them, the shadows cleared, by what had happened in the night and by Josie's going. He found himself inhaling and releasing breath as a way of nourishing that space, and he breathed in hard for a second at the thought that nourishing it like this was maybe all he would ever be able to do with it.

The Street

Malik stood in the corner by the drawer where the cash was kept while Baldy counted the day's takings. He tried to look humble but also alert as Baldy, without once looking up, spoke to him for the first time since his arrival. He told him that he could have a half-day free every week until he was trained and then maybe a whole day. Malik nodded and stayed still and then nodded again in case Baldy turned in his direction, or in case one of the other barbers in the Four Corners was watching. They all claimed to dislike Baldy, but Malik did not think he could trust any of them.

Baldy was gruff. When they had met at the airport in Barcelona a few weeks earlier, he had not even said hello to him. When Malik had tried to explain the long delay in Madrid, Baldy had not paid him the slightest attention, he had turned and walked away, having brusquely indicated that Malik should follow him. Then he had walked impatiently out of the airport building towards the car park. As he drove into the city, Baldy had talked business into a tiny mobile phone that he attached to his ear and in front of his mouth and had not said a word to Malik.

Malik remembered how dark and frightening the city seemed. Baldy had eventually pulled up outside a tall old building in a narrow street and motioned to Malik from the front seat that he should take his bag out of the car. With

Malik standing on the pavement beside him, Baldy rang a bell beside one of the doorways and shouted a name when someone answered through an intercom. Then, without a word, he got back into the car and drove away. Malik had waited alone in the street until a man came down and accompanied him upstairs to his quarters. The time waiting had frightened him even more than the arrival in Madrid.

Malik was surprised at the idea that Baldy thought he would ever prove himself as a proper barber. Although he was becoming more confident at the practice sessions, the others still laughed at his awkwardness. He found the machines difficult. One night the previous week, for example, they had let him give a full haircut using the electric shears and Salim had taken photographs of the result to amuse everyone. Some of the cut was far too tight, but in places Malik had left tufts of hair uncut.

Malik began sweeping until the floor was clean and then moved towards the door and stood close to it. He found a newspaper on a chair and folded it neatly. He wondered if he should do something else and tried to look busy, even though it must be obvious, he thought, that he was not busy. Baldy, he saw, was adding up the number of customers who had come to the Four Corners that day and what each had paid. When he had finished this, he put the euro notes into his back pocket and left the coins in the drawer. Then he walked out of the Four Corners without speaking.

The atmosphere changed as soon as Baldy left. One of the barbers went to the cassette player and turned up the sound. Malik thought for a moment that he might go and sit down, but then he worried that Baldy might suddenly return and catch him doing nothing. He went into the back room and checked the towels and then came out again into the shop, where there were still two clients having haircuts. The other barbers were chatting and cleaning up. He leaned against the wall and watched them. He thought that some of them resented his sullenness, his silence.

He wondered what they all did with their day or half-day free. He had never heard anyone saying that they went any-where or did anything. It struck him that the only thing he could do was spend his free half-day sitting beside Super at the cash register in the supermarket a block away on the same street as the Four Corners. He had met Super on his second day in the street, when he was sent to get tea. Super was the first person to call him by his name and ask him questions about himself. If Super was busy, he thought, he would help him out; if the supermarket became quiet, he would sit and listen to Super's commentary on those who passed in the street, or on his regular customers, or on what was happening in the world.

Later, as the shop was getting ready to close, he was glad when no one suggested that he continue his training. He waited with them until the last customer had gone; then he joined them as they walked back to the house, being careful to say nothing, and not seem to listen too closely to any of them, in case they picked on him or laughed at him. He looked forward to getting into bed and feeling alone there in the darkness; the very thought of that pleased him and made him feel almost comfortable and happy.

One day he explained his fears to Super that he could not seem to learn as the others had learned and he noticed how atten-tively Super listened, how much he wanted to know the names of all the barbers and what each one had done or said. He waited for Super to give him advice, or predict what was most likely to happen, but Super said nothing, just looked out the shop window into the street. Since the supermarket was open late, he went there sometimes for a few minutes after work but Super was not always free to talk to him, as there were other men, who looked up in surprise when Malik approached and grew silent as Super indicated that he was busy and suggested that Malik return some other time. The men, most of whom had beards, did not seem like customers and Malik wondered who they were. They were older and seemed serious, like business-men or mullahs.

Malik did not move beyond the street and he liked how gradually he was becoming known as he made his way to the supermarket to buy milk or soft drinks or tea. He enjoyed being greeted and saluted. And there were other things too that made him feel comfortable. Even though eight of them shared the room, for example, he learned that he would not need to lock his suitcase, he was assured that no one would touch it. One night, when one of the other lodgers wanted to move his suitcase for a moment, he came and asked permission. He realized that they all kept money and photographs and other private things in their cases, fully confident that no one would go near them.

He noticed too that each of them had something special, a camera, a Walkman, a mobile phone, a DVD player, that set them apart and that they lent out as a special favour, or at particular times. Only Mahmood owned nothing. Mahmood worked hard and spent no money because he wanted desper-ately to go home. Some of the others, he told Malik, spent half their earnings on phone calls home. He had never called his wife even once, he said, not even for a second. He would not waste the money and it only made him sad.

Each morning, except Saturday and Sunday, Mahmood left early to deliver *butano*. He carried the heavy bottles of gas up narrow staircases. And then in the afternoons he took care of all the laundry in the house, leaving clothes clean and folded on each bed, never making a mistake. And in the evening he cooked, charging less than even the cheapest restaurant in the street.

Malik liked Mahmood from the beginning and liked having his clothes washed by someone he knew, and laid on his bed as though he were equal to the others. He also liked the food Mahmood cooked. But more than anything he was intrigued at how single-minded Mahmood was, how determined he was to go home.

It was Super also who warned him not to wander in the city. The locals were not the problem, Super said, and not even the tourists. It was the police you had to be careful of. In this street and the few around it, Super assured him, they would stop only blacks, but in other streets they could easily mistake you for a Moroccan.

"Why do they not like Moroccans?" he asked.

"I don't know, but they don't," Super said. "They just don't. And they don't like Africans either. They like us because we just do business, that's all we're here for."

Under the counter Super had a collection of magazines with photographs of the prisoners the Americans held in Iraq. Malik had seen the pictures on television; he had noticed that no one wanted to talk about them. Each time the television in the house had shown the naked figures being tormented by the American guards, for example, his fellow lodgers had watched in complete silence. When the news moved on to some other item, they still did not speak but simply stared straight at the television for a while.

When he went through the pages of the magazines with Super, neither of them said anything either; instead, they looked at each picture slowly, letting their eyes take in every detail. It was the one with the big black dog that Malik remembered most; that was what made him most afraid. At night sometimes he thought about it, and the sharp teeth of the dog and the crouching prisoner tied up made him shiver.

Super reminded him of men in his village at home who could be found after prayers at the mosque gathered in a small group having earnest discussions, or who would visit a house if someone was in trouble. He had a way of becoming quiet and looking serious.

One day as Malik and Super observed Mahmood banging a piece of metal against the *butano* cylinder to let customers know he was in the street, Malik told Super how great it was that Mahmood would have plenty of money when he went home because he worked so hard. Super listened and said nothing for a moment.

"No, he won't have a penny when he goes home," Super said. "Not a penny. They did all the paperwork for him and got him his visa and paid his fare. He is saving to pay them back so he can go."

"Pay who back?"

"The same people who paid for you," Super said.

"You mean Baldy?"

"Baldy works for them too."

At night sometimes Malik lay in the dark thinking of the vast city around him, its night sounds seeping in. He had learned some words of the language and wondered how he might learn more. Even if he never became a barber, he thought, they would always need someone to sweep and clean. He would never go too far beyond these few streets, he was sure, but he relished the idea that other, different people lived in the city, people whom he would never meet or even see. Maybe in a while he would try just the next street. He imagined taking one street at a time, just as he imagined learning a few words every day. And maybe after a month or so, he would summon up the courage to ask Baldy which half-day he could have. It was not too bad, he thought, as he curled up in the warm bed and waited for sleep to return.

Once a month he went to the *locutorio* the others used and phoned Fatima, as he had arranged to do before he left. She owned the stall that sold live and dead chickens in the market and she knew his father, who often passed by. Malik asked her always if there was any news and she said no, and then he told her what news of his own he could think of, but it was never much. Then he said that she must be busy and she said she sometimes was. And then he asked her to pass on the news to his father and his sister that he had phoned and that he was well. And she agreed that she would. The phone call cost him less than five euros if he stayed on for under three minutes.

Malik looked forward to the quiet time when everyone was asleep and he was woken by some stray noise. It could be anything: the noise of a motorbike on the street below and then that noise fading into the distance, or one of the others who shared the room groaning in his sleep or saying a few words that made little sense, or someone talking or shouting below the window, or the men who came to hose down the streets or the truck that came to collect the garbage. On nights like this he thought that, despite the trials of training to be a barber, he was glad to be in Barcelona, happy to be among strangers and away from everyone he knew.

And when the morning broke in Barcelona the eight in

Malik's room, and the three in the room at the back, had to use the single bathroom. They never queued, and there was never a rule about who went first or who waited until the end. If someone was in a hurry or late, however, he could make that clear to the others and he would be let go next. No one ever stayed too long in the bathroom, just time enough to use the toilet and the shower and maybe shave and then dry off and come back and dress. Everyone kept their underpants on, or their pyjamas, or a towel around their waist, as they got ready for the day.

Some of them had their own prayer mats and they prayed in the mornings while everyone moved busily around them. But Malik did not pray. Since his mother had died, there had been no one in the house to tell him to pray and so he had got out of the habit.

But Super, he knew, prayed and sometimes Super would read him a few lines of the Koran and ask him to repeat them and he would do so. He liked the words and often tried to remember them.

Some days were slack. There was usually a strange empty hour in the morning when there were no customers and they all had to watch out in case Baldy pounced on the place. He would demand that the barbers stand behind their chairs as though waiting at that very moment for the arrival of a customer. But mostly Baldy was too busy, they all said, selling mobile phones at the lowest price.

Malik usually kept his eyes on the door and the window. Although he knew some of the people who passed, because they were customers at the Four Corners or they came to buy groceries at the supermarket or consult with Super, he was careful never to greet them with anything more than a nod of recognition. He did not want to be seen not working even though he had nothing to do most of the time.

They had given up for the moment, it seemed, trying to teach him to cut hair; he was hopeless, they said. The fun of watching him make a mess of someone's hair and the pleasure of laughing at him as he grew more nervous and agitated had lost its initial charm. One or two of the barbers treated him now with blunt indifference or mild irritation and soon, even Super agreed, his utter uselessness would come to Baldy's attention and no one knew what might happen then. But, for the moment, Baldy seemed to notice nothing, and when Malik waylaid him one day and asked him if he could have Tuesday afternoons off as his half-day free, he agreed immediately.

Although Super had warned Malik not to go too far beyond the street, to stay close to where there were other Pakistanis, Malik worked out that it was safe to wander one block on each side. He moved carefully, often doubling back and stopping, noting the number of stores selling mobile phones, hoping not to bump into Baldy and ready to veer into the shadows if he did. He wished he had a phone of his own, because no one minded you standing on the street staring at them or their store as long as you were talking on a mobile phone.

One day when Baldy arrived in the Four Corners, he came right up to him as all the customers and barbers watched.

"What are you looking at?" Baldy asked him.

"I'm not looking at anything," Malik replied.

"Well, don't. Don't look at anything, you little maggot. Get on with your work! What do you do anyway?"

Malik did not reply.

"What do you do anyway?" Baldy repeated. "I don't know why we have you here. We'll have to deal with you one of these days. Do you hear me?"

Malik did not reply.

Later, when he told Super what had happened, Super said that he thought it sounded serious. He or one of the other men would try to talk to Baldy, he said, but he was not sure what the result would be.

Malik concentrated on small things so that he would not worry too much about Baldy. He made sure now that he did not linger in the streets even on his half-day free in case Baldy spotted him.

One day soon afterwards Baldy came into the Four Corners looking for him.

"Where are you?" he asked.

"I am here," he said.

"I know where you are," Baldy replied.

Baldy went over and checked the ledger and the drawer where the cash was kept.

"Super says you are intelligent," Baldy said. "But I have never seen any sign of it."

If Baldy had called him lazy he would not have minded. He might seem lazy because he usually had nothing much to do. But he did not want Baldy to say that he was not intelligent.

"I don't see the slightest sign of intelligence," Baldy said. "In fact, I see only stupidity."

Malik moved closer to Baldy and looked at him steadily, evenly.

"I am not stupid," he said.

"Can you count?"

"Yes."

"How many pockets do you have?"

"In my trousers I have two at the front and two at the back."

"Right. So I am going to give you phone cards to sell. You put the cards in your left pocket at the front and you put them nowhere else. And you put the money in the right pocket at the front. And these cards work only for mobile phones and they are the cheapest anyone will get. Five hours' talking for ten euros."

He handed Malik a bunch of phone cards. Malik immediately put them in the left-hand front pocket of his trousers.

"If I find you cheating, you won't have any trousers," Baldy said. "I'll use your trousers to wring your neck."

Malik did not reply.

"Do you understand?"

Malik nodded.

"And be here when I come."

Malik was going to ask how anyone would know he had the cards but he decided to say nothing.

Baldy left the Four Corners as though in a bad humour.

Salim came over and slapped Malik on the back.

"You're in business," he said and smiled. One of the customers smiled as well. Even Abdul, the most serious of the barbers, smiled.

Later when Malik went to the supermarket, Super said that he would work out the terms with Baldy, but he thought that Malik might soon be on a percentage of the money he took in if the sale of the cards went over a certain figure. By the time he said this, Malik had sold only two or three cards, and these to the actual barbers in the shop. They might have bought them just because they felt sorry for him. But in the days that followed, people began to stop by the Four Corners asking for Malik, saying that Baldy had sent them, and by the end of a week he was able to inform Super that he had sold more than thirty phone cards at ten euros each.

"Did Baldy take all the money from you?" Super asked.

Malik nodded.

"I'll talk to him," Super said.

A few days later as Baldy was collecting the money, he spoke to him again.

"Keep an account of how many you sell every week. And you're on ten per cent. You get it every Friday."

Malik understood that this was business so he knew it was important not to smile or say anything in reply. He nodded his head gruffly in a way he thought Baldy might appreciate.

It was clear to him then that Baldy might realize that he was both intelligent and honest. And he had something more to do than sweep the floor and keep things clean and get sheets and towels. Men came looking for him by name, and a few women too, and they recognized him on the street and they saluted him if they saw him.

Sometimes when he woke in the night he no longer worried about the possibility of being sent home, or of being given even more menial work. He liked selling phone cards. As he lay in bed in the dark in the great strange city, taking in the rank air of the room, the thought came into his mind for the first time that maybe everything was going to be OK.

On Fridays and Saturdays he usually went to the supermarket after the Four Corners had closed and sat listening to Super or helping him if he needed help or having some food with him. Sometimes Super spoke about the Koran and picked a longer passage from the book and ran his finger along the lines of the page, reading out the words as Malik listened. If anyone came into the shop, however, he put the book away immediately. One evening a man came to buy some razors and soap; Super spoke to him politely for a while before he left the supermarket.

Super seemed worried for a moment and then told Malik

that he should look out and not be seen talking to that man because he was a police spy.

"He tells them everything," Super said, "and they pay him and that is how he lives. He will tell them we were reading the Koran. He saw it before I put it away. No one in the street minds him, because there's nothing wrong here. It's just business here. We make sure of that. As long as he doesn't tell them lies, we are happy. But you have to watch what you say, and what you let him see, all the same."

"Where does he live?" Malik asked.

"Near you," Super said.

"But does he sleep in a room with other men?"

"He does everything the same as us, except for his job. When the bomb went off in Madrid he was gone for a week. We were all worried in case he might make up things just to please them, might tell them things that weren't true about people in the street. They would arrest anyone. It wouldn't matter to them. We don't know where he went or what he said, but nothing happened here. He just came back and things were normal."

"Where did he go?"

"To Madrid, I suppose. Maybe they needed him there. I don't know. But they didn't arrest anyone on this street. So that was good. It had nothing to do with us."

Baldy instructed Malik to tell anyone buying the phone cards that he also sold mobile phones from a booth in a side-street and from a larger shop that had all the newest models. A few times Malik went and looked at the shop windows, one on each side of the entrance door. He noticed the lights, how bright they were, and how each model of phone appeared perfect and beautiful.

At the end of each day, he was able to tell Baldy how many cards he had sold and then how much money he had taken in. There was never a problem with the money. It was always exact. Sometimes, he also mentioned to Baldy that he had directed customers to the booth and the shop, but he was careful not to do this too much as Baldy often grew irritated if he spoke out of turn. Baldy preferred him to speak only when he was asked a question.

One night he could not sleep, because Abdul in the bed opposite him was coughing. He asked himself how the others could manage to sleep, because at times Abdul's cough was rasping and loud. Maybe they were awake too, he thought. Abdul gasped for breath and wheezed and then became quiet before the coughing started again. Malik wondered if Abdul smoked and tried to picture him with a cigarette, but of all the barbers who worked in the shop he was the one who paid closest attention to his work, concentrated hardest on shaving or cutting hair, and seldom looked out the window, or even joined in the conversation in the shop, except to ask them sometimes to change the music. It was impossible to imagine Abdul taking time out for a smoke. Abdul was the oldest of them, Malik realized, and maybe there was a period in the past when he had smoked, or when he had damaged his lungs, or maybe it was just a cold he had now and it seemed worse because of his age. Malik tried to think what age Abdul might be, but he was not sure; he thought that he could be forty.

As the coughing continued, Malik quietly left the room and went to the kitchen on the floor below, where he found a flask of cold water in the fridge. He filled a glass from the flask and tiptoed back, approaching Abdul's bed and whispering to him that he had brought him a glass of water. When he put his hand on him, he felt Abdul's skin covered in sweat and realized that he must have a high temperature. As Abdul reached for the glass, he touched Malik's hand for a moment and then held it briefly as a way of thanking him. He sat up then and drank the water. Malik could hear him gulp. He did not know whether he should wait and retrieve the glass or let Abdul put it on the floor when he had finished. He whispered to him that he would get him more water if he needed. Abdul did not reply, but squeezed his arm and then moved his hand down and caressed Malik's thigh. It was just two or three seconds, but as Malik made his way back to his bed, it made him feel warm and comfortable, more than if Abdul had said anything to him. Soon, he fell asleep, but in the morning, as he heard one of the others say that Abdul was too sick to go to work, he felt a bond with him, felt that something had happened between them.

He waited the next day until his break at lunchtime and went quickly back to the house. When he opened the door of the room, he saw that Abdul was asleep. Since Abdul was taller than the rest of them, nearly too tall for the bed, his feet were sticking out from the sheets. His feet, Malik saw, were angular, the toes all bony. He sat on his own bed watching him. When Abdul opened his eyes he did not smile; he appeared tired, weary, as if in some distress. When Malik asked him if he was all right, he nodded but he still did not move. Without asking him, Malik went to the kitchen and returned with the flask of cold water and a glass.

Abdul was covered in sweat and the sheets were almost wet. Malik saw that he needed a fresh pair of pyjamas and fresh sheets. He knew where Mahmood kept spare sheets, but did not know how he would find fresh pyjamas. In the room below, where Mahmood did the ironing, he found two single sheets and a pair of his own shorts that had been freshly washed. He found a small plastic basin in the kitchen as well and took them all upstairs. In the bathroom, he filled the basin with cold water and fetched a sponge.

Abdul was lying with his eyes closed. Malik moved towards the bed and set the basin down. He knelt and gently opened the top of Abdul's pyjamas and whispered to him that he was going to sponge him with cold water. Abdul nodded slightly and lay quietly as Malik began to sponge his chest; then, having made him sit up, Malik took off the pyjama top and slowly sponged Abdul's shoulders and back. Abdul looked as though what was happening caused him mild pain. His shoulders were broad and the skin on his back had a shiny smoothness broken by the shape of his spine. The warmth coming into his hand from Abdul's shoulder as he held it made Malik want to keep it there for as long as he could.

He did not know if Abdul would allow him to lower the top sheet and sponge him on the stomach and around his crotch. But Abdul lay back as though he did not notice or care. As Malik opened the button on his pyjama bottom, he was surprised to find that Abdul had an erection. He glanced nervously at Abdul's face; he had his eyes closed partly from exhaustion, but also from a mixture, Malik thought, of embarrassment and something else, something that Malik could not be certain of as he sponged him slowly. He kept an eye on the door and listened carefully for a footfall on the stairs, but there was no sound. He was sure that they were alone in the house, but he was ready to cover Abdul quickly at the slightest hint that anyone was coming.

He rubbed Abdul's legs with the sponge and then suggested that Abdul should stand up and change into the shorts while he put new sheets on the bed. Abdul stood up with difficulty, moaning softly to himself and shivering. It was only when Abdul was standing that Malik could see how long the penis was, much longer than his own, he thought, and far too long for the shorts to cover. As Abdul lay down again on the clean sheet, Malik whispered that he had to return to work before Baldy noticed his absence, but that he would be back later if Abdul needed anything. He took the basin and emptied the water into the shower in the bathroom and then left the sheets and Abdul's pyjamas downstairs in a pile beside the ironing board. He would explain to Mahmood later, he thought, that he was the one who had done this.

In the days afterwards, as Abdul got better, and was able to take soup and then solid food, Malik noticed that he began to ignore him. Before he was sick, Abdul was often silent, seldom making jokes or contributing to the night-time conversation. He was often to be found lying on the bed with his hands behind his head, making clear somehow that he was content to be left alone, happy to remain unnoticed in his own world. A few times now, both in the barber shop and at night, Malik tried to make him acknowledge his presence, give some hint that he remembered what had happened between them, but Abdul often stared at him as though he did not know him. One night when he returned from work, Malik found the shorts that he had given to Abdul lying on his bed. They had been washed, but nonetheless when he put them to his nose he could smell something faint that he thought might be the smell of Abdul. He put the shorts in his suitcase, and a few times over the following days he took them out and smelled them again.

One evening when Baldy was counting the money he suddenly turned and looked at him.

"You're a bit of a fool, aren't you?" He was almost smiling as though he did not really mean what he said.

"What?" Malik asked. He did not like it when Baldy said

anything other than the usual. He wished this could stop now and Baldy would just count the money, make sure it was correct, and then look around the room before leaving.

"Yeah, you," Baldy said, accusingly.

Malik did not reply. He glanced down at the money, hoping that Baldy would finish his business and go.

"OK then," Baldy said as if speaking to himself, "that's enough of that. Do you know how to use a mobile phone?"

Malik nodded.

"Good. You'll be selling them from tomorrow. Don't come here in the morning. I'll get some other fool to sweep the floor and sell the cards. Come to the bigger shop. At nine on the dot."

As he left, Malik noticed the barbers who were finishing up looking at him as though something grave had occurred. As he passed Abdul, he tried to catch his eye, but Abdul was busy, working with fierce concentration as he clipped at the hairs around a customer's ear. He did not lift his head as Malik left the shop.

Almost every single person who came to buy a mobile phone already had one. He knew that it was not his job to tell them that there was very little difference between the one they were already using and some new bright and more expensive model on display. Often it was just a brand name, or model number, and the packaging. And yet, when his customers came in ones or twos and asked to see the latest type, there was something so serious, so earnest, about them that it was clear to him that nothing more important would happen to them in months, maybe all year, than this purchase, this exchange of a perfectly good model for a totally new one.

Every one of them knew about phones; it was one of the subjects for easy discussion at night between the customers who came to the Four Corners and the barbers there, and the people who came to the supermarket. They could argue about brands and systems, as though they themselves had been involved in their manufacture or design.

They touched the new models with reverence and awe, but also with expertise. Malik needed only to stand back and let them study the model they were looking for and let them know what colours were available. The prices were all written down. He emphasized to them that they could not take the actual phone they were going to buy out of its packaging unless they had already paid for it. They could look at a sample of it, however, hold it, test for themselves its properties, how it took photographs and how the keys might be slightly easier to handle than some other model only a year old, which could be discarded or given away, as no one seemed interested in owning a second-hand mobile phone.

A few times he was tempted to say to men who came in shabby jeans or in thin kurta pyjamas or in worn shoes that they should spend the money instead on clothes or in a shoeshop. Their time with him, he slowly realized, had nothing to do with need, or value for money. It was how men at home thought about cars or trucks or houses, the same seriousness, the same sense that the newest thing would be good for their reputation, would make their neighbours respect them. These men away from home would never have enough money for a car or a truck or a house. This small object so filled with modern tricks had come to stand in for all of that.

Abdul began to talk to him. It started one evening when the others were watching a cricket match and Malik had retre to the bedroom and was busy putting his newly laundered clothes into his suitcase. He noticed that Abdul was hovering in the room, moving back and forth between the window and the door and then sitting on the bed. At first Malik was hesitant about speaking to him, and it occurred to him also that perhaps Abdul had come back here to be alone, or to open his suitcase when no one else was watching. He was almost ready to leave the room when Abdul spoke.

"Are you selling many mobile phones?" he asked.

Malik turned to him. Abdul seemed nervous now, as though he had made a request of some sort, such as a loan of soap or shampoo, and was uneasily waiting for the answer.

"Some days it's good," Malik said and smiled, "and some days it's quiet."

Abdul nodded and looked at the floor.

"I'd say you don't miss the Four Corners."

When he had spoken he looked up; the expression on his face, Malik saw, was sad. Malik did not reply, but sat on the edge of his own bed.

"You're not watching the game?"

"It's no use," Abdul said. "It's just a video. I know the result."

"Do you like cricket?" Malik asked.

"I used to play," Abdul replied, then lowered his eyes again. Soon, he seemed lost in thought and Malik judged it best not to break the silence. He lay back on the bed and put his hands behind his head as he had often seen Abdul do. After a while he heard cheering and clattering and he knew that it must be the end of the match. It was not long before a few of the others came into the bedroom laughing and talking and beginning to get ready for the night.

On most evenings after that if Malik made his way into the

bedroom immediately after supper he found that Abdul would follow him. Sometimes they would be alone for a while and Abdul would sit on the edge of the bed and ask Malik questions or remain silently watching him. Malik wanted to ask him questions in return but he was too nervous and thought he would wait. If anyone else arrived, Abdul would stand up and pretend to be busy, rummaging in his suitcase or going into the bathroom or back to the kitchen. He would never join in the general conversation.

Abdul would always begin by asking him how many mobile phones he had sold that day. A few times when Malik tried to go into detail about a customer or about a new model that had arrived, Abdul would look down as though embarrassed or bored, and he did not know whether he should go on talking or not. He told Abdul that his mother was dead and that his brother had died just the previous year and all he had at home were his father, who had married again, and his sister, who was also married. When he added that he called home once a month but did not speak to his father but instead to the woman who ran the chicken stall, Abdul nodded sympathetically and said it would be good if his father and he both got mobile phones and then he could text. Malik did not say that his father already had a phone but he did not think his father would send him texts since he had not even suggested that Malik should use his number when he phoned home.

When he saw Super, he mentioned Abdul's name and listened in case Super had any comment to make on him. But Super simply asked him if Abdul was the tall one and when Malik said that he was he remarked that Abdul was very quiet. Malik noticed that Super seemed to approve of this. Super had nothing else to say about Abdul and it was hard for Malik to mention him again although he was eager to find an excuse to do so.

Sometimes he lay on the bed knowing that Abdul was opposite sitting on the edge of his bed. At first Abdul's silences made him uncomfortable but slowly he became used to them, believing that Abdul was shy, or was someone who kept his thoughts to himself. He would not, Malik thought, follow him into the bedroom unless he wanted to be friendly. It was not unusual for the lodgers in the house or the men who worked in the barber shops or the other shops on the street to have a friend, someone they had known at home perhaps, someone they could be seen with or could depend on. Abdul, he realized, had no such friend; nor did he.

Abdul was more distant than any of the others. None of them ever commented if he stood up from the table even before the meal was over. But they must notice now, Malik thought, that Abdul was often to be found talking quietly to him. Even though Malik learned nothing about him in the conversations, he learned to trust him and came to like him and looked forward to returning each evening knowing that Abdul liked sitting close to him at the table when they were eating and seemed to want to be in his company later.

One evening when he arrived back at the house, Malik found that all of the Pakistani businesses on the street had received the same flier as he had with news that a band called Wooee from Pakistan was to play in a square nearby the following Wednesday night at ten o'clock. Salim insisted that the lead singer was a brother of Ali Azmat of Junoon and that he had seen them on television. No one else had heard of the band and Mahmood said that he would not go to the concert as it might be just a cheap way to check everyone's papers.

"They could do that any day just by walking along the _et," Salim said.

_he following evening Salim announced that he had Googled

the name of the band and he had watched them on YouTube and he was right, the lead singer was Ali Azmat's brother and he was great. He had shown the clip to other people in the *locutorio* and all of them had agreed with him. Soon, he said, everyone would know their music. They were young, he said, and that was why no one had heard of them, but it was going to be a special evening and he was tired of listening to music on bad cassette players and bad CD players. At home, he said, his brother had a stereo with speakers, and it was like being in the room with the music. He was not going to miss the concert.

Later, Malik asked Abdul if he was going to go, but Abdul said that he was not sure, that he did not finish work until ten and would need to eat something and there might not be time.

The next evening Mahmood said that he had seen the clip on YouTube too and he agreed with Salim and he was going to go and see Wooee. As the week went on and there was much discussion about the band, Malik waited for a sign from Abdul. A few times he almost asked him again. Since it was clear that all of the others were going, Malik knew that the building would be empty that evening. He began to imagine Abdul and himself in the room alone preparing for bed, Abdul slowly undressing, maybe talking more than usual. He imagined him moving across the room to turn off the light, and then both of them lying silently in the dark, aware that they would have this room to themselves for an hour or maybe more, and aware too that they would easily hear the others coming back. Malik did not think in any detail about what would happen between them in the dark; it was almost enough for him that they would be alone together and almost enough for him to know that Abdul would be lying on his back and Malik would be able to hear his breathing.

On the morning of the concert as he prepared for the

Malik still believed that Abdul would make some sign to him about his intentions, but instead Abdul seemed even more distant than usual. During the day as business was slack he found himself watching the door. Abdul could, in his break, walk to the shop and let him know what he was doing later. But Malik knew that Abdul was unlikely, in fact, to approach the shop. He went over in his mind the nights when Abdul had followed him into the room; he wondered now if he had done this to get away from the others, and if he was not actually making an effort to be his friend, and if the time he had washed him with the sponge had meant nothing, and if he himself was thinking too much about this.

When the shop closed at nine he had an hour to spare before the concert began and before Abdul usually arrived home. As he walked back to the house slowly, he felt almost happy that nothing about the evening had been resolved. Either Abdul would come back to the house, or he would go to the concert. Whichever it was, it would be something new, and it was this very newness in all its vagueness and uncertainty that made Malik smile as he walked up the stairs of his building and decided that he would have something to eat while he waited to see if Abdul would come home.

There was not a sound in the house, and even the noise from the street seemed strangely muted. He sat at the kitchen table and ate some cold chicken curry and bread that had been left over from the night before. And then he strayed into the bedroom. Having the room to himself like this made him acutely conscious that this was also Abdul's room, the room where Abdul slept, the room where his lungs took in the air, the room where his suitcase held his clothes and whatever special things treasured. Malik went over and touched Abdul's pillow and hand along the shape that he would make were he to come now and lie on the bed. Malik looked at the suitcase in the corner but he knew not to touch it, let alone open it. Instead he lifted the pillow and carried it over to his own bed. He could smell some shaving lotion and maybe some hair oil or tonic from it, but there was also something stale or earthy that belonged to Abdul, that came from his breath, his mouth. He put the pillow right up against his face and tried to breathe in the smell so that it would belong to him too. He then moved it against his chest and hugged it, keeping his eyes closed and pretending that he was someone else and that it was a dark room and that he was alone with Abdul, who was softly pushing against him.

When he put the pillow back, trying to ensure that there was no sign it had ever been removed, he saw that the time was nine forty-five. He decided that he would wait for half an hour or maybe thirty-five minutes to see if Abdul would come, and then, if he did not arrive, he would go to the square where the band was playing and hope that he could find him there. He wished now that he had some way of being able to read Abdul's mind, or even know where he was, what he was doing, so that he would not have to wait like this, moving from the bedroom into the kitchen and then into the bathroom to check himself in the mirror, and then back again to the hallway, standing close to the door, ready to go into the bedroom if he heard a sound that might be Abdul approaching.

He waited and no one came. As time passed slowly, seemed almost suspended in the shadowy bedroom, something came to him from a dream he had had, a scene that he had vividly remembered when he woke a few mornings earlier, as if it had really happened.

After his mother died, his father's sister had spent a in the house and had talked a lot about when he was and his mother was sick and she had taken care of him and his brother and his sister. She had sung songs to them and looked after Malik when he cried in the night. Now, as he waited for Abdul, he had a sense of her deep voice, its softness and kindness. It was a voice he had always known. Even though he could not actually remember it from the time when he was a baby, he had a sense that it had always been with him.

This voice, he thought, was not in the dream, but his aunt herself was, his aunt who had been dead for five years. She was a silent presence in the streets of Barcelona, streets where she had never been. In his dream, she was in the supermarket, she was passing the window of the barber shop, she was passing him as he walked from the apartment to the shop where he sold mobile phones. She never spoke, but always smiled, moving easily as though she belonged to the place, or had been there for some years. It was strange, he thought, to dream about her like this now when he had never dreamed about her walking the streets of home, when he had never, in fact, dreamed about her before at all, or did not think he had.

Once it was ten fifteen he presumed that Abdul must have gone to the concert, but still he waited, going through in his mind the streets between his street and the square where the concert was being held. Since he had decided to wait until twenty past ten, then he did, even though in the last minutes he could not think how he had not guessed that Abdul was never going to come back here. He would have gone with the others; that is what he would always have done. Malik, as he made his way down the stairs, wished he had realized that earlier in the evening.

Even when he was only halfway there he thought that he ⌐ hear the music, but then it faded and he did not hear it ⌐ntil he was two streets away. It was a song he recognized but it was being played faster. And either there was cheering coming from the sound system or the crowd was really cheering, he could not be sure. The first entrance to the square was blocked off; he stood and listened for a minute as a song came to an end and then, when the applause began with cheering and shouting, he moved quickly back and made his way into the square by another street, which was open. As soon as he saw the stage he realized that the lights were too bright for him to be able to look clearly at the tightly packed crowd of men. He moved towards them, trying to find a place where he could stand and get a view of the stage as the group started up again to wild cheering. No one else was moving, everyone seemed settled, standing with their friends. No one had any patience for someone distracting them from the action on the stage.

It struck him that he had never known that there were so many Pakistanis in Barcelona. He wondered where they all lived, what they did. Up to now, he had thought that they all lived in the same street, but then he remembered that there were figures who had come just once to the barber shop or the mobile phone shop. Their being gathered together should have made him feel at home, but it somehow made the city seem stranger, almost more foreign than it had seemed before.

Quietly, he pushed his way between two men and managed to stand in front of them without blocking their view. He wished that he had not been worried about Abdul and had not spent that time alone waiting for him. He could not relax now and enjoy the loud sounds coming from the stage or watch the lead singer and the changing lights. He found that he was already wondering when it would be over. Suddenly, he began to watch a lone seagull hovering, as though staking the square out for food. As the lights moved from red to yellow to b the underbelly and underwings of the bird seemed to b even more white. He closed his eyes and started to take in the music, keep everything else out of his mind except the music, but no matter what he did he could not stop thinking that it would soon be over.

He edged along the front of the crowd wondering if there was a place he could sit on the ground and still see the stage. He watched one of the band playing what looked like a small piano; he was surprised by the sounds that seemed to come from the instrument, as though the man had a small orchestra at his command. And then he saw Abdul, the expression on his face glowing and happy; he was clapping his hands to the music. Malik moved quickly towards him and embraced him, the way all friends embraced when they saw each other on the street. Abdul smiled and pulled him near to him so he could say something, but the music was too loud to hear. He felt Abdul's breath on his face and saw the light in his eyes but had to shrug to intimate that he could not understand. Abdul laughed and looked again at the stage. He seemed younger when he smiled like this. Malik stood close to him but he could not get a view of the stage so he moved away a bit and concentrated on the music as best he could, happy that Abdul was here, happy also that he knew to leave him alone with the music, not to look at him too much or try to speak to him.

As the crowd shifted, Abdul pulled Malik closer until he found a way of standing in front of Abdul, keeping his head to the side. This, he realized, was what he had waited in the apartment for, and why he had come to the square. It was like being alone because no one noticed them, and maybe, Malik thought, it was better than being alone because they could concentrate the music as Abdul began to pull Malik against him, put-his arms around him and letting them loose again.

lead singer began a slow song about love; it was about

a woman who did not notice the man who really loved her. The chorus sang of how her eyes did not see him and her mind did not think of him and how he hoped that would change, and then repeated the words "would change, would change, would change." The voice of the lead singer rose tenderly into the night air as the crowd stood still and Abdul held Malik, his arms around his chest and his crotch tight against him, moving tighter and tighter against him as the song went on.

When the concert was over, Abdul and Malik walked together out of the square into a side-street. Malik was sure that no one who knew them had spotted them leaving and was sure that in the excitement and crush of the last few songs no one had noticed how closely Abdul had embraced him and how much both of their hands had strayed. Malik knew not to talk, knew just to move slowly alongside Abdul. He would have been happy to walk home with him, to get ready for bed in the room with him and the others without saying anything, just knowing what had happened between them at the concert. And then lying in bed going over it in his mind while Abdul across the room from him fell asleep.

He presumed that they were walking towards their building and was surprised, once they had walked through a number of side-streets, to find that Abdul was leading him away from the flat towards the barber shop. Abdul did not speak even as he produced a set of keys as they neared the shop. Malik walked alongside him silently until Abdul motioned him to walk behind him. As the door was opened, Malik stood back and then checked the street before darting in through the doorway. Abdul shut the door and locked it from the inside with his key. Then Malik followed him into the room be the shop where there was a sink and where the towels and sheets were kept.

Abdul closed the door so that this room was now entirely in darkness. Moving towards him and putting his arms around him as Abdul opened his own belt and unzipped his trousers, Malik put his hands inside Abdul's shirt, touching the bare skin on his back and allowing his hands to move under the elastic of his underpants. He kept his hands there and then pulled the underpants down so that Abdul's penis was free. He held it with one hand and cupped the testicles with the other until Abdul began to apply gentle pressure to the crown of his head, indicating that he should kneel down, as he did now until his face was at the level of Abdul's crotch. He could smell his sweaty flesh as he took Abdul's penis into his mouth and wet it with his saliva. He released it and licked it and took it again full into his mouth as far as it would go while reaching in between Abdul's legs with his hand.

At first Abdul let his arms hang loose by his side, but slowly he began to put his hands on Malik's head, touching his ears and his face, lingering there, and then gripping his head, urging him to allow his penis in and out of his mouth, speaking only when he told him not to put his tongue too much against the top of the penis as it was making him too excited, just move his mouth up and down as he had done before. Malik did as he was asked.

As Abdul began to moan and Malik knew that he was soon going to come, the light was switched on. Malik did not move, did not look behind as Abdul pulled up his trousers and set about zipping up his fly and buckling his belt.

The voice that spoke was Baldy's, who whispered something before he shouted. Malik found himself hoping that this not really happened when a blow came across the top of his legs that made him fold over. He could see then that Baldy had the leg of a chair in his hand and was now hitting Abdul with it as he crouched in the corner. He was shouting again as he moved towards Malik, shouting curses and obscenities as he began to kick Malik in the ribs, causing him to stand up and back into the corner to protect himself, with his hands guarding his face.

Soon Baldy moved away and began to kick Abdul, whom he pulled to his feet by the hair and beat on the back and on the legs with the piece of wood. Abdul screamed in pain. Malik wondered now if he should risk crossing the room quickly and making for the door but he thought that he would stay where he was for the moment until he was certain that he would be able to slip by Baldy, who seemed in an even greater temper now. He was hitting Abdul still and had pulled him closer to the centre of the room. Malik asked himself for a second if it would be best to pretend he was dead or unconscious, with his eyes closed, but he did not have time to make a decision about this as Baldy came towards him again and pulled him to his feet and gave him a knee in the balls that made him double up and cry out. As he lay on the ground Baldy hit him a number of ferocious blows on his arm and his leg with the piece of wood. He saw a flash of red and thought that he was going to faint with the pain as more blows came.

As soon as he opened his eyes he could make out that Baldy was standing in the middle of the room. His eyes were almost bulging out of his head as he looked from Abdul to Malik and then back again. Malik was unsure now if he was going to use the leg of the chair on his shoulders or his head, or hit h' again on the leg and the arm. He could hear Baldy breat' For a second Malik had the urge to move towards him he could and grab the chair leg from his hand and '

Abdul would be agile enough to get him onto the floor holding his legs so that he could not even kick. And then he supposed that they would leave, but he did not know what they would do after that. As he was thinking about these possibilities Baldy walked out of the room. Malik could hear the keys turning in both locks that led to the street.

He wondered if Baldy had gone to get the police, if there was a special police force for this. He wished Baldy had turned off the light so that he would not have to see Abdul pulling himself across the floor and then crouching in a corner crying. Slowly, he began to feel an intense crushing pain in one side of his body and he lay back, afraid to move or think.

Later, when he tried to stand up to turn off the light he realized that he was injured. His ribs made even the slightest move very difficult and one of his legs seemed not to have any power. Then when he moved his arm he realized that something was wrong with that as well. He could not lift it without excruciating pain. Suddenly, he began to vomit; he tried to make it to the sink but could not and a stream of vomit came out of his mouth onto the floor all around him. The heaving made him almost cry out because of his ribs and made him see black spots. He managed to stand by leaning on his left leg and using his left arm to lever himself up. Propped against the wall, he stood there on one foot trying not to breathe in too deeply. And slowly he hobbled across to the light and turned it off and then sat down. Across the room Abdul was whimpering and then gasping for breath and whimpering again.

He had time now to think, to weigh what might happen
d wonder if there was anything he could do. Since he could
eally walk and since his rib-cage on the right-hand side
ercely every time he took a breath and since his right
ed to be broken, the idea of walking out of here and

through the streets was impossible. In any case, he realized, the door was locked from the outside and he was not sure that Abdul's keys would work from the inside. Maybe they were trapped here and would have to wait until morning, or maybe someone would come and take them away in the night. He supposed that there would be a special place for them, for men who had been caught as they had been caught. They could try to deny it but it would be hard to think of a convincing excuse for being in the barber shop together after the concert.

He went through all the people he knew, including Super and the others who shared the room with him and Abdul, including Mahmood, who did the cooking and the laundry, and he realized that none of them would want to help him, that all of them would feel that he and Abdul deserved their punishment, whatever it was. Maybe they would be sent home. He did not know whether that would be better or worse than here. He imagined himself and Abdul being led from a plane in handcuffs and pushed into a truck. He thought of the figures he had seen crouched in fear with a dog's teeth bared in front of them but that, he knew, had been done by the Americans. He thought about Baldy, how angry he was usually, how no one could talk to him and how everyone would support him now when they found out what had happened.

Abdul's whimpering had stopped. The silence was broken by the sound of an alarm in the distance. Malik realized that the best chance they would have with the police would be if they denied everything. He tried to think now of an excuse they both could use. They could say that Abdul had left his wallet behind so that it would be safe during the concert and they had come back for it and been brutally attacked for reason by Baldy. He hoped that Abdul had his wallet wit' and he hoped too that he would wake soon and make so that they could talk and agree to the same story. Maybe the police would still believe Baldy but it would be worth a try. They could ask why Baldy did not go to the police in the first place, and why he had taken the law into his own hands. Others would confirm that Baldy was a bully. If he and Abdul denied everything vehemently and convincingly enough, then at least the police would have to think about it. On the other hand, he thought, Baldy was not stupid, and he would want no trouble, so he might easily just put them on the next plane home. But who would buy the ticket? He tried to think about it from Baldy's point of view, and he realized that if he were Baldy he would not want people like Abdul and Malik working for him. It struck him then that maybe he was wrong, maybe Baldy did not care about things like that, he cared only about money, but then, of course, it made no sense that Baldy had been so angry. Maybe he was just angry that they had been in the shop without permission, but no, Malik thought, that would not explain why he had hit them so hard.

Abdul was asleep now. Malik could not understand how he was able to sleep. He hoped that he was not unconscious, but he did not think he was. He knew that there was nothing he could do but lie awake until Abdul woke and then talk to him about what they should do.

Malik was dozing when he heard the keys turning in the front door. He could feel his arm throbbing with pain. He listened to see if he could work out if Baldy was alone or if he had come with the police. But he heard no voices. Suddenly, he had an urge to disappear, to check if there was a cupboard he could ▪ide in, or if he could lock himself into the bathroom. He ▪ld tell by Abdul's heavy, even breathing that he was asleep. ▪ still and waited. When the light was turned on he pre- ▪that he was asleep. He presumed that it was Baldy and wondered, as he heard Abdul begin to stir, why Baldy had not spoken. He was tempted to turn and open his eyes but he realized that it would be a mistake.

"Get him up," he heard Baldy saying, "and get him out of here."

At that point he turned and sat up, wincing at the pain in his ribs and his arm. He lifted his other arm to shield his eyes from the light. Baldy was standing over him and Abdul was already on his feet. Baldy, he saw, was no longer angry, but seemed preoccupied, almost worried.

Malik tried to stand up and faltered, so Baldy had to help him.

"Get him out of my sight," Baldy whispered to Abdul, who moved towards Malik without looking at him, allowing Malik to lean on him as they both made their way out of the room into the main part of the barber shop and then out to the street.

They hobbled back to the apartment, Malik having to stop sometimes because the pain in his side was so bad. He saw that it was early morning; the shops were still closed and there was almost no one on the street. He realized that Abdul did not want to talk and felt so distant from him that he could not find a way to begin to ask him what they should tell the others in the room. He could not rest his right leg on the ground, but even though he put all his weight on the other leg, the right one began to throb. He could not move his arm and every time he took a breath he almost cried out in pain. He would not, he knew, be able to go to work, and he did not think, from the way Abdul was walking, that he would either. And even if they could work, he thought, Baldy would not want them near him.

They managed the stairs of the building bit by bit and quietly they went into the room. One or two of the others stir in their sleep but none of them woke as Abdul and Malik off their shoes, trying not to make a sound, and got into bed with all their clothes on.

Later, when everyone was awake and moving in and out of the room, Malik heard Abdul explaining that he and Malik had been working late helping Baldy move boxes and they would not be going to work until the afternoon. He knew that the story must sound strange, as they must know that Abdul had been at the concert and they might even have seen Malik there, but everyone seemed too busy getting ready for the day for any of them to question what Abdul had said. As soon as they were both alone in the room, Abdul fell asleep again.

An hour or more passed before Malik heard the door into the apartment open. He lay still, ready to close his eyes and pretend to be asleep. He waited. The bedroom door was opened very quietly. He did not move as someone approached his bed.

"Wake up, the two of you!"

The voice was unmistakably Baldy's. As Malik turned he checked immediately that Baldy did not have anything in his hands. What surprised him now was that Baldy appeared even more nervous than he had earlier that morning. Now he looked almost afraid. He wondered for a second if Baldy had the police outside but then as Baldy whispered to him to get up he guessed that Baldy was alone.

Malik tried to get out of the bed, but his ribs pained him very badly and then his arm. He used his left arm to lean on as Baldy came close to him and pulled up his vest and, as Malik winced, asked him if he was hurt. Malik nodded.

"Where?"

Malik pointed to his right arm and leg and then to his ribs on the right-hand side.

"Try to walk," Baldy whispered.

Malik attempted to move but his right leg was too stiff. He

cried out as Baldy touched his arm. He sat on the edge of the bed as Abdul woke and turned around.

"Get out of the bed," Baldy whispered to Abdul.

"Not for you, I won't," Abdul replied.

"Come on. I want to see if you are all right. I won't hurt you."

Slowly, Abdul sat up and stood out on the floor. As Baldy moved towards him, Abdul put his arm out to prevent him coming too close. Baldy went to the window and looked out. When Malik glanced at Abdul he saw that he was angry. He seemed uninjured. He wondered how Baldy had managed to hurt him so badly and not Abdul so much. Abdul was bigger, he supposed, and perhaps knew how to defend himself from the blows, or else Baldy had not hit him as hard.

"Can you walk?" Baldy asked Abdul.

"I can walk. No thanks to you," he replied.

"Are you hurt anywhere?"

"I'm probably bruised," Abdul said in a tone that was dry, almost disengaged.

"I'm going to take this fellow to the hospital," Baldy said.

Malik suddenly began to cry. He wished it could be an ordinary day and he could be at work, showing someone how to use a new model of phone. He had been in hospital once before when his brother was dying, and he remembered the long ward and the smells and the moans and cries. He did not want to go to a hospital; he knew now that he would have to do something to prevent Baldy taking him away. As he tried to stand up he leaned for a moment on his right leg and screamed in pain and felt that he was going to faint.

"Put your shoes on," Baldy said to Abdul, "and get his on as well, and help him down to the car."

Baldy left the room as Abdul worked at putting Mali

shoes on, but the right shoe would not go on, as the foot was limp and swollen. Abdul showed no sign of worry. Malik was going to ask him what would happen now but held back, knowing that Abdul would not reply. He seemed even more withdrawn than usual. Malik leaned on Abdul as he helped him to stand. He was reassured by Abdul's closeness to him and by his calmness. Surely he must know how much trouble they were in? Or was it possible that they were in no trouble at all now that Baldy's rage had subsided?

But he still had to face the hospital. He did not know who would feed him, or what would happen to him. He began to say something but Abdul immediately put his hand over his mouth to stop him and led him gently and slowly out of the room towards where Baldy was waiting.

Baldy spoke only once as he and Malik were driving across the city, having left Abdul standing in the street.

"If they ask you how this happened, you must say you were attacked and they ran away, and if they ask you what they looked like, say they were black, say they were Africans."

Malik turned and studied Baldy carefully because he had noticed once again how nervous he sounded. It struck him that Baldy did not want anyone to know what he had done, and this meant that he would not easily be able to tell anyone what he had seen. Maybe attacking people like this was illegal in Spain, enough for the attacker to be deported, or maybe going to the police would cause them to come and ask questions, and there were surely things about money and visas that Baldy and those he worked for did not want anyone to know.

Baldy made him wait in the car as he walked into a mod-
n building with a garden somewhere on one of the hills at

the edge of the city. Eventually, he emerged with a man wearing a white coat pushing a wheelchair. The man helped Malik out of the car and manoeuvred him into the chair, nodding as Malik pointed at his right arm to indicate that it could not be touched.

They used scissors to remove his vest and then stronger scissors to cut his trousers open. They took his clothes away in a black bag. For the next hour he was examined closely by two doctors, put lying on a table with just his shorts on as they shone bright lights on him. Then he was moved to a bed with wheels on it and pushed through the hospital. At the beginning, Baldy had spoken to the doctors but now, as he followed, no one asked him any more questions. It struck Malik for the first time how poor Baldy's clothes were and how strange and ill at ease he looked beside the young doctors and nurses in the clean, shiny corridors of the hospital.

Later, he remembered that he was given an injection in the arm and then he remembered nothing else until he woke in a room with a window, everything painted white. He was alone. When he tried to move he found that his leg was in plaster and so was his arm and there was a tight bandage around his ribs. He wanted to go to the bathroom but there was nothing he could do until someone came to help him. There was no sign of Baldy.

Over the days that followed, he was given food three times a day and helped to the bathroom any time he rang a bell. He liked the noises in the corridor and the doctors who came and spoke to him and gave him injections. Even though he could not understand them, he pointed to his arm and his leg in plaster and they responded with reassuring gestures and left him once more in the white room with the window. He was able to sleep and think and then sleep again. All the worry about

Baldy and the police seemed to have faded, to be replaced by the image of Abdul and what had happened between them at the concert and in the barber shop before Baldy arrived.

They gave him a frame with wheels after a while so that he could push himself towards the bathroom without leaning on his right leg. At first it was difficult to use because his right arm was in plaster but slowly he learned that if he leaned hard on it with his left arm he could stabilize himself and then push himself gently to the bathroom. When the doctors came and saw him moving of his own accord, they gave him a thumbs-up sign and left without giving him an injection.

One night when he woke he found that he was suddenly afraid of the silence and afraid of the closed door and afraid of the cupboard. He turned on the light but the brightness in the room frightened him even more. At least, he thought, his brother had been in a long open ward as he died and there was never silence like this, even if there was always pain, or fear of pain. It frightened him now to think that he could call and a nurse would come and she would be clean and dressed in white but she would not understand a single word he was saying, it would sound like gibberish to her. He wondered now if prison cells in Spain were like these hospital rooms, all white and perfect and locked, and no one there would understand him either. Again and again it came to him that there must be some way to get to the airport, some way to get clothes and money and buy a ticket, some way to get his passport back. He realized that this was all he wanted and that everything he did from now on would have to aim towards going home. A ticket. His passport. He whispered the two words to himself as he turned off the light.

In the darkness he tried to think about Abdul but all that came to him now was Abdul's indifference to him, which was there all the time. Even making him kneel in front of him and take his penis in his mouth was part of it. And it was Abdul who had led him to the barber shop, who had put him in danger. He tried, for a moment, to pretend that he was Abdul, to put himself in Abdul's mind, and he wondered if it was possible that Abdul missed him or worried about where he was. But all that came into his mind were images of blankness, Abdul's face expressionless, his attention fixed on other things.

In the morning when Malik woke, Baldy was in the room. He moved closer when Malik opened his eyes.

"Did they ask you any questions?" Baldy enquired.

He still seemed nervous. Malik felt he could smell him, some perfume, but also something stale like unwashed clothes.

"I don't know," he said. "I don't understand anything."

"They didn't send in an interpreter?"

"No."

"I have the car outside. As soon as they check you and say you are OK I am taking you home."

"Home?"

"Out of here. And what will you tell the others when you see them?"

"I was attacked."

"By whom?"

Malik sighed and closed his eyes.

"I know what to say."

"By whom?"

"By black fellows, Africans."

"How many of them?"

"I don't know. Two or three."

"Three. You say three."

"Three."

"And, by the way, you're not going back to the house. I have another place for you."

"Am I going home? You said home."

Malik closed his eyes.

"I have new clothes for you," Baldy said.

"Where am I going?"

"Don't ask questions. You won't be far."

Malik used his left elbow to help him sit up. He looked at Baldy, let his eyes linger on his face and his frame. Then he held his gaze until Baldy looked away.

"No one knows what happened," Baldy said. "I lost my temper, that's all. I don't tell, you don't tell, but my advice to you is—"

"Leave me alone."

Baldy waited there silently until the doctor came and examined Malik and said that he could go, but that he would have to take the walking frame with him and not put too much pressure on his right leg. They could pay a deposit on the frame, the doctor said, and then return it on his next visit in a month's time, when his arm would probably be strong enough for him to use a crutch.

He hated being dressed by Baldy and could smell the staleness from him even more powerfully now. In the lobby of the hospital he sat in a chair as Baldy went into a side office. He supposed that Baldy must be paying the bill, but he did not ask and they did not speak as they drove into the city through busy traffic. Malik's leg was throbbing from the short walk to the car. He knew that he would not be able to use it for a while. He wondered for how long.

As Baldy parked the car in a side-street that Malik knew not far from the mobile phone shop, he seemed almost fur-
His eyes darted back and forth as he helped Malik from

the passenger side and then fetched his walking frame from the boot. As they moved along the street, he walked a few steps ahead of Malik, who watched him with care as the expression on his face grew close to panic at Malik's slowness and the idea that anyone passing might notice they were together.

At a doorway, Baldy fumbled for a while with keys, trying and failing a few times to select the correct one from a number of bunches of keys he had in his pocket.

"You know something?" he asked Malik. "You have been nothing but trouble since the day you arrived."

Eventually, having opened the door, he helped Malik up the stairs while impatiently pulling the frame behind him. At every landing Malik stopped, presuming that they had arrived, but each time Baldy indicated to him that they would have to go farther. Finally, when they reached the top floor, Malik saw that one door, which was ajar, opened onto a roof. Baldy fumbled with keys again and opened the door opposite, which led into a small hallway. There was a door into a larger room into which they went.

"You'll be all right here," he said. "There'll be food every day and I'll have keys cut for you. And I don't want any more behaviour, do you understand? You're lucky—"

"That you hit me?" Malik interrupted. He had found a stool and was sitting down.

"Yes, that is exactly what I was going to say."

"Is there anyone else here?" Malik asked.

"No," Baldy replied. "It'll keep you out of harm's way."

He moved quickly to the hallway. Malik could hear him locking the door from the outside.

There was a bed with a bedside table and a sofa near the door with a table and two chairs near the window. His suitcase was on the floor beside the bed. Someone must have carried from the other house. There was a television in the corner. Outside, off the dark hallway, there was a bathroom with a washing machine, and a small kitchen with a cooker and a fridge. There was nothing in the fridge. Neither of these rooms had any window. The window in the main room was long and led out to a rooftop that was bright with sunshine. There were a few rotting plants in bowls. He opened the door to the rooftop and, with the help of the frame, made his way out.

It was a small space enclosed by three walls, but it was overlooked only by his room. There was a low wall on the fourth side that looked over the back of some buildings below. No one, he realized, could see him on this rooftop. And no one, he imagined, could hear him if he screamed. He was at Baldy's mercy here. If Baldy decided to forget about him, or if a car ran over Baldy in the street, he would languish here, he realized. No one would ever find him. He looked around him but all he could see were blank walls and the sky. There was a hum of traffic but it was faint and distant. He sat and waited to see if he would hear a voice, or any human sound, until he noticed a shadow moving gradually across this open space. The day was waning. He was hungry and thirsty and, as the shadow edged towards him until he was sitting in the only square of sunlight, he was afraid.

He wondered now what he would have to do to convince Baldy that he should be sent home. It hardly mattered that they would not want to see him at home. If he had the number of his father's mobile phone he could call to say that Baldy had injured him and he would deny that he had done anything to deserve it. But he knew that his father would not insist that he come home. His father would probably say instead that he would find one of Baldy's brothers and threaten him, or warn him that Baldy was his boss and he should learn to get on with him.

When the sunlight disappeared from the small rooftop, he

moved inside and lay on the bed. He was dozing, half dreaming when Baldy came with a bag of supplies that contained bottled water, rice, some legs of chicken, ground garam masala, oil, beans, onions, a bag of salt and some tea and sugar.

"You'll have to learn how to cook," he said. "Can you stand up?"

Malik nodded.

"Well, just boil the rice and fry the chicken and onions in oil."

"How long do you boil it for?"

"Until there's no water left."

"How much water do you put in?"

"How would I know?"

Baldy handed him a box of matches.

"There's a full bottle of *butano* and there's a frying pan and a saucepan."

"Did you get the keys?"

"What do you want keys for?"

"If there was a fire or something I would need to get out."

"If there's a fire, you can jump off the roof. Someone will catch you."

"I want keys," Malik said.

"Look at you. You're useless, worse than useless. I'll bring you keys tomorrow."

Over the next month Malik cooked chicken and onions and rice every day. He slowly worked out how much water to put into the saucepan for the rice. The television had only Spanish stations; sometimes he watched them, but mainly he did nothin
He sat in the sun and when the sun disappeared he lay on
bed. Baldy brought him a set of keys and took away his cl

and returned them washed and folded. He kept the keys safely but he did not want to risk the stairs on his own or go out into the street. At night he thought of things he might say to Baldy or to his father on the phone, angry things, or demands, but in the mornings he knew that he would never say anything to either of them.

Baldy brought him soap and shampoo and he kept himself as clean as he could. Sometimes, his arm and his leg grew itchy under the plaster and he tried to think about Abdul and this made him excited but soon he had to be careful because after the excitement he grew depressed and angry again and felt like banging his fists or even his head against the wall or going out onto the rooftop to scream.

Some days he was content and liked the idea that nothing would happen except that Baldy might come with a bag of food. Baldy, when he arrived, would never stay long or say much. He knew that Super must miss him and wondered if there were something he should say to Baldy about Super, or if he should try to find out what Baldy had told Super. And then there were all of the others in the bedroom, and Mahmood, and the two who worked with him in the mobile phone shop. All of them must miss him and must have asked about him. And then there was Abdul. Even in the morning, when most of the thoughts he had had seemed heated and exaggerated, he still felt free to imagine that he had a bond with him and that Abdul often thought about him, and that what occurred on the night of the concert was not an accident or a mistake or something that had casually come to pass. Abdul, he believed, had wanted it and planned it, even if he had done everything not to show it.

When Baldy took him back to the hospital, they examined leg and his arm and removed the bandage from his ribs. more, he noticed how cowed Baldy was in the presence of the doctors, how badly shaved he was, and how large his hands seemed, the fingernails all bitten to the quick. Beside him, the doctors appeared almost delicate, everything about them perfect and sleek, like rich men. Malik watched them, enjoying how they moved and spoke, even though he could not understand a word they said.

"Another month," Baldy said as he drove back into the city. "Another month and they'll take the plaster off and you can go back to the shop and make yourself useful."

"Does Super know where I am?"

"He's in the mosque day and night."

"Is he not in his supermarket?"

"Of course he is, but he has more to think about than you. He thinks about his prayers, him and his friends. You'd think they were the government the way they go on. He gave me the holy book to give to you."

"Where is it?"

"I forgot about it. I'll bring it tomorrow. Don't tell him I forgot or I'll get a long lecture from him."

In the days that followed, the temperature in the city went up. Instead of wind, there was humidity. Whether the long window was open or closed made no difference, the room was a small oven, and this did not change even when night fell. Malik's arm and leg began to itch so that he could not sleep; at times he would have pulled the plaster off if he could. He asked Baldy for a fan but it took him a few days to deliver it. He brought it, Malik believed, only because he himself needed to cool down after his long climb up the stairs, which left him sweating and panting.

When Malik asked him when they were to go back to the hospital, if he had an actual date, Baldy shrugged and said that it would be more or less a month from the last visit. W

Malik said that he would like to have the plaster removed sooner, Baldy said that he would call the hospital but he did not mention it again. Malik was worried that Baldy would tell him not to overuse the fan and thus cause expense so he did not draw any further attention to his discomfort but waited, hoping that the temperature would go down or that a breeze would blow from somewhere.

By the time Baldy drove him to the hospital again, he had not slept properly for weeks. On the journey, each time they seemed to be coming close to the car in front Malik braced himself, certain that they were going to crash into it. For the last part he fell asleep and had to be woken by Baldy in the hospital car park. In the hospital itself, he noticed only the air-conditioning and kept looking around to see where it came from so that he could move closer to its source and bathe himself in it. Once more, as he waited for the doctor, he fell asleep and wondered when he woke if he might be kept overnight, or even for a few days, as they took the plaster off. But it was all done quickly and, as he waited in the lobby while Baldy went into the office with cash in his hand to pay, he realized that he could walk, he could go where he liked in his spare time and this meant he could pass by the barber shop and look in at Abdul, or he could visit Super. And soon, he hoped, the heat would go. He touched his leg and his arm, the skin seemed raw and foreign and almost exciting to him. In the car, as Baldy told him that he would be starting work again the next morning, he wondered about Abdul, he saw him in his mind as he stood working on someone's haircut glancing out the window for a moment and seeing Malik on the street. He would, he thought, walk by the Four Corners as often s he could.

Now that he had learned to cook rice and chicken, he could is own shopping, look at different cuts of meat in the butcher's shop and talk to Super, when he went to see him, about types of vegetables and varieties of couscous.

When he appeared first Super made no comment on his absence but one evening as they both sat at the cash register and Baldy passed by the window Super told him he knew what had happened on the night of the concert. Malik froze for a moment and then looked at him, saying nothing.

"He's a big bully, that's what he is, and he loses his mind when he smokes, but he won't be smoking any more," Super said. "He was told to give up the hashish. We had a meeting with him. It was turning him into a maniac. We don't want any trouble in the street. If the police found out that he was smoking and then blaming what he did on other people, they could close us all down. So he was told to keep you out of sight until you would not be noticed. The police would have heard. He was lucky not to be sent home."

Malik wanted to ask Super what he had been told about the night of the concert but instead he listened closely as Super put all the blame on Baldy.

"Baldy is lucky that you and Abdul don't make a complaint about him. He knows that. So if you have any more trouble from him, just let me know."

Malik nodded.

"What were the two of you doing that night anyway?" Super asked him.

"Nothing," Malik said.

"I told Baldy I didn't want to hear anything about it," Super said. "That he was to quit the smoking and control his temper."

Malik nodded again and looked away.

"But then he told me," Super said.

For a second Malik thought that he should run out of the shop, go back to his room and curl up on the bed.

"He gave me a description of what he saw."

Super's tone was cold and factual. They sat at the cash register in silence. Malik could not tell whether Super was angry or not. As a customer came into the shop, Malik turned his head away. Super stood up eventually as the customer came with a full basket of groceries, and keyed the prices in. Slowly Malik filled two plastic bags with the groceries and the customer, having paid and waited for his change, left the supermarket.

"I asked him if he had told anybody else," Super said. "And he told me that he had not. So I warned him that if he told one other person what he had told me he would get more than a beating with the leg of a chair. And he knew I meant it."

Malik glanced at Super; he saw that he was smiling.

"And as for you . . ."

"What?"

"Oh, nothing. You know what."

Malik looked at him and nodded.

"You're lucky I heard it before anyone else," Super said. "That's all."

He stood up and walked to the door.

"No one else has a clue what happened. They all think Baldy smoked too much before the concert and lost it. They all blame him. But Abdul knows I know."

"Did you say something to him?"

"No. I looked at him. That was enough. I looked at him long and hard."

day a week later when he came back from work during his -break with a bag of groceries, Malik saw that another bed had been moved into his room. He checked his own suitcase to make sure it had not been interfered with and then he checked the fridge to see if anything had been taken. There was no sign of anything missing or anything strange. Just a new bed placed parallel to his. No sheets or blankets or anything. He wondered if anyone else besides Baldy had a key but realized that he did not know. This room had been his alone for so long that he found himself panicking at the idea that someone else had been here, or that someone else was planning to move in. He hated the idea of someone intruding, maybe even two or three people carrying in the bed and looking around the room. He shivered as he stood there and went back to work feeling almost angry.

Later, he saw Baldy but said nothing about the bed. Baldy was busy as usual and Malik knew that he would get no information from him if he asked why it was there or who had carried it up the stairs.

For a week it stood there like a ghost, like something he had imagined in the night. He looked at it in the morning and smiled at the idea that it might have come into the room of its own accord.

One night soon afterwards when he came back in the evening and was getting ready to cook, he saw that Abdul's suitcase was on the new bed and there were also sheets and blankets and pillows with white pillowcases. It seemed like a joke. Just the previous day Abdul had studiously and openly avoided his gaze when he had passed the Four Corners. Surely, Malik thought, he was not arriving now to share the room with him! If it was a joke, Malik thought, he could not imagine who was playing it. But still, it could not be serious. The only person who could authorize Abdul's coming here was Baldy, and Malik knew that this was the last thing Baldy would want to do. He touched the suitcase for a moment and then edged it open. He knew from the clothes at the top that it was definitely Abdul's. Abdul would be finishing work within an hour.

He began to boil the rice and fry some lamb he had bought. It was a warm night and he had opened the door onto the rooftop. As the food cooked he walked into the main room as though he were Abdul. He turned off the main light and switched on the lamp beside the bed and then he made his own bed properly. He watched the time. He would be able, he knew, to eat before Abdul finished work. He wondered if Abdul had actually been in the room already and supposed that he had since his suitcase was here.

Once he had eaten he went to the rooftop, where he had made a seat for himself with old cushions that Super had given him. He was determined not to look at his watch or think any more about what was going to happen next. Nonetheless, he remained tense enough to start when he heard voices and a key turning in the lock. As soon as he looked into the room, he saw Abdul and Baldy entering from the hallway. They both studied him suspiciously and it looked for a moment as if they were expecting him to offer an explanation for his presence or indeed for theirs. Both of them appeared uncomfortable and he realized slowly that they were staring at him because they could not face each other.

"So this is it," Baldy said.

Abdul did not say anything.

"I'll get you keys tomorrow," Baldy said.

Abdul's skin was darker than Malik remembered and he appeared taller in the low-ceilinged room. The top buttons of his shirt were open and Malik could see his hairy chest. Abdul was sweating. As Baldy turned to go, Abdul swung towards him but then he stopped himself. Malik noticed that he took up a lot of space in the room. He stood against the wall, breath-

ing heavily as though trying to control himself. Baldy slipped
out of the room and could be heard closing the door that led to
the stairs.

"Are you hungry?" Malik asked.

"Do you have keys?" Abdul replied.

"Yes."

"Give them to me."

Malik handed over his keys. Without speaking, Abdul
walked out of the apartment.

Malik woke up to the sound of Abdul undressing and then
heard him getting into bed. Soon Abdul was asleep. Malik
could make out his body in the bed. Abdul's back was turned,
but even so Malik felt almost happy that he was there beside
him, if still puzzled at why Baldy had sent him. In the morning
before he left Abdul handed him back the keys.

Over the following days Abdul came and went without
speaking to him or even catching his eye. A few times at night
when he asked Abdul if he was hungry, he responded by walking out of the apartment and not returning until late. In the
morning, he took his clothes into the bathroom, had his shower,
dressed himself, and went to work without coming back into
the room where Malik was.

When Super asked Malik how things were going, he
shrugged and said that they were going fine.

"You have company in the room?" Super asked.

Malik nodded. He did not know what Super was going to
say next.

"I thought that you were lonely there on your own," Super
said.

Malik glanced at him sharply.

"So I told Baldy that he was to move Abdul in there."

"And what did Baldy say?"

"He asked if I would promise to leave him alone about smoking hash if he did that and stop accusing him of disturbing the peace of the street."

Malik said nothing.

"So I said I would at least for the moment if he moved Abdul in."

The next day at lunchtime Malik went to a *locutorio* and gave them Fatima's number. Once more, he was surprised by how quickly he was put through and how clear her voice was.

"There's no news here at all," she said. "Except business is bad. Your father is well and your sister is well and all her family are well."

"And will you tell them that I'm well?"

"Oh I will, Malik, and they'll be glad to hear that you phoned as usual."

He waited in case she would say something else. He could hear the chickens squawking in the background and other noises too. He began to speak but he hesitated.

"Did you say something?" she asked.

"No, no," he said.

"So there's no other news?"

"No."

"You sound as though you're just around the corner."

"It's a good line."

"Well, I'll tell your father you called."

"Thank you very much. I hope you don't mind me calling."

"Of course I don't. And it's great to hear your voice."

"Goodbye now," he said.

"Goodbye."

* * *

At work they received a new consignment of phones that included not only models with built-in cameras but also iPhones. One of his colleagues made a deal with Baldy that he could have one for a reduced price and thus have his own music downloaded onto it, which he could display to customers. He offered to sell Malik his cassette player and his cassettes for a very low price. Malik thought about it during the morning and went home at lunchtime and got the money from his suitcase.

That night when Abdul came in, Malik had music playing. For the first time Abdul went onto the roof and sat on the cushions and accepted a cup of tea and a glass of water. When he came back into the room Malik showed him the cassettes; he examined them closely, going through them one by one, leaving a few aside.

"Do you want me to put one of those on?" Malik asked.

Abdul nodded and handed him one. It was the soundtrack of *Kuch Kuch Hota Hai*.

"You like Shahrukh Khan?" Malik asked.

"I like the film, but I like the music more."

As the music played Abdul lay on the bed with his hands behind his head. For the first time he seemed relaxed.

The following evening when they had turned off the light, Abdul asked Malik quietly if he would put on the cassette again and let it play out while they fell asleep. Without switching on the light, Malik managed to put the cassette on, turning the sound down so that it was not too loud. Before he got back under the blankets, he asked Abdul if it was all right, or if he wanted it louder.

"No, it's fine," he said.

He was aware of Abdul lying awake.

"Abdul?" he whispered.

"Yes?"

He left silence and then was sorry he had spoken.

"Yes?" Abdul said again.

"Can I come over to your bed?"

"Is the door locked?"

"It is. But I'll put a chair up against it as well."

"Will you do that?"

Malik found a chair and placed it against the front door of the apartment. Before he went back into the room he listened to the sound of the music. Slowly he approached Abdul's bed. Since the night was warm he had only a sheet and a light blanket over him. Abdul was on his side so Malik moved in close to him, letting his face rub gently against Abdul's hairy chest. He put his left hand on Abdul's back and then edged his other hand down between Abdul's legs. He listened to the music and to Abdul's breathing and felt his own heart beating and Abdul's heart beating. The window onto the roof was open and he loved the idea of the hot humid night outside in the city, people walking through the streets, traffic moving, the world awake, while he and Abdul lay still and the music wafted towards them.

He wondered would they do this every night, or what had been going on in Abdul's mind until now, but then he tried not to think. He snuggled in closer, put his lips hard against Abdul's chest. He desperately wanted to open his mouth and lick Abdul's neck and chest and his face but he had decided that he would make no further move until Abdul did. He knew that the cassette would come to an end, and when it did and he heard the click he moved his hand towards Abdul's hand and squeezed it and then got out of Abdul's bed and slipped quietly into his own and lay there happy until he fell asleep.

* * *

He could never be sure what Abdul would do. Sometimes, if he put the music on after the light had been turned off, Abdul would turn on the light again and cross the room and turn off the cassette and put it back in its case. Twice, when Abdul came home and did not speak and did not want any food, he tried to ask him what was wrong, but Abdul responded by walking brusquely out of the flat and staying away for several hours. A few nights, however, they lay naked together for hours and he could feel Abdul's need for him and he knew by his touch and how close he wanted to be to him that Abdul had been thinking about this, that it was not casual, or a mistake in any way.

He wanted to whisper to him, ask him what was wrong and why they could not lie like this together every night, but he knew that he must wait. He simply did not know what the reason was. It must be that Abdul was ashamed or afraid, and he wondered if he would change or if the shame or the fear were fixed in him as the silence on bad, brooding nights seemed fixed in him. On one of those nights together he had for the first time since the episode at the Four Corners put his mouth around Abdul's penis and played with him between his legs and moved his mouth up and down on him. When Abdul had gasped, he could feel the spurts of sperm firing through his penis and he took the sperm in his mouth and held it there for a few seconds before spitting it out. Then he changed his position in the bed so that his face was against Abdul's chest. Even though the music had stopped he lay there with him for a long time before going back to his own bed.

One evening when he came back to the apartment he found a brand-new mattress near the window and new bedclothes on the floor beside it. He wondered if this was a new way for Baldy to torture him, or if Super also knew about it. He went throug' all of the men who worked for Baldy and realized that any s' gle one of them would disrupt his life with Abdul, which now had its own rhythms, which included Abdul's absences and his bad moods. He felt that Abdul was slowly getting used to being alone with him and that what was happening could only improve with time. He did not want any outsiders witnessing Abdul's sudden departures or listening to the same music as he and Abdul listened to on the nights they slept together. Whatever they did would have to be furtive but would most likely not happen at all if a stranger came to live in their room.

It did not occur to him that the mattress had arrived with Abdul's knowledge and approval until Abdul came home that evening. He had, he admitted, helped carry it up during his lunch-break.

"Who's it for?"

"My cousin Ali is coming here. He's a butcher."

"Why is he staying here?"

"Because he's my cousin."

"Does Baldy know?"

"Of course he knows."

Malik went onto the roof and sat on the cushions. Abdul soon followed him.

"There's nothing I can do. He's my cousin. What should I have said to his father? They live in the same building as my family."

"You could have said that there is no room."

"No one in my family has ever said that."

Later, they ate in silence. As he got ready to turn off the light, Malik asked Abdul when his cousin was coming.

"Next week," Abdul replied.

"Do you want me to tell Baldy that I want to go back to the room where I was before?"

"No, I don't."

"Are you sure?"

"Yes."

"So what will we do when your cousin's here?"

"I don't know."

Malik almost asked him then if he cared that they could no longer be alone with each other, but instead turned away from him and tried to go to sleep. After a while, he regretted that he had not asked. He was sure that Abdul was still awake and wondered if he might do it now, but he could not think of a way to start the conversation again and he also realized that he was not sure he wanted to hear the answer that Abdul might give.

The image he had in his mind of Ali the butcher was of a man the same age as Abdul, or even older, so he was surprised when he saw Ali for the first time. He seemed young, almost innocent, and he was very polite and shy. He smiled softly when he spoke but he mostly listened as Malik described the street. He was puzzled that they had no video recorder attached to the television and that in the kitchen they had only one saucepan with burn marks on it and one frying pan. He asked if they had their meals on the roof and appeared amazed when Malik said that they had never once moved the table from its place in the main room.

It struck Malik that Ali made Abdul look old; against his freshness Abdul seemed tired, and then as he lay in the bed with the other two sleeping he realized that this made him want to be with Abdul even more. It made his strength, his height, his hairiness, his solidity more real and present and caused Malik to feel proud of the life they had before Ali came. Even his silences now did not make Malik uneasy; if he noticed Abdul beginning to withdraw he smiled at him and shrugged.

Ali, it emerged, was not only a butcher but a cook. With the small amount of money they had, he made Abdul and Malik buy a big saucepan. He himself bought spices and some days would bring home meat that was left over in the butcher's shop and cook for all of them.

The problem was that he left in the morning at the same time as they did and was home in the evening at the same time as Malik, before Abdul. Since they had never yet arranged to have the same day or half-day off, this meant that Malik and Abdul were never alone together. In the first few weeks Malik found himself at night lying in bed thinking of Abdul's body, imagining that he was running his hand over and over along the wiry hair between his legs. In the mornings as soon as they heard the shower going in the bathroom and they knew that Ali would not appear for some time, Malik moved towards Abdul's bed and held his hand for a while or kissed his chest, but they always had to be careful in case Ali came out of the running shower for some reason.

One evening as the three of them were having supper Ali produced a wallet of photographs from his suitcase. He wanted to show them pictures of himself with his six brothers. The photographs were sunny and bright; the seven boys looked alike and, Ali explained, since there was just a year between each of them, people often could not tell the difference between them.

"We all have the same clothes," he said. "No one knows who owns what."

He then began to flick through the rest of the wallet.

"Look, Abdul," he said, "here's you and Nadira when the twins were born."

Malik saw Abdul lowering his shoulders; suddenly he

seemed afraid. The photograph was obviously of a man and his wife and their two babies. They were all smiling. The man was Abdul, thinner and not as bald, and the woman was beautiful, with long hair and shiny white teeth. Malik glanced at Abdul but he had his eyes cast down.

Malik then stood up and went to the bathroom and waited there for a while before returning to the main room and announcing that he was going out. Abdul did not even look up.

"I need some fresh air," he said, "and a walk but I won't be long."

Ali, he thought, might be reassured by what he had said, but Abdul would know that he had never gone out like this before in the evening. He would know also that Malik had nowhere to go, no knowledge of the street at night. It was the only thing he could do, he thought, as he went down the stairs, and even if he had to stand looking at a shop window, he would stay on until the lights had been turned off in the room and he would not have to look at Abdul again.

He realized as he walked up and down the street that he should have guessed that Abdul was married. A good number of the older men were married, so it would make sense. Even if he had not guessed, he should have asked. But Abdul in all their conversations had never mentioned it, had never talked much about his family at all, just as Malik seldom had. He had never heard Abdul even mention making a phone call. Also he had presumed that Super knew about everyone in the street, anyone who passed his window or anyone new who arrived. He wondered now if Super knew and had decided not to tell him.

He pictured Abdul when he saw him first, how silent and self-contained he was, how unlike all of the others. He could not imagine him married. One or two of the married men wore wedding rings or showed people photographs of their family, but Abdul had never done this. And then suddenly it struck him that everything about Abdul, his silences, his way of being alone, his reticence about himself, and how he was always careful not to give the impression that he would come looking for Malik, everything pointed back to the photograph, to the man pictured happy with his wife and his young children, the man sad now to be away from them. And it would explain too how unhappy he was when he arrived first in the room alone with Malik, his presence having been organized by Super and Baldy. How eager he must have been to have his cousin come and break up whatever might happen between them!

Malik had twenty euros in his pocket, so when he found an open-air bar at which there were a few Pakistanis having coffee he sat down and ordered a Coke.

He pictured Abdul in the mornings as he lay in bed holding hands with him. He knew Abdul waited for this and liked it. But these were just images and moments. He was a fool for thinking they amounted to anything. Soon they would amount to memories because he would not hold Abdul's hand again or put his hand on the bulge in Abdul's crotch or be patient with him when he became silent.

Whoever he knew or remembered was not a real person, that much was now apparent. He did not know Abdul, who had made sure of that. He had remained unknown, unknowable. Everything about him could be explained by the fact that he missed home, everything including his sporadic tenderness towards Malik, his wanting and then not wanting to be held and made excited. All of this was simple now. As he sipped his drink Malik understood it all.

Soon, he thought, he would talk to Super; he did not know yet what he would say, but he would make clear that he did not want to be in the room with Abdul and his cousin. He might make the reason sound religious and this would please Super. But he knew that he had to take care not to blame Abdul for anything or make Super suspicious of him.

He imagined Abdul and his cousin Ali rolling out Ali's mattress now and both of them carefully and modestly preparing for bed. He wondered if Abdul would ever have actually told him about his wife, and if he had more children than the twins. He knew that it was not nothing for Abdul that Malik was aware now that he had a family. He knew also that, despite Abdul's being often withdrawn, there was, or had been, a bond between them, but even though it had been based, or Malik thought it had, on something half understood, it was the more real for that; it had been based on the idea that they had sometimes wanted each other, that Malik was not merely a way for Abdul to relieve his loneliness, or a temporary substitute for the young woman in the photograph.

Over the next few days he avoided being alone with Abdul. He had his shower first and left the apartment first. In the evening when Abdul was there, and if Ali was in the kitchen or the bathroom, he went and stood on the roof or rummaged in his suitcase or arranged his clothes. When his half-day came he went back to the apartment as usual. Since he had not been sleeping he thought that he might wait until the sun had moved from enough of the roof to allow him to stretch out on the cushions and sleep. He also thought that he would wash his clothes in the machine and then leave them out to dry.

He was surprised to find Abdul in the apartment. As soon as he saw him he went into the bathroom and stayed there for a while, hoping that Abdul might soon go. When he came out he found that Abdul was in the main room facing him. Abdul looked at him sadly and put out his hands and shrugged.

"Sorry," he said. Abdul held his gaze and seemed to suggest that Malik should come towards him.

"No," he said.

"Please," Abdul said.

"Did you say please?"

Abdul nodded and sighed.

"Yes, I did. Please."

When Malik moved towards him Abdul held him. At first he thought this was Abdul's way of saying sorry, of recognizing that they would not be together again, but soon he realized that Abdul had an erection and that his intentions were unmistakable. He had to decide what to do.

"Maybe we should talk?" he whispered.

"Can we talk after?"

Malik waited for a moment before he replied.

"Just say one thing now."

"You're not to imagine . . ."

"What?"

"I promise I'll talk to you."

"But say one thing now."

"Can I do something?"

"What?"

Abdul leaned towards Malik and kissed him. He pushed his tongue into Malik's mouth. Malik put his arms around Abdul's neck and smelled his breath and felt his tongue in his mouth moving against his own tongue. He did not know what this meant. It was something that they had never done before. He pulled back only because he felt that he was going to ejaculate. He stood gasping in front of Abdul.

"That's the first time I have done that," Abdul said.

"You've done that with no one?"

"No one."

"What are you saying?"

He saw that Abdul was close to tears.

"You are with me," Abdul said.

"I can't."

"You are with me."

Malik shook his head. Abdul went towards the door of the apartment carrying a chair to block it and then came back into the room.

"We can't," Malik said.

"Come and lie beside me and listen to me."

He put out his hand and guided Malik to the bed.

"Just talk?" Malik asked.

"Just listen," Abdul replied.

He pulled Malik towards him.

"I'm sorry I didn't tell you before," he said. "I'm sorry. I couldn't believe when Ali produced the photograph."

He sighed and they both lay still.

"There were nights when I came back and I tried to say something and instead I had to walk out and go up and down the street and hope you'd be asleep when I came home."

"It's all right. Now that I know. It's all right."

"It's not all right," Abdul said.

"Why?"

"You are with me. That's why."

"I'm not with you."

"I want . . ."

"What?"

"I want the two of us—"

"We can't."

"Do you want to?"

"What?"

"Be with me?"

"Yes."

"Then it's fine. When I go home you can come with me."

"And be what?"

"It's a big family and now you're a friend of Ali's as well. We will have to be careful and it won't be perfect, but it'll be worse if we don't. Look, I have thought about it every night. People often come and stay with my family and there are always friends and cousins. It's not like it's just a small house with me and the woman you saw in the photograph."

"She's your wife?"

"Yes."

"Do you have more children?"

"There's a girl as well as the twins."

"What age are they now?"

"The twins are eleven and she's nine. And all their cousins live around and my brothers have friends who stay. Ali's brothers have friends who stay."

"Friends like me?"

"No. But no one will think it strange that you are staying."

"But your real family is your wife and your children?"

Abdul looked away and was silent for a while. Then he whispered something that Malik could not catch.

"What did you say?"

"I said that my real family is you."

In the weeks after that, no one noticed that Malik and Abdul took the same half-day, or maybe, Malik thought, Baldy and Super did but decided not to comment on it. He did not know what to think about what Abdul had said. He watched him and saw how relaxed he seemed now when he came in at night, how he loved lying on the floor with a cushion under his head after supper listening to music.

A few times Malik raised the subject of Abdul's family with Ali and he learned that what he had said was true, but he still did not know what it would be like to live in a house with other people who did not know why he was really there, until he realized that this was how he lived now.

He waited in the apartment for Abdul to come. It had been a quiet morning in the shop. He opened the window and stood out on the roof and felt that the season was changing, that it was warm now only in direct sunlight. He had put some cold food on the table and made a place for himself and Abdul. When he heard the key in the lock he moved out to the hallway to greet him. Abdul kissed him on the forehead when he came in the door. He pulled two cassettes from his pocket.

"These are new," he said. "Salim recorded them for me."

Malik smiled and gave him a mock punch in the stomach.

"When we get the CD player, what will we do with the cassettes?"

"Ali can cut them up and cook them."

They sat together eating in silence and then, once Abdul had put the chair to guard the door into the apartment, each of them went in turn to have a shower. Then they made love quietly on Abdul's bed. Later, as Abdul slept, Malik went to the roof in his shorts and T-shirt and sat on the cushions in the sun.

When he heard Abdul moving, he looked up. He heard the shower going again and was standing at the open window when Abdul came back naked, drying himself. He put on fresh clothes. As Abdul put his finger to his lips and left the apartment, Malik had a shower and dressed himself. After a while, when he himself was on the street, he followed the directions that Abdul had given him some weeks before. He moved casually on the shady side of the street until he was on another street where he was sure no one would know him. Then he walked in the sun. Soon, he could see a huge ship in the harbour that was there some weeks and not others; it was, he thought, like a city in itself. He knew now to cross the street and turn left and head down to the waterfront. He ambled slowly, as Abdul had told him to do, looking at the small fishing boats and the palm trees and trying to pretend that there was nothing special about this.

When he came to the end of the walkway he crossed another street when the lights went red for the cars and green for the pedestrians. He followed the line of the waterfront until he saw Dino's ice-cream shop. He made his way to the opposite side and then down a side-street, walking in a straight line until he came to a boardwalk with palm trees that looked over a beach and the sea. Even though he had seen seagulls every day and had heard the foghorn at night, until he began to come down here he had never realized how close the apartment was to the sea.

Abdul was sitting on a seat as arranged. He stood up when he saw Malik coming, and as Malik put out his hand Abdul slapped it and smiled as though they were ordinary friends meeting. They walked along by the sea, stopping sometimes if there was anyone on the beach they could look at, or if there was a boat or ship coming into port they could examine.

Although Abdul did not talk as they walked along, there was, Malik felt, no tension in his silence. He was amused by things, by people who passed, or by anything Malik said. He knew that they would walk as far as they could and then turn back and walk together to the seat where they had met and part there, Abdul going ahead, Malik leaving twenty minutes and then following him. Abdul, he knew, would collect some meat from Ali's shop and they would both follow Ali's cooking instructions and have supper ready for him when he came in. Since they had a DVD player, they would finish supper early and watch a film before they went to bed.

But all of that was hours away, the hours after darkness fell. Now it was still bright. And all Malik wanted was for this walk to go on, for him to say nothing more and for Abdul to leave a silence too, for both of them to move slowly by the big strange bronze fish, both of them looking at the tossed sand and the small waves breaking and being pulled out again, out to sea. Both of them were on their afternoon off, away from all the others, away from the street; both of them were slowly walking away from everything as though they could, but not minding too much when they had to turn back and face the city again. Brushing against each other, they both knew that they should do that only once or twice, and only when no one was watching them.

Acknowledgements

I wish to acknowledge the following publications where some of these stories first appeared: *The New Yorker* ("One Minus One" and "The Colour of Shadows"); *The Dublin Review* ("The Pearl Fishers" and "Barcelona, 1975"); *Boulevard Magenta* ("Silence"); *The Financial Times* ("Two Women"); Vija Celmins: Dessins/Drawings, Centre Pompidou ("The Empty Family"); *Brick* ("The New Spain"); *McSweeney's* ("The Street").

I am grateful to Angela Rohan for her careful work on the manuscript; to my agent Peter Straus, to my editors Mary Mount at Viking/Penguin in London, Nan Graham at Scribner in New York, and Ellen Seligman at McClelland and Stewart in Toronto; also, to Catriona Crowe, Deborah Triesman, Brendan Barrington, Enrique Juncosa, Javier Montes, Jonas Storve, Vija Celmins, Dave Eggers, Paul Whitlatch, Jennifer Hewson, Aidan Dunne, Robert Sullivan, Marie Donnelly, Edward Mulhall, and Pankaj Mishra.